MW00334582

SAY MY NAME

A TRUE CRIME NOVEL

JOE CLIFFORD

SQUARE fire™ books

Copyright © 2023 by Joe Clifford

All rights reserved.

No part of this publication may be reproduced, distributed, or transmitted in any form or by any means, including photocopying, recording, or other electronic or mechanical methods, without the prior written permission of the publisher, except as permitted by U.S. copyright law. For permission requests, contact joe@joeclifford.com.

The story, all names, characters, and incidents portrayed in this production are fictitious. No identification with actual persons (living or deceased), places, buildings, and products is intended or should be inferred.

Square Tire Books, Austin, TX.
Book cover by Christian Storm

Author contact: joe@joeclifford.com

First Edition 2023

This book is dedicated to my dear friend Jack Lotko.
Rest in peace, brother.

AUTHOR'S NOTE

When the Rodgers Twins, Annabelle and Ava, were reported missing the summer of 1985, we expected they'd be found. Of course they would. Kids didn't go missing from Berlin, Connecticut. Berlin, like the one in Germany, but pronounced with the accent between syllables, like "pearl" and a preposition. And God forbid local residents hear you pronounce it the other way.

Ours was a nice, little New England town ensconced from such horrors as kidnapping and murder. That was the stuff of books and movies. Annabelle and Ava must've forgotten to tell their parents about plans; they had to be at a friend's house, went somewhere for lunch, lost track of time. The girls would return home soon, safe and sound. It would all be one big misunderstanding. Except the girls never came home. Police were called in, search parties sent out, eyewitness testimony taken. There were several suspects but no arrests made. Now nearly forty years later, their bodies still haven't been recovered.

I'd like to say nothing changed after that summer; that our quaint, charming New England town remained an idyllic village where young families moved to escape the scourge of the big city. I'd like to say that my best friends at the time—Jim Case, Ron Lamontagne, and especially Jack Lotko—weren't forever affected, life courses permanently altered. I wish I could tell you that the girls going missing, in no way, played a part in my moving west, or in my staying gone as long as I did, just as I'd like to tell you that my return has brought solace and peace, a reconciliation with the past.

From a certain point of view, maybe I could sell that narrative. I write fiction after all. It's not like I've sat around in a dark room for decades, slowly drinking myself into oblivion, consumed by the unknown fates of a couple girls I knew a few years when I was twelve. And, yet, there has been an element of that summer in everything I have done since. My interactions with people in the industry. My interpersonal relationships with friends and lovers. Pushing fifty, I have made many bad decisions, most of which I can't blame on that hometown tragedy.

But their abduction certainly played a part in my decision to write crime novels.

With over a dozen books published I've enjoyed success as a mystery author. I've hit several bestseller lists; my books have been optioned and translated into foreign languages—I was able to tour Italy a couple winters back. That was fun. Writing earned me a big house on the hill, critical acclaim, money. Life, for me, has gone on. Still, despite these reassurances, the horror of that summer continues to haunt; and its lingering specter has become a permanent part of who I am.

I may've left that town. But that town never left me.

So much of our fears is rooted in the other. This is particularly true in small, insular towns where everyone looks the same, acts the same, believes the same. I still remember the story my mother, God rest her soul, shared when I was a boy, about that poor woman from a tiny town not unlike ours who was visiting New York City. There, in a subway bathroom, a gang of thugs confronted her, demanding her wedding ring. When the woman refused to surrender it, the gang cut it off, finger and all. It wasn't until much later I realized that, like the uncle or family friend who lost his arm by dangling it out the car window, the story wasn't true; it was make-believe, a cautionary tale designed to scare us into behaving, living in fear. This is how I viewed the big city growing up, as a dangerous, Godless place filled with dangerous, Godless people. It's why we stayed hidden in the suburbs, concealed by the lush green valleys of summer long after winter days turned them cold and barren. I've spent most of my life in the big city. And, sure, it's hard to be a saint there. But its evils and transgressions pale in comparison to the sinister elements that can lurk in a small town, where everyone knows everyone's secret, but somehow no one sees a goddamn thing.

It's not 1985 anymore. Annabelle and Ava Rodgers' bodies most certainly will never be recovered. Like my mother, like my friend Jack Lotko, those young girls are dead. My mother and Jack died of cancer. My mother was fifty-three, Jack my age, late forties. Still, their passing was natural. Sad and premature, but natural. What happened to the Twins was not. Their story is an abomination, an anomaly, an aberration, a thing that should not be but is. Growing up I never would've believed it possible. Even as a crime fiction writer who mines the darkest depths of the human psyche, I never could've conjured something as ghastly as the truth I uncovered writing this book. I'd feel better if the final product were the result of my twisted imagination.

Except it is true, all of it.

What I discovered writing this book I wish I could unlearn. I long to go back to that original spin, that "fear of the other" instilled by my mother, go back to believing that monsters hide in closets and live under beds. But they don't. They reside in our hometowns, hiding in plain sight; they shop at the same stores, eat at the same restaurants; we pass them every day.

We don't recognize them.

Because they look just like us.

SAY MY NAME

CHAPTER ONE

I once started a book by having a lonely handyman boxing up the belongings of a dead packrat in the cold winter mountains up north. The old farmhouse had been abandoned, no heat or electricity, a treasure trove for a rag and bone man who makes his living sifting through trash. By introducing this character, estranged from the world, wounded—physically, emotionally, spiritually—I was attempting to mirror the fragmented psyche of the broken. He's seeking to scavenge the worthwhile from the worthless, recycle scraps from the wreckage, and in the process find meaning in his fractured life. Looking back, maybe it was heavy-handed, this treatment too obvious. But so much of our person is attached to, as Tim O'Brien so eloquently writes, the things we carry. We do not define our possessions. They define us.

Late October is a lovely time in Connecticut. I'd been back for a couple weeks, uprooting my life in San Francisco; the things I carried didn't amount to much. My meager material goods spoke less to frugality and more to an utter lack of sentiment. When I left the Bay Area, I didn't want to strap my world on my back. Newly single, Diamond Heights condo sold, money split, thanks for the memories, maybe I'll see you around, I longed for a fresh start.

Being in Northern California so long, I had avoided the seasons for close to a quarter century. The Bay Area seldom got rain, to the point

1

thunderstorms felt exotic. Come a Connecticut winter, I might feel differently with the onslaught of sleet and snow, the ice-weighted branches snapping off from on high, shattering overloaded roadways, the raw, howling winds that hurt any exposed flesh. I'd spent a childhood with chapped cheeks and cracked lips, warming aching bones beside the fire. Nor'easters translated to a prison sentence, power out, grocery store shelves raided and left barren. All you could do was hunker down, playing board games by candlelight. Of course that was my youthful recollection, and memory fails as a reliable source of information. These nuclear fallout landscapes of the frozen and inhospitable were hallmarks of my books, my author website defined by bleak winter backgrounds, a telling marker of the impression cold left on me.

But for now the balmy temperatures and dank humidity of an Indian summer was welcome relief from the never-ending autumn of San Francisco, a land of perpetual cable-knit sweaters, pumpkin-spice flavored everything, temps hovering in the high sixties and low seventies regardless the time of year.

This morning, I had the windows open. Birds were chirping, far-off church bells ringing, and I didn't feel so old.

I had moved back home to teach at the local college, Central Connecticut State University, my alma mater. Fresh off the break-up, I needed a new start. I was planning to take a break from writing, dedicate myself to sharing all I'd learned about craft. The teaching gig didn't start until spring semester. Still, I hadn't reached out to old friends, hadn't left the house much, save for the occasional run to Stop & Shop. The need to eat aside, you have to get outdoors once in a while, remind yourself you are part of a greater collective. So much of writing is living in your head, having conversations with imaginary people. Without actual human interaction now and then you start seeing invisible bartenders at the Overlook Hotel.

I didn't plan on remaining a hermit. I was, however, a creature of habit, with a strict sense of order. I needed to reestablish what that order would be. When your head is a cluttered mess, you seek to control your intimate environs. That meant setting up my work area. Which I had yet to do. I didn't own much that mattered to me, but that still left nailing ducks to the wall. Pots, pans, books on shelves. The prospect of slicing open boxes and dumping contents was daunting. The project represented more than where I hung a picture or stacked my black V-neck tees that came in a ten-pack. Once I set up shop, the new chapter would officially begin.

For years I'd been churning out two novels a year, which might not sound like much but for an author is a frantic pace, constantly dredging up new worlds and stories and turns of phrase. Spending that much time inside your own head can turn your brain to mush. A writer is always writing. Even when he isn't—he is still dreaming, plotting, and scheming. If your brain is a muscle, your subconscious is a gym rat.

The house I was renting sat atop Worthington Ridge, the historic older section of Berlin where bronzed placards boasted George Washington spending the night. Many of the homes were several hundred years old, the region a stop on the old Revolutionary War trail. This particular house belonged to my friend Rich Rice, who like I had moved west after college. Through the years, he'd dipped his toe in the real estate market in our hometown, where his cousin was a realtor and property came cheaper. Rich's mother lived down the street. Which helped Rich act as landlord three thousand miles away. I think Rich was relieved to have me as a tenant. He knew I wasn't going to bother him with complaints about leaky faucets or creaky stairs.

I brewed an espresso and primed to get to work. I'd managed to take care of the bigger ticket items—setting up a couch, putting together the bed, screwing bookshelves, getting the internet up and running. You can't write or do anything these days without being plugged in, Timothy Leary be damned.

I dropped in my cushy rolling writing chair, gliding across the room to the boxes labeled and stacked in the corner, Sharpie scrawled across the tops—"Kitchen," "Bathroom," "Mementos," "Books."

The very first box I opened, right on the top: my divorce papers.

The doorbell rang at the same time my cell phone buzzed in my pocket, my blade still stuck in the box. I hadn't told people I was back—Amazon was probably delivering more things I didn't need. There I sat, bathed in sunshine, pinching the bridge of my nose, trying to convince myself that the reason my eyes were tearing up was due to allergies and not because of marital failure.

The doorbell and cell buzzed again. Pushing aside regrets, I side-stepped burnt bridges to accept my postal delivery.

It wasn't the mailman.

CHAPTER TWO

I fumbled for the cell in my pocket, choking on heart meat. I saw my uncle's face pressed to the glass. Given the heightened senses, the anxiety that had jumped onto my back like a monkey, I didn't see him clearly, his features distorted, creating both a comical and ghastly effect. I'd have recognized Uncle Iver, even if he didn't have his phone pressed to his ear and his name wasn't on the Caller ID.

My mother's younger brother Iver had always been larger than life. Which had less to do with his size or personality than it did the vital role he played in my growing up. My last living relative, Iver had picked up the mantle of my absent father. Being several years younger than my mom, Iver also landed in that sweet spot in between: part dad, part cool, older brother. He was the first one to give me beer, the first person I smoked pot with. When I got into trouble at school, he was the one I had them call.

The disparity in age between us played out differently when I was a boy. At fourteen, I looked up to my uncle, sought his advice and followed his rules. Opening my front door, a different picture confronted me: we were just two old men, each broken in unique ways. Life has a way of doing that. You live long enough, all you have is the regret.

He held up his cell phone. "Why did you make me use this? You know I hate these damn things." Iver was the last person I knew to get a cell. And the one he had was, no lie, a flip-top.

Iver presented two Dunkin' Donut coffees on a tray. "You didn't think to tell your uncle you were back in town?" When I didn't move fast enough, Iver grimaced, extracting his cup and taking a sip. "What's the matter? Been out in California so long you've gotten too good for Dunkin' Donuts?"

I chuckled politely. Dunkin' Donuts was a regional, obligatory novelty, a form of East Coast nostalgia. But their coffee was terrible, little more than hot weak bean water. I had espresso on tap, the good stuff. The truth was I hadn't eaten. I hadn't been eating much lately. Didn't have an appetite. Two of the three greatest stress producers? Divorce and relocation. And the other, career change, lurked on the horizon. Normally a stout two twenty-five, I'd lost weight, leaving me hovering around the Mendoza line.

"I haven't told anyone I'm back," I said, relieving my uncle of the coffee, looking over his slovenly appearance. "Who dresses you?" I plucked at the ketchup or salsa stain on his ill-fitting shirt. He jokingly slapped away my hand.

I attempted a grin. It *was* good to see him, even if I hadn't been in the mood for company. It was hard not to be happy when you saw Iver, who, even in his sixties, possessed a vivacious personality and infectious humor.

"Was out at West Farms," Iver said. "Had to pick up a couple things. Then I thought: why not see the boy? I know how much you writers like your coffee."

"How'd you even know I was here?"

Uncle Iver pointed out the window, in the vague, general direction of the center of town, where the businesses operated. "Ran into Marilyn Asal at Stop & Shop. Said she saw you picking up groceries."

I didn't recall seeing Mrs. Asal. I certainly hadn't shared my new address with anyone. Then again, my head had been stuck in the clouds of late. Perhaps a conversation so banal had slipped my mind. When I ventured into public, I switched to autopilot. I was barely present even when I was somewhere I wanted to be. Another joy of being a writer: perpetually lost in thought. You walk around with that vaguely cognizant, dull-eyed, befuddled expression as you orchestrate the fates of invisible people. Drove the ex nuts.

"You know you can't keep anything from your uncle," Iver said, groaning and reaching for his lower back, a constant source of pain. The poor guy's entire body was a wreck. "Besides, what other choice do I have but to hunt you down? You don't call. You'd think a writer could be bothered to *write* once in a while." He beamed that familiar playful smile. This time, however, I thought I detected a hint of sadness behind it.

"Are you going to ask your old uncle to have a seat?"

I apologized for my lack of manners. Surveying the scant décor, I pointed toward the couch, the only place to sit other than the bed. I knew how hard it was for Iver to stand for long.

I couldn't recall if we'd spoken since the divorce. I leaned against the nearest wall and began recapping the past year. I told him about the break-up and teaching gig. When you're younger, you never go long without speaking to those closest to you. Now it wasn't uncommon for months, years to pass. One of the side effects of social media, which my uncle was not on.

"I'm sorry to hear that," he said, referring to the divorce. "Maybe it's just as well I didn't get to know her better."

"She didn't like the East Coast. Thinks everyone here is aggressive and mean."

"She's not wrong." He laughed.

"And you hate to fly," I said, a weak attempt to alleviate the guilt.

"Can't stand those tiny seats." Uncle Iver glanced out the window as if distracted by a birdsong. I didn't hear anything. "I'm surprised you'd come back here," he said, sipping his coffee. "Given how much you hated this town growing up." Iver moved his whole body toward the window.

"I didn't *hate* it here. I …" I followed his gaze out the open window, wondering what had him so rapt.

No robin or blue jay perched on a sill. Perhaps it was the brightness. I hadn't gotten around to hanging blinds or drapes. The vibrant view outside was more enticing than the white walls of my place. Cherry blossoms budded with creamy dogwood flowers; scents of warm vanilla and lemon curd lingered in the soft air. Worthington Ridge was the busy section of a town that didn't get very busy.

"I had to make my own way," I said.

"Huh?"

"Why I left Berlin. It was … time." The pat answer was easier than dissecting the intricacies of wanderlust. I'd been young, headstrong, and had to learn things the hard way. The oppressive arms of Berlin's religiosity also had a stranglehold. This town was governed with a repressive, conservative edict that was tougher to stomach at twenty. I hadn't grown any closer to their god. But it's easier to accept differing points of view and belief systems when you get older, especially when viewed through the lens of academia, which embraces inclusion over exclusion. Though the underlying ideology still irked me, I understood why kitchen walls around here were adorned with white, blond-haired, blue-eyed Jesus. He looked like them.

"Talk to any old friends?" my uncle asked.

"Not many of them left."

My uncle's face drained color, betraying feelings of sorrow. "I heard about Jack Lotko." His gaze shifted to the floor. "Cancer. That young…"

"Hit Mom about the same age."

We left that hanging there, the loss of my mother, Iver's only sibling, the tie that bound us together. I was in my early thirties when she died, living out west. Her passing still hurt but not as bad as if she'd died ten years earlier. By that point I had my own life, career starting to take off, and it had been a while since my mother was a daily part of my life, which sounds rotten to admit. But that's the point of being a writer: going places others won't, even when they paint you in a less-than-flattering light.

"Tell me more about this job," Iver said, delicately navigating the melancholy of mortality.

"CCSU. Spring. Fiction."

"Giving up on the writing?"

"You never stop," I said. "I'm writing now. You just don't know it." I winked. "I live in my head."

"That's a poorly kept secret, my son." My uncle smiled and stood, swatting his lap, as if to rid it of crumbs, though he hadn't been eating anything. He ambled toward the door. I waited for him to tell me he had to be running. But he didn't move, standing there, gazing out that window.

I hadn't seen my uncle in a while but didn't recall this particular, pensive trait. I felt a tremendous weight pressing on his mind. I was probably projecting, creating a character sketch to later use in my work.

"You always were a daydreamer," he added softly. An odd remark, since I could've said the same about him right then. The way he said it, though, carried the gravitas that could've sunk a fully loaded steamer bound for Cleveland. Perhaps it was the fond remembrance he held onto, charged with helping raise a young boy, cat's in the cradle and silver spoons.

"How about you?" I asked. "Isn't it time for your yearly trip to see the leaves change?"

Uncle Iver laughed. Ever since I could recall, Uncle Iver traveled north to watch the leaves change. When I was younger, watching leaves change seemed lame, and I teased him about it endlessly. Now that I was older, I saw the appeal. These days, I got excited about taking naps. New England is lovely in the fall.

"Not sure it's in the cards this year." He didn't say more than that but I could feel the remorse. Something was wrong. I worried he was ill.

My cell buzzed in my pocket and, honestly, I was grateful for the excuse to cut short the conversation. I'd slipped into a funk, a down-hearted mood washing over me. I didn't know if it was seeing Iver or the divorce certificate, or my gut growling for food and me with no appetite whatsoever. Didn't matter the impetus. I was often at the mercy of my moods.

"Take your call," my uncle said. "We'll talk soon." He made for the door, opening a bright day. I caught the smell of new-mown grasses. He walked off the porch, leaving me alone. I felt relieved.

Until I looked at the phone.

CHAPTER THREE

AMBER Alert
West Hartford, CT AMBER alert: VIC/ two 15-year-old sisters SUSPECT LIC/ (CT) White Acura. Refer to local media. 10:04 a.m.

The sisters and their age caught my attention. I grabbed my laptop, pulled up Google, and typed in "missing teen girls," "Hartford County," narrowing the search to within the last hour. A bunch of headlines popped up across various websites and Twitter accounts for local TV affiliates, WFSB, WTNH, FOX 61. A recent development, the abduction didn't afford many details. Two sisters, Bethel and Brielle Paige from Avon, another upscale suburban enclave a couple towns over, were last seen at the West Farms Mall, the big shopping center in the middle of the state. Police said to be on the lookout for a "newer white SUV," CT license plate partial: B, 7 and 4. Which narrowed it down somewhat. I drove a white vehicle with one of those numbers. Although my new Honda was a sedan and not a gas-guzzling SUV. I felt my heart race, the onset of a panic attack. It didn't take much for my anxiety to kick in. I could tell I wasn't going to be able to ride this one out without chemical assistance.

Making for the medicine cabinet, I sifted through the plastic orange treasure trove until I found the Valium, toppling a pair of 10mg tablets. I sucked on them sublingual, grinding to dust, sucking harder to hasten the sedative process.

Two girls, so young, same age, similarities striking. Sisters. Taken from a mall. Then again, was it that strange? Kids went missing all the time—it's the unfortunate reason Amber alerts were necessary in the first place. But this time was different, wasn't it? The initial report had been wrong. The Paige Sisters were actually a year apart, fourteen and fifteen. They were not twins. Different mall. This was not 1985. I was an adult, not a teenager. Most of all, I did not know these girls.

I hated thinking, "What is this world coming to?" Because it was such an old-man thing to think. But missing sisters from a neighboring town evoked a parallel too chilling too ignore. Once that connection sparked, it fired up neurons and synapses, my brain chugging cerebral gasoline; I knew I'd have a hard time powering it down.

Rifling through boxes, I pulled out old clothes and letters, important papers like car registration, social security card, and closing condo statement, until I found what I was searching for, the old Berlin High yearbook from 1985. I graduated in 1988. The same year we all should've. Everyone received a copy of the 1985 yearbook.

I sank back to the floor and cracked the old pleather cover, turning to the back page and the dedication made on behalf of the entire school:

This yearbook is dedicated to Annabelle and Ava Rodgers. Please come home soon.

Of course, they never did.

❊ ❊

What I remember most about that summer, the summer of 1985, even before the Rodgers Twins disappeared, was how everything was changing. My world was coming into focus, events switching from the frivolous activities of youthful indiscretion into something harder, more concrete. Childhood's end.

Annabelle and Ava Rodgers had arrived three years earlier, the occasion momentous. It was a big deal, two pretty blonde-haired girls, twins no less, moving into our little town. You sometimes got stragglers landing on the outskirts. I hate using words like losers or nobodies or nerds. Maybe these new kids were nice or smart, but they didn't move the needle. In baseball parlance, these were utility infielders, long relievers. The Rodgers Twins were top-tier talent, the best free agents on the market.

At twelve years old, baseball was my life. Future plans included right field for the New York Yankees, despite a decided lack of talent or ability to hit a curveball. When I wasn't practicing for a dream that couldn't come true, I was drawing my pictures and writing my stories, running off for adventures with Jim Case, Ron Lamontagne, and Jack Lotko, my best friends. It's not like we didn't notice girls at that age—we all had crushes, gossiping about who "liked" whom—but at twelve, we were still boys, as content to roll around in the gravel pit at the end of the cul-de-sac or hurl snowballs at passing cars in the winter. We noticed girls but we weren't under their spell.

By 1985 that had changed. That summer, I was closing in on fifteen. Not like fifteen or even sixteen is a "man," but the jump between twelve and fifteen, physically and mentally, is huge. I had my own friends, my own interests. Music started to matter. In a year I'd ditch baseball and learn how to play guitar, aspiring to the highest, holiest of goals: starting a band and becoming a rock star. I discovered Pink Floyd and Bruce Springsteen, whose words spoke to my specific plight of existential suburban ennui. It was also around this time I began to leave behind the Christianity forced upon me, which created a rift with my mother because she was the religious one. Uncle Iver never outright disrespected her faith but he never went to church, and during the weekly Bible study groups Mom hosted he managed to make himself scarce. I followed his lead. In eight years I'd be gone.

The summer of 1985 was the first time I fell in love, a short, mostly unrequited relationship with Annabelle Rodgers but one that still ached if I let myself think about it too long. I also recognize the big bang of events, the age and hormones, the strong, pure conviction of right and wrong, and the fiery, unwavering pigheadedness that comes along with it. That age affords the passion and clarity you only get when you are young. You see the way the world is and weigh it against the way the world should be, and you start to realize everything you've been told is a lie.

Things could've turned out much different for me without Uncle Iver in my life. He was the one who opened my eyes, getting me to reject the spoon-fed for what was real. This was Reagan's America, which most of Berlin ate up, the rah-rah chanting and misinterpretation of "Born in the USA" lyrics, rabid xenophobia, patriotism on steroids. I didn't know better. Life is simple in a small town. Drug problem? Don't do drugs. Don't want to get shot by a cop? Don't break the law. Duh. Iver was a thinker. During my Christianity conflict, he said something I'd never forget: "I can't believe in a God who would grant me intelligence and then punish me for using it."

My parents married in miserable Schenectady, New York. I had zero recollection of that city or my father, a man I never met. They weren't married long. Shortly after I was born, he moved north, the greater Buffalo region Mom thought. He never wanted kids.

And my story might've ended there, had my mother allowed herself to slip into the same vicious cycle as her mother, collecting welfare checks and government cheeses, finding solace in a bottle, forced to care for a child, bitter and resentful over the fact.

Except Mom had Uncle Iver.

Around the time my father was hightailing it for greener, childless pastures, Iver was living in Connecticut, where he'd come into money, a lot of it, if the hard way. Shortly after turning sixteen, my uncle broke his back in a motorcycle accident. Almost died. One inch higher and my uncle never walks again. He was laid up in the hospital for a month, stuck in a wheelchair after that. It took a while, but after a couple years of grueling physical therapy he made a full recovery. The accident affected his gait. He walked with a slight limp and often needed a cane if he was on his feet for a long time. He couldn't work, though. A subsequent lawsuit meant he'd never have to.

I don't remember any of this of course, these assembled snapshots of that rough start. My first memories are of Mom and Uncle Iver in plush Berlin, Connecticut, at our house on Old Farms Place, a two-acre plot watching fat cows grazing lazily in nearby pastures. I never knew poverty or what it was like to go hungry. I had a few hardscrabble years after grad school, partying too hard, the usual growing pains. I'd bounced back fine.

There's a reason all my books, in one way or another, take place in Berlin. No matter where I set my work—New Hampshire, Northern California, Minnesota, Upstate New York—I use Berlin landmarks. The Dairy Queen. The Great Taste restaurant. The high school squad is always called the Redcoats.

In 1985 I was entering high school, where I'd started noticing girls more, until, like most boys that age, they became all I could think about. I could run down the list of girls I thought I was in love with, year by year; girls, who, in one way or another cracked the veneer of my heart. Lisa Blake, Jen Colaresi, Heather Richotte, Tracy Bartlett. But Annabelle Rodgers was the first one to truly break it. Maybe because of that, she was the one girl I never wrote about.

I spent a lot of time with Annabelle in the summer of 1985, and we'd been growing closer. Something was happening between us. Maybe if she and her sister don't go missing, I convince her to take a chance on me. Maybe we officially date, the relationship plays out, and a permanent scar is erased or takes a different shape, a badge instead of a wound. Honestly, probably not. Like her sister Ava, Annabelle was out of my league. But the heart wants what the heart wants. Annabelle never led me on or gave me much hope we'd be more than friends. That didn't stop me from saving up the three hundred dollars for the necklace I bought her. At fourteen, that is not easy money to come by.

❋ ❋

I put down the yearbook. Outside, light traffic dawdled along Worthington Ridge as the wheels of my brain raced. What I'd said to my uncle earlier, how a writer is always writing, wasn't a lie—every daily occurrence is potential fodder. It's lousy to admit, especially in the face of such horrific circumstances, but as soon as I read about those two missing girls in Avon, a part of me braced for where the revelation would next take me: the idea for a new book. I didn't want to exploit tragedy. I hoped and prayed those two young girls in Avon were found—I really did—but it's not like I could do anything about it three towns over. I was a writer without an ounce of investigative acumen. The world can be a cruel, rotten place.

I couldn't deny the powerful association created by reading that Amber alert.

And like that everything started to slide into place, what I should be doing.

I would write a true crime novel about the unsolved disappearance of Annabelle and Ava Rodgers in 1985.

Though known primarily as a mystery author, I was intrigued by the prospect of tackling real life. No urgency, no rush. More hobby than certifiable project. The plan was still to teach at CCSU, take it slow, write during downtime; though I knew that was a lie. Once the seed took root, the book had started to grow. I wouldn't be able to stop it from blossoming into whatever wild thing it would become.

I also knew my interest in the Twins' disappearance was more than professional. Like many, I'd been at the Meriden Square that day. What I reported seeing was the truth. In light of the circumstances—which involved a mystery man using a newfangled tape recording device to interview kids—I ought to have rethought my testimony. Saying I saw my friend Jack Lotko and his stepfather, Kurt Shaw, was particularly damning. Kurt had a criminal record. Physically, he matched some of the descriptions given of the tape recorder man (though to be fair, descriptions were all over the board). The bigger problem was saying I saw Jack, who I didn't talk to, only spying from afar. You couldn't mistake Kurt, though. The guy was never without a cigarette in his mouth—this was back in the '80s when you could smoke anywhere. I was down the corridor by the music store. Kurt was always dressed the same—jeans, sleeve rolled with Marlboros, like a 1950s hood. I didn't care about Kurt. But Jack already had a reputation with the police for being a troublemaker.

Jack was eventually cleared of any wrongdoing, as was his step-father. I was glad since it removed Jack from the path of the storm. Though suspicion still hung over both, at least in the court of public opinion. In the midst of summer, the Meriden Square saw tons of traffic. There were many more customers—suspects—young and old alike.

Still, the allegation drove a wedge in my friendship with Jack. He and I never talked about what I said to the police, and Jack wasn't the kind to hold grudges. But I could feel it, the needless strain it created. I never had the chance to make amends. I'm not sure how I would've done that anyway. Jack had other demons tormenting him; I was out west with problems of my own. Since Jack passed away from cancer, I'd come to terms with the fact I'd never be able to fix my mistakes or repair the damage.

But I was wrong.

This book was my chance to make things right.

CHAPTER FOUR

"Can I have hair this time?"

"It's a book, Ron. Not a magic show."

"Har har. You gave Jim hair last time."

Jim glanced over his beer, unable to hide hopes for a second hirsute miracle.

In one of the books in my mystery series, I named a character "Jim Case," making him a gung-ho muckraker in tireless pursuit of the truth. I also graced him with a gorgeous head of luxurious locks. An inside joke.

"Guys, it's going to be *non-fiction*," I said. "I can't guarantee you'll make the final cut." I didn't have an outline or anything plotted. This was initial stages, verbal processing, as my ex-wife used to say, a favorite expression of hers, one of the many quirks that used to irritate me but that I now found endearing. I'd told them I was going to write another memoir, focusing on my youth and growing up in Berlin, avoiding the specific subject matter.

"If you're writing an autobiography," Jim said, "obviously we're in it. We're your best friends." He caught himself, the hard stop highlighting the profound absence of one.

Ron raised the glass first.

"To Jack," he said.

"To Jack," we all agreed before downing a toast.

A few locals streamed in, beer bellies and can-I-talk-to-the-manager haircuts, flannel guts for the men, frosted wedges for the women. More than a few red hats. I fought against condescension, trying to rise above the liberal coastal elite stereotype.

"Anyway," I said, snapping back to the conversation. "Non-fiction means everything as it is. So *if* you make the final cut, you'll have to appear as you are now."

In high school, going bald ranked among my biggest concerns. I know how silly that sounds but that's not hyperbole. I'd stand at a mirror, compulsively checking my hairline, gripped by a paralyzing fear, convinced it was receding at an unredeemable rate. At almost fifty, I was playing with house money.

We were sitting at Sliders, the townie bar I'd shoehorned into several novels. Not sure why I felt such loyalty to the place. Unlike the Turnpike diner or Chinese restaurant next door, I seldom came here when I was younger. Wasn't much of a drinker in those days. As far as bars go, Sliders wasn't much. Too bright, mediocre food, lousy selection of beer, though at least that part seemed to have improved, even if the predominant pour was still Coors and Budweiser. Sliders was strictly townie, populated by guys and gals who rarely ventured beyond borders. Sidled up to the bar, you couldn't help but feel you'd somehow slipped into a Springsteen song.

"Hey!" Ron waved a hand in front of my eyes.

"Huh?"

"Did you start pregaming before you called us, buddy?" Jim's gaze lingered on the almost empty third pitcher. "Nobody gets that drunk from a few beers."

"One," I said, correcting him. "I don't drink often. Two, I'm not drunk. I was thinking." I could lose huge chunks of time; it was true. I was eager to start teaching so I could play the absent-minded professor card.

"Man, you're never really here, are you?" Jim said.

"What do you mean? I just got back."

"No, like, you're never present."

"You sound like my ex-wife."

Jim laughed it off. I did too. Still the comment stung. I *did* live in my head. I couldn't explain the mental meanderings that disengaged me from the present. It was a form of cerebral purgatory, a fugue state, like lucid dreaming, half awake, half asleep, wandering through a strange land populated by second-rate actors and B-movies, the dates of obscure wars and meaningless batting statistics.

"Man, if I had your life..." Jim started saying.

He didn't have to finish. To them, two men slaving away at the nine-to-five grind, my life seemed glamorous. I blamed Hollywood, the depiction of the professional novelist nestled behind his typewriter with his scotch on the rocks, inspired words pouring out at a fevered pitch. The gig might not have been as revered as rock star, but writer rated sexier than working at the phone company like Jim or being the director of a public school like Ron. Perception is nine-tenths of the law.

Reality can never live up to the expectation. I don't care how successful you are, a writer always wants more. More books, more readers, more accolades. Movie options, TV, cold hard cash. Being a creative, you are your job; negative feedback stings sharper, any criticism an indictment of *you*. Maybe guys like Jim and Ron had it right. Work a day job, put in your time, and then punch out, go home, enjoy a few hours *off*.

"He's doing it again."

"He's drunk."

"I'm not drunk," I said, perhaps too boisterous. "It's these lights," I added quieter. Sliders had to be the brightest bar on the planet, three thousand watts sucking your eyeballs dry.

I couldn't recall how much more we had to drink after that—might've been another round (or two or three)—before I blurted my idea in full: a true crime novel about the missing Rodgers Twins. I'd look at the town, then and now, back and forth in time, like Vonnegut's *Slaughterhouse Five* (I'd always said that if I had a son I was naming him Billy Pilgrim), with linear jumps, parallel arcs, and writerly ruminations; instead of the bombing of Dresden, I'd focus on the decimation of Berlin, at least as I perceived it. What Berlin was like then. What it was like now. How one tragedy could shape a generation.

Maybe I was laying it on thick. But copious amounts of alcohol on an empty stomach—they ate; I didn't—can render one waxing philosophical. After the Amber alert, I'd spent the day on the computer, researching the old Rodgers case, mentally outlining themes and angles, and a center had begun to emerge. I couldn't contain my enthusiasm. I hadn't been this excited about a book in ages.

"Are you out of your fucking mind?" Jim said.

"Jesus," Ron said, "that's a terrible idea."

"Why? The specifics of the case are fascinating!" I launched into my elevator pitch, a honed skill. "A mysterious man with a tape recorder? Lurking around the mall, talking to a bunch of kids." Kids we must've gone to school with. Yet, no "kid" came forward. Not with anything useful. Who was this man? Descriptions had him anywhere from twenty to sixty. "And you can't rule out the sex angle. Sad. But tantalizing."

I waited for them to say something positive, pat me on the back, congratulate my willingness to do the heavy lifting, for having the stones to delve into such darkness, which for me was nothing new—I made my living extrapolating unsavory topics: sexual perversions, gruesome murders, twisted fates. I was kicking myself for not coming up with the idea sooner.

Except no one lauded anything. Ron remained silent as if exercising his right to do so. And Jim looked livid. I couldn't understand their lack of excitement, their unwillingness to appreciate the role they would play in all this, never mind the hostility and apprehension. So I stoked the flames, firing them up to see this was *our* story too. "*We* were there that day."

"I wasn't there that day," Jim said.

"I don't mean literally—"

"You were there that day," Ron said.

"Yeah, I was. And what's your point?" I might've said it more heated than I'd intended—alcohol can do that to you, tease out underlying feelings of guilt, cause you to flash hostility. I felt attacked. The elephant in the room: Jack. Or more to the point how my statement to the police about seeing Jack and his scumbag stepdad contributed to Jack's already hard lot.

I didn't kill Jack. I didn't cause his drinking and drug problems. But I needed their absolution.

"I saw Jack and his stepfather. What did you want me to do? Lie to the police?"

"No one is saying you should've lied."

"Then what *are* you saying?"

"We aren't saying anything. You're getting defensive. I get it, buddy. You feel bad about Jack. But writing a book about the Twins isn't going to wash away those feelings or bring him back. All it'll do is piss people off."

I fell back, indignant. "It was almost forty years ago, guys. When Capote wrote *In Cold Blood*, he was five years removed from the murders."

"What's *In Cold Blood*?" Ron asked.

"Are you serious? How have you never heard of *In Cold Blood*? It's one of the greatest American novels, books, works of non-fiction! It's about these murders in Kansas, and . . . forget it. Never mind. Pretend I didn't bring it up." How does someone live their whole life never hearing of *In Cold Blood*?

"I think the Rodgers still have family in town," Ron said.

"No, they don't," Jim replied. But he didn't say it in a way that exonerated me. Instead, he snapped the words off, the backhanded slap of some dandy's glove in a Dickens novel, the ultimate gentlemanly slight.

"I'd think twice before you write about that summer, is all." Ron postured tough. Beneath those harsh lights, he bore a striking resemblance to *Breaking Bad*'s Hank Schrader right before he slugged Walter White.

I strove to feel indignant—I wasn't doing anything wrong. This was my job. My friends weren't objecting to a finished product, bristling at an unfavorable portrayal. They were shooting down the mere idea, chastising the jerk who dared trample a grave at midnight.

"You left," Jim said. "We stayed." The declaration of this consistent presence granted authority and final say on all matters Berlin.

"No one around here talks about that summer."

"But it happened," I said. "And they never caught who did it. Never found Annabelle's or Ava's bodies." Hearing my words aloud, they sounded hollow, selfish.

Jim reached for my arm, aggressively enough that I jerked it back. But he didn't flinch, standing his ground even though I was the bigger, more imposing man. He searched the bar, making sure no one could hear what he was about to say next. Few patrons remained on a Wednesday at 1 a.m., jukebox stuck on an endless loop of terrible new country songs, which is redundant. But no one played Lydia Loveless, Sturgill Simpson, Tyler Childers, Jason Isbell, Travis Meadows, the good stuff. Jim's secretive gesture made me want to blurt out laughing. We were all drunk. When I looked in both their eyes, however, I didn't see anything funny.

"Closing time," the bartender bellowed. Besides some guy at the end of the bar, we were the only ones in there.

"It was just an idea," I said, waving for one last beer.

I don't remember who said goodnight first—Jim, Ron, or me—but we bro-hugged it out in the parking lot, said our goodbyes, schlepping off to respective rides. I wasn't unhappy to see a couple old friends. But like my uncle's unannounced visit, the encounter brought up emotions I wasn't ready to unpack, leaving me rattled and uncomfortable, melancholic. Beneath a million blinking stars, I shivered in the chilly air. I didn't know what I'd been expecting. It was more than approval for a prospective book, which I may or may not even get to. I had ideas for a thousand books, ninety-nine percent of which I'd never write. The alienation cut deepest. Coming back, I'd taken for granted I'd have a place to belong. For so long I hadn't felt right. Not at home, not in my marriage, not in San Francisco. My skin too tight, I could never relax. They say wherever you go, there you are. And like most clichés, I never got that one. Until I did. And then I couldn't run far or fast enough to get away from me.

CHAPTER FIVE

Leaving the bar, I took Episcopal Road, toward Christian Lane—no one ever accused Berlin's founding fathers of going easy on the religious overtures, its Puritan edict alive and well. Blue laws still kept liquor stores closed on Sunday. Because Jesus. At the intersection, I passed this dilapidated old house. Rusted wrought iron, water damaged and decayed, peeling paint and exposed beams, bars covering shattered windows that whispered of horrible secrets, the kind of weather-beaten monstrosity that would've landed right at home in an old black-and-white Hitchcock. When we were kids, we used to say it was haunted. The house was still ugly and decrepit, swallowed by tall grasses, garlic mustard and porcelainberry, shoulder-high weeds. No one lived there. And it was clear no one had bothered on the upkeep.

Heading back toward a tiny town illumined by all-night gas stations, I reflected on those scary stories we'd tell each other as kids. Bloody Murder and Headless Mary, calling names backwards in the mirror to make apparitions appear. I had no idea what kids today did. Outside of trends on social media. Sewer alligators and backseat killers giving way to Slender Man and Momo, a modern generation of horror ushered in, a brave new world of terror passing me by. Like Billy Joel says, it's just a fantasy, a healthy imagination, however dark. The macabre compels us. Seeing the return of the House of Usher, I told myself it was just a building, with walls and a roof, but its lurking menace left me unable to separate childhood fodder from bona fide evil.

The Rodgers Twins going missing was an isolated event. I wanted to believe that, wanted to take Jim and Ron's words at face value. A lot of time had passed. Revisiting that summer *was* a waste of time. Who'd be interested? I hadn't pitched my agent. No publisher was lined up. How did I know anyone would even read it? Why did I still care? Was it any different than glancing up at that old house, knowing it wasn't haunted but still allowing rumor to feed the fear in my bones? These neuroses are too ingrained. Because we birth them into existence. To maintain otherwise is hubris. Who was I to say ghosts and demons didn't exist? That the undead didn't walk among us?

Yeah, I was still drunk. I shouldn't have been behind the wheel. I should've driven straight back to my house, which was only a couple miles away. Everything in town was a couple miles away. Instead I found myself cruising old streets. It had been a while since I'd lived in Berlin, the exact geographical center of the state, an odd source of pride for residents—there was even a plaque commemorating the dubious honor. It sat between two benches and a mulberry bush next door to the Dairy Queen and Webster Bank on Main Street. I didn't need GPS. The town's road map was burnt on my brain. Plus, this place never really changed. They might erect a new supermarket, a restaurant might change hands, but you could still get a house here for about the same price you could when I was a kid. Berlin was a land in which time stood still, part of its charm, and a larger chunk of its stagnation.

I passed the old farm I'd worked on in high school, a three-week, backbreaking gig I survived before realizing I was not meant for manual labor. Continuing on, up Four Rod, back into Kensington, hooking a left down the long and winding road, then over the crest and down dale to the house where I used to live with Mom and Uncle Iver.

My childhood home shone in the pale moonlight. It used to be gray. Someone had painted it canary yellow. Whoever lived there now kept the giant old milk can on the porch. I wondered if they stored a spare key under it too. That was if they even locked the door. After the Twins went missing, in the immediate aftermath, there'd been the expected panic. Don't talk to strangers. Everyone in before dark. Avoid candy and vans. Over the years that worry ebbed until complacency reclaimed. I toyed with the idea of letting myself into that old house, taking a look around at these things that used to be mine.

Of course I didn't. I didn't go home either.

I drove out to Gribbard Pool, the old community pool where I first met Annabelle and Ava Rodgers. That's the biggest problem with alcohol, the way it paints poignancy on the mundane. What was I doing at the old Gribbard Pool? Place was closed down, tool shed overrun with weeds, the pool itself a dry bed filled with dirt, leaves, and, for some reason, a plastic chair. But I didn't want to go home or call it a night. Sleep didn't come easily these days. Because I knew it would be worse when I dreamt, when my own mind, unencumbered by self-imposed limitations, was free to explore and dip deeper into the madness. All artists are mad, and writers are the worst. These reminders—architecture and alcohol, being twelve, fourteen, seeing Annabelle in that bikini, forever burned on an oversexed teenage brain.

I didn't know how long the cruiser had been sitting behind me. But my internal monologue and storytelling ceased when the lights started flashing. When I saw those swirling blues and reds, my heart seized up, rearview alighted.

Fumbling in the center console, I fished for gum or mints, Tums, anything to mask the booze on my breath, except it was pointless; I hadn't bought any gum, mints, or antacids. They weren't going to magically appear. The clock read two fifty-eight a.m. Stupid. Cars don't sit on the shoulder of Berlin forests at that hour. This was an invitation to be stopped. Although technically I hadn't been driving. I tried to recall how long I'd sat in the bar with Jim and Ron—and moreover how long I'd been tooling around town, resurrecting my childhood, fragment-by-fragment, bone-by-bone, alcohol being absorbed into my bloodstream, flushed out by the aged organs still tasked with the handling the job, however less efficiently with time. When was my last drink? An hour, two? How many had I had? Five? Nine? An hour per drink, the math wasn't working out in my favor.

Watching the swirling lights in the rearview, I didn't truly feel the panic until I acknowledged I hadn't signed any paperwork with the university. Meaning CCSU had time to change its mind. A DUI would be plastered all over the papers. Even if I kept the job, this wasn't the city. Bus routes didn't run with regularity, public transportation out here little more than a gesture.

When the cop appeared outside my window, he didn't ask for my license or registration. He stood there, staring, flashlight leveled. Shielding my eyes from the glare, I couldn't see much.

Then the flashlight snapped off. "I thought that was you," the cop said with a perky upbeat. "Heard you were back."

I didn't know this cop, but I wasn't going to blow the opportunity. "Yup, it's me."

"Still haven't gotten around to reading the book."

"It isn't going anywhere." I chuckled. I didn't ask which book he was talking about. I smiled and prayed he'd tell me to have a good night.

"The one with the cop?" he said.

"Yup. People like that one."

All of my books had a cop in them. My portrayal of law enforcement wasn't favorable. I didn't have anything against police. I used them as a means to an end, peripheral vehicles to help propel narrative. I didn't like the professional investigator angle, preferring the amateur sleuth pursuing justice, a purpose higher than a paycheck.

"Is it true?" he asked, leaning in, violating personal space, like we were old high school pals. "That he's based on me? The cop. In your book?"

I didn't have any cop based on a real person. The closest I'd come was using the singer and bassist (from an obscure band I liked). And because of this, I didn't answer fast enough, and I could see I'd hurt his feelings.

"Wayne?" he said. "Wayne Wright?"

"I know," I said, as if he'd told me there's no air in outer space. "Obviously." I remembered a kid by that name back in high school. We weren't friends. We weren't *not* friends. We weren't anything. He didn't look like the kid I remembered. Then again, this was thirty-whatever years later; people change.

Wayne glanced through the thicket, up the road, in the direction I'd come from. "Ran into Jim Case at Sliders a while back. Said you wrote a book with a cop." Wayne scrunched his face, probing deeper thought. "Said you'd based him on me?"

"Kind of," I answered, now knowing the book he was talking about, which was part of a series. But, no, I hadn't based the cop on him. I'd based that particular character on a restaurant in Colorado, which served the most mediocre breakfast food. After grad school, a friend and I had attended the AWP Conference in Denver and this restaurant was located en route. We kept stopping there because it was cheap and fast, even though the meals were, at best, edible. So we'd started riffing slogans, like, "When you don't care to try any harder" or "When good enough is good enough." Which was funny for about eighteen minutes, until we arrived at the most pretentious writing conference in America. When I was writing that book, I realized that was the type of cop I'd created: woefully average, serviceable, unremarkable in every way. So I'd used the restaurant name. Not a compliment.

Wayne eyed me with suspicion.

I turned toward the backseat. "I have a bunch of copies," I said, even though I knew I didn't have any books in the car. People feel better with action sequences. Too much dialogue bogs down a story. "Darn it. Looks like I don't have any with me. Tell you what. How about I drop one off at the station? Free of charge, of course—"

"Have you been drinking?"

"Excuse me?" I tried to level my response as both surprise and affront, as if the sheer proposition of one's being drunk at three in the morning at an abandoned community pool were tantamount to seeing an elephant and desiring to drain its blood to paint your boathouse. Kiss, kiss, bang, bang.

"You smell like a brewery," Wayne said. Gone was the old high school chumminess, replaced by the bravado of the lawman. This was why I never portrayed police favorably in my novels. It was the act, disingenuous, little kids playing grown up.

"A few *hours* ago," I said, stressing the time, "I may've had *a* beer with dinner."

Wayne ran his hands over his face. "This is not good," he muttered, shaking his head.

Motivation. It's the key to everything. Writing. Life. Getting out of drunk driving tickets. Everyone has buttons to push, means by which they can be manipulated. It's what I did for a living, after all, examining the whats and whys. I wasn't a psychiatrist, though I'd been in therapy, in one form or another, most of my life. I'd picked up valuable skills. Let people talk to fill the silence. Prompt when needed. Listen. Most of all, you need to make people feel as though they matter, especially when they feel small, and being a cop in Berlin, CT, had to leave one feeling as small as humanly possible.

"You know I'm working on a new book. About police officers. How hard a job you guys have. I'd love to interview you. What your day is like? The ins and outs, the perils. Of course I'd make sure you got thanked in the acknowledgments—"

"What are you doing?"

"I'm trying to … I'm working on a new … I thought maybe we could talk. Now. Later. I'd be sure to thank you in the acknowledgments."

"Yeah, you mentioned that."

"Who knows? Maybe this is the one that gets optioned into a summer blockbuster—"

"Stop," he said. "You can't be driving drunk around here." He craned his neck, surveying the empty roads. "This is serious shit."

"I know. Sorry. I was hanging out with Jim Case and Ron Lamontagne. I guess we got caught up in the old days."

"Where you staying?"

"Worthington Ridge. Just moved in. Still have to finish decorating. To tell the truth, I just got the divorce papers. It's been a rough time—"

"If this was another cop—" Wayne stopped himself. "I'm not going to bring you in. I'm not gonna write you a ticket either."

"Thanks, Wayne. Thank you so much. Won't happen again."

"How drunk are you?" he asked. "The truth."

"Closing time was one?"

"Think you can get to your house without crashing into a tree? Driving the speed limit? No swerving."

I nodded. "No speeding, straight line, got it."

Wayne shook his head once more for good measure, before returning to his cruiser.

I threw back my head, relieved at the bullet I'd dodged.

"Hey," he said.

I glanced up.

"But I will take you up on that offer. The free book? My wife is gonna get a kick out of me being in a book!"

I gave a hearty thumbs up, slipping it into reverse, and turning the wheel with deliberate precision.

Wayne followed me all the way to my house.

You have to love the communal bonds with small-town cops.

CHAPTER SIX

Bright sunshine smacked my face like an insult. I had a vague recollection of driving back to my house, Wayne, like a good dad, making sure I got there safely. After that? Nothing. No memory of opening the door, brushing my teeth, drinking water, or passing out on the couch, which told me I was far more inebriated than I would've liked to admit. I often wrote about alcoholics—my best-known material featured elements of addiction. I'd known quite a few alcoholics and addicts in my lifetime. I had a few wild years myself. I wasn't that guy anymore. These days, I was a glass of wine at dinner, couple beers on the golf course kind of guy, last night an outlier. Waking up so disoriented, with vague snippets of what had happened proved disconcerting, challenging this image I had of myself. The shame I felt, however, was complemented by a tinge of pride for having gotten so many alcoholic details right.

You only need to be hungover once to never forget it. And I never wanted to be this hungover again. My mouth tasted like hairy caterpillar ass. Staggering to the sink, I pounded a couple glasses of water, dehydration pulsating my temples and throbbing the tiny veins. I braced for the imminent stroke. I hadn't felt *that* drunk but clearly I had been.

And I felt like an asshole getting behind the wheel. I could've killed someone. I wanted to believe I was being hyperbolic, piling on shame to beat myself up, another favorite pastime of mine. There'd been no one on the road. I made it home fine. But, no, I'd been an irresponsible jerk, who without Wayne's break could've landed in jail.

I retrieved a copy of that book I'd promised Wayne, scribbled a heartfelt inscription, and set off for the Berlin Police Department. More than gifting the book, I wanted to apologize in person. He'd done me a huge favor.

The Berlin PD was actually located in Kensington, the two towns indiscernible, interchangeable. Train tracks separated them, which might've led to one being called the wrong side of the tracks if Berlin and Kensington were the kind of towns that had a wrong side. The closest we came to that was New Britain. Growing up, we'd viewed the industrial hub to the north as the rough-and-tumble section, a gang-infested warzone. Now it was another delightful suburb. New Britain hadn't succumbed to gentrification. We were just sheltered.

I steered up the tortuous road to the police station, which shared its real estate with senior housing, a community center, and a library where I'd often come back to read. Your average book event in the city? You're lucky if you get a dozen people. And that's if you include the hobos who show for the free wine. Each reading at Peck Memorial was packed, half the graduating class of '88 coming out to lend its support.

Today I found the dreary, overcast parking lot deserted. Most seniors didn't drive or have cars, and the middle-aged men who took advantage of the free gym in the community center had day jobs. I locked up, a pointless precaution, and headed for the precinct's reception. I planned on leaving the book with a secretary and was surprised when the desk sergeant told me to give it to him myself.

"Oh boy!" Wayne said, emerging from a back room to relieve me of the book. If he held any resentment about last night, he didn't show it. He flipped right away to the inscription. I'd played up his being an inspiration. "My wife is gonna flip!"

I leaned in, whispering, "Thanks." Hoping he got my meaning.

"Gotta hit the streets," he said, motioning outside, brushing off effusive praise.

I wasn't sure what "hitting the streets" meant in Berlin, other than stopping for coffee at the Whole Donut. But I wasn't making that joke at Wayne's expense.

We exited together, descending to the lower lot. The clouds blotted the sky, a muddied swirl of black, charcoal, and concrete. Indian summer retained seasonal heat, the day muggy and humid, but you could feel the threshold threatened, as if one good lightning crack could usher in the fall. The air tasted familiar, carrying the weight of a thousand juvenile days. Sprinkles drizzled. How had almost half a century passed? I felt so old. When was the last time I woke without a crick in my neck, spine wrenched, muscles strained, bones aching for nothing more than being used up, worn down, and awake?

"I had a question for you, Wayne." I hadn't come with an agenda—drop off the book, say thanks, be on my way—but as soon as I arrived I realized I had ulterior motives.

Wayne's face squirreled up.

"I can call you later, if that's better?"

Wayne checked his phone. "Nah. I got time. What's on your mind?"

"Well ... the Rodgers Twins."

Wayne's reaction was strange. It wasn't like Jim's or Ron's, as if I'd broached a taboo topic and was treading on the thin ice of good taste. More like ... reconciliation with the inevitable? The fugitive relieved when the law catches up with him because he is sick of running.

Far away, thunder cracked and showers fell harder. No one broke for his car. A little rain never killed anyone.

"Right," Wayne said, stopping short of chastising his oversight with a good slap to the head. "Of course they'd want to talk to you."

They?

I had no clue who "they" were but I nodded anyway.

"Called last week," Wayne said. "Strange. After this much time. Who'd you talk to?"

I pretended to probe for a name I'd never heard.

"What was his name?" Wayne said. "The cold case guy?"

Cold case guy?

"The one who reopened the Rodgers Twins case?"

I was confused but knew nothing I said was helping my cause. So like I'd learned sitting on countless panels at endless writers' conferences when I was overwhelmed and didn't know the answer, I kept my mouth shut, hoping my silence would be construed as intelligent pondering.

"Jerry," Wayne said.

I shrugged, neither in the affirmative nor negative.

"Gary!" Wayne shouted, self-correcting. He seemed so proud of himself. I clapped my hands. "Gary St. Jean, Hartford PD."

A car pulled into the parking lot of the community center down below, and a frighteningly skinny man emerged, the kind of guy who'd have to run around in the shower to get wet.

The skies ventured beyond overcast, dark sands layered in a glass jar, Jupiter swirls and never-ending Saturn turbulence. The rain continued to fall, picking up pace; temperatures felt ten degrees colder. A chilly breeze scuttled over cracked asphalt, rustling lush green leaves in the forest. The thunderstorm was getting closer. You got a lot of these in Central Connecticut. When the clouds burst, you didn't want to be without shelter. I also didn't want to miss out on a possible lead.

"Maybe it's not that weird," Wayne said, as if talking to himself. "Not with those sisters taken from Avon the other day."

"I heard about that." The Amber alert that dinged on my phone. "They find them yet?"

"The Avon Sisters? Not that I know of." His apprehension gave me pause.

"You don't think there's a connection—"

"With the Rodgers Twins?" Wayne scoffed. "I doubt it. That was thirty-five years ago. Sad, though, isn't it? Do you know how many kids go missing every year?"

"No."

"I don't have the specific number," he said. "But it's a lot. You stop noticing after a while."

I didn't want to believe I'd grown numb to such horrors. Then again, maybe Wayne was right. Shootings. Murders. Kidnappings. All the horrible things man is capable of, broadcast daily, a feed forever scrolling on our computers. Perhaps I had become desensitized.

"Wasn't like that for us growing up," Wayne said.

"Except for Annabelle and Ava."

"Yeah. Except for that."

The rain dumped buckets. Wayne called for me to follow him to his squad car.

Felt weird sitting in the cruiser. I never got in *that* much trouble when I was younger. Still, I wasn't used to the front seat. Wayne shivered, shaking the rain from his bare skull, a mangy dog unable to break the habit. Like Jim and Ron, Wayne didn't have anything up top.

"Maybe that's why the cold case guys are poking around again," he said. "Seems bizarre we'd get a copycat so long after the fact."

"They never found much that first time," I said, which was true, and one of the enduring elements that continued to fascinate, the lack of evidence recovered, how inconsistent the eyewitness testimony was, the way Annabelle and Ava seemed to vanish without a trace. Other than the tape recorder man, who was never identified, details were scarce.

"That's what I wanted to ask you." I started patting down pockets. People comprehend better with visual aids. "I lost … Jerry's … number. The cold case investigator."

"Gary," Wayne said. "Gary St. Jean."

"That's what I meant. Jerry, Gary. Easy to mix up. Must be in one of my boxes I have yet to unpack. I'm working on a new book." I waited for him to make the connection, professional quid pro quo. "Do you have it? Gary's number? I'm under a tight deadline."

CHAPTER SEVEN

Driving along Route 9, scanning for the I-84 connection, skies pissing rain, I tried to reconcile yesterday's Amber alert with the police reopening a decades-old cold case. If Gary St. Jean contacted Wayne "last week," could there have been another inciting incident? Maybe there wasn't forty years between abductions. Maybe this latest tragedy was just another in a long string of atrocities. Heading to Hartford to speak with the cold case detective, I attempted to think like the investigators do in my books. One event triggers another; nothing happens in a vacuum. Action can't move forward without cause and effect. *This* happens so *that* occurs. Without understanding this fundamental relationship, you can't have a mystery, and you sure as hell can't write one.

The rainstorm ended almost as soon as it began. A ten-minute monsoon that washed everything clean, whisking away lingering heat. I felt the jolt of autumn cold as I stepped from my car into the police department parking lot.

Hartford County's operation towered over my hometown's rinky-dink efforts. I'd written so many interrogation scenes, and, again, I was struck by all the details I'd gotten right. The position of the clerk, the marching uniforms, importance and insignificance, heroes and villains, good guys and bad, who was who a point of view.

The clerk had me take a seat. A few minutes later, a man in a blazer that couldn't cover his belly walked across the room, extending a hand.

"I'm Gary St. Jean."

The man who stood before me projected a commanding presence, an underlying air of superiority, which I supposed was a prerequisite for the profession.

"Right," he said. "One of your boys called and said you'd be stopping by." By "boys," I assumed he meant Wayne Wright, who'd I'd asked to phone ahead. I'd invented a story for Wayne, how I'd actually spoken with an assistant—if he could explain who I was, it would save time. The worst that happens, the guy says he has no idea who I am, but then at least Wayne could vouch for me.

Landlines rang relentlessly as last night's drunken arrests were paraded across the bullpen floor like scarlet letters. The stiff scent of cheap liquor and bulk coffee clogged the air.

"You're writing a book about the Rodgers disappearance?" Gary St. Jean said.

I nodded, firm enough to instill confidence that I, in this journalistic capacity, should be entitled to see whatever material he had on the subject.

Gary St. Jean checked the big clock on the wall. "I have to be somewhere," he said, thumbing toward the door. "Closer to your neck of the woods, down the Turnpike. Mind if we meet over a quick bite while we talk about this?"

A local staple, the Olympia Diner was an old-school dinette on the Berlin Turnpike, which we used to frequent back in the day after rock concerts and football games, all gleaming tin, flashing neon, and Edward Hopper aesthetic. I didn't think Gary St. Jean noticed my eyes go wide when he suggested it. Maybe he'd read my books. How else could he have known? I used the Olympia for key scenes throughout my mystery series. I'd transplanted the restaurant to Northern New England and tweaked the name but everyone around here knew what I was talking about. Could've been a coincidence. Central Connecticut is intimate. There aren't many can't-miss breakfast spots. Personally I liked Mo's Midtown in Hartford. If Gary St. Jean had a meeting around here, the Olympia made as much sense as anywhere.

The Hartford detective was already seated when I arrived.

"Great choice," I said, as I slid opposite him. "One of my favorites." I waited for acknowledgement. By now he'd at least looked me up online, read the back jackets of my more popular works; I'm sure I mentioned the Olympia in an interview. But Gary St. Jean didn't look like he had any idea what I was talking about. I added, "Eat here a lot?"

"Couple times." The terse response bordered hostile. Gary St. Jean, who had been pleasant enough when we spoke at the precinct, now scowled as if beset by the sudden onset of gas. He poured a thick stream of cream into his coffee. "A writer, eh?"

To the average person, the job seems romantic. The truth was, like that of a real-life private investigator, the job wasn't that interesting. Time spent "researching" translated into procrastinating without pants on social media, sidetracked by bear attacks, endless snacking, and caffeine on tap. Gary St. Jean did not appear impressed.

On the way over, I'd prepped an intro, puffing up accomplishments, prepared to toss in the proven sound bites guaranteed to titillate. Publishers, possible big pay days, exposure. Point out my Wikipedia page. I'd be sure to sprinkle in words like "bestseller" and "movie option." Language is fluid, malleable; we can mold it to say anything we'd like. Before we began, I reached into my bag, extracting several hardcovers, which I'd already signed, passing them over. But Gary St.

Jean didn't take my offering, leaving me awkwardly extended, the over-zealous priest holding up a cracker to the non-believer.

"What do you want?" Gary St. Jean asked.

"I'm writing a book about—"

"The Rodgers Twins. I know. Your cop friend told me. You're wasting your time. I'll tell you right now, those girls will never be found."

I wanted to ask if the situation was so hopeless why had the case been reopened. I decided to keep the conversation cordial. I could already see I was grinding his gears.

Instead I asked, "Have you heard about the missing sisters from Avon?"

Gary St. Jean returned a dead-eyed stare.

"Of course you heard..." I gathered my thoughts. The unchecked animosity had me reeling. "How long has the Rodgers case been reopened?"

"One, it's not 'reopened.' We're looking at a couple things. And, two, I'm not at liberty to say."

"Was it before the Avon Sisters?"

"Like I said," he repeated, extra slow and aggravated, "I am not at liberty to divulge that information with the public."

"Understood, but my being a journalist—"

Gary St. Jean cut me off. "What paper you work for? You're not a journalist. You write those smoky boy in the cold months books." Before I could object to the slight, Gary St. Jean hoisted a meaty hand. "No," he said. "The Rodgers case has nothing to do with Avon or any other copycat."

I tried not to get frustrated. He could've told me to get lost at the precinct. Why drag me here only to clamp up?

"Some new information must've come in," I said. "To warrant assigning the additional manpower?"

Remaining civility now erased, Gary St. Jean checked the time on his phone. "What is it you want?"

"I was hoping I could look at the case files? I'll be sure to give you credit—"

"No."

I waited for more. But no more came. Gary St. Jean sat there, steadfast, resolute, dismissive. I'd entered the diner on a high note, thinking we were equals, professionals sharing a common goal. Gary St. Jean did not share my assessment.

The waitress arrived to interrupt our conversation. I still wasn't hungry. The thought of food made me nauseated. Not that the Olympia Diner was revered for its cuisine. What I recalled most were the waitresses, an endless parade of exotic, high-cheek-boned beauties.

Maybe I'd been like every other teenage boy, oversexed and horny, viewing all women through the bar light at two a.m. Maybe those pretty young women simply got old like me. Whatever the case, the woman taking our order today, God bless her, did not come from the same stock.

The detective's appetite was not lacking. He ordered half the menu, melding a hodge-podge of breakfast, lunch, and finger foods, with no respect for culinary pairings—omelet, toasted turkey sandwich, pudding, bacon, mozzarella sticks, Danish, bowl of Italian wedding soup.

After the waitress left, Gary St. Jean stared at me, unblinking. If I were writing this scene in a novel, I'd add a toothpick, giving him something to do with his hands. In fact I *had* written this scene. Many times. Except in my work when the amateur investigator seeks the expert's help, said authority, in a show of solidarity, passes along a file, which contains a vital clue. It's usually a manila folder. Gary St. Jean passed along nothing.

In my work, I often juxtaposed the solitary blue-collar hero against a cold, uncaring world. His refusal to surrender, to not give in; to soldier on in the face of hopelessness, maintaining grace. Outside, I spied semis barreling up the boulevard. There was no poetry in their movement; big diesel engines lacked poignancy. Along the Turnpike, garbage swirled in the drift, wet tires spraying rainwater gasoline rainbows.

Maybe I hadn't worded my request right. Maybe Gary St. Jean misunderstood what I could bring to the table. Trying to remain optimistic, I decided to resume the conversation under that pretense.

"True crime is very popular at the moment," I said. "A book like this, Detective St. Jean—it can—I'm not saying it *will*—but it *can*—gain traction, and—"

"I can't let you look at evidence," Gary St. Jean said. "We don't have *a* file. We have boxes and boxes, forty years of wingnuts who spend all day bending blinds, late-night cable TV psychics—because this shit started so long ago there were still—"

"Miss Cleo," I interjected, proud to recall the name of one of those late-night '80s shysters. The bond I'd been hoping for did not form.

Gary St. Jean checked over his shoulder for the food that still wasn't there. I made a mental note. In my books, food always arrived much quicker. Gary St. Jean signaled to the waitress. "Can I get that to go? And the check."

"The tape recorder man," I said, throwing out the word like boiled spaghetti, hoping it stuck to the wall.

No response. We sat at an impasse, silent.

The waitress slapped down the check and Styrofoam container with his boxed-up meal. Apparently, conversing with me cost him his appetite. I tried not to take it personal.

"I was there that day, too," I said. "My uncle dropped me off—"

"Everything you know I know," he said. "And anyone of interest has been interviewed. If they were at the mall that day, if they had contact with the Twins, we had contact with them. Kurt Shaw and Jack Lotko, Danny McPhee, Melissa McPhee, the Meriden pep squad." He stopped, caught my eye, made sure to annunciate with perfect diction: "*Everyone* there that day. Nothing. Now as for why this is being re-looked at? The way it goes sometimes. A politician wants to appear proactive, a commission gets a hair up its ass, pick a name out of a hat. There's no movement on this case. In a week, I promise you, my bosses will pull the plug and reassign resources."

Gary St. Jean stood and started toward the door, stopping by my side.

I peered up. For a moment I thought there *was* a connection, the shared remorse of failure and lament for the mishandling of justice.

"Listen," he said, "you seem like a nice kid."

Kid? I was almost fifty years old.

"I were you? Find another book to write."

CHAPTER EIGHT

When I left the Olympia Diner, I was beaten. I resolved to give up the idea of trying anything new. I wrote mysteries. *Stay in your lane.* They did all right, my mysteries, well enough that I was about to be teaching at my alma mater. No, Central Connecticut State wasn't Harvard or Yale, but it was a legitimate collegiate institution. Moreover, I was indebted to the mystery and thriller genre, where I had built a loyal fan base. I had a brand to protect. Why bother reinventing the wheel? Or to pick the more apt cliché: why should this old dog learn a new trick?

I wish I could say I stayed true to my word, that by not having those fictional investigative Xeroxes in front of me, I wised up and walked away. But after forty-nine years—thirty-five of them mired in mystery—I returned to the conversation with the irascible, tight-lipped detective.

And I remembered the name.

Detective Gary St. Jean said he'd interviewed everyone at the Meriden Square that day. He mentioned Jack Lotko and his stepfather, Kurt Shaw. Danny McPhee, my older neighbor who was forever in trouble and the first guy police questioned whenever something went wrong around here. Talking to Danny made sense. I knew all that. But Gary St. Jean added a name I hadn't heard mentioned in conjunction before.

Danny's cousin, Melissa.

My neighbor growing up, Mel McPhee lived next door to Danny. Talking to Danny's family made sense. But Gary St. Jean specifically mentioned Mel. Not her parents—not Danny's parents, Ken and Barbara—just Mel, who at the time was so much younger, she barely registered on my radar. When I was about to turn fifteen, sneaking beers with Jim, Ron, and Jack at Swede's Pond, Mel wasn't even ten. Rail-thin and odd, the girl was a lurker, forever staring up through googly-eyed glasses. Because she lived next door, Mel would often show up at our house, chatting with my mom, the neighborhood den mother. At fifteen, I had no reason to talk to a ten-year-old girl.

Then after the Rodgers Twins went missing, Mel and her family moved away. And I never would've given Melissa McPhee a second thought were it not for a random college party senior year.

I was up at UConn. It was almost summertime and we were hanging out in someone's dorm. It was late, we were getting stoned, when in walks this beautiful girl. Long brown hair and penetrating emerald gaze. She's staring at me, nonstop. I'd exchanged flirty smiles with pretty girls plenty but this felt different; she was being *so* obvious. If I were in Vegas, I'd swear she was trying to sell me company for the night.

Of course, it turned out to be Melissa McPhee. The glasses were gone, so too the gawkiness, leaving only elegance.

We caught up in a corner. She was laughing, touching my arm. Envy emanated off every guy in that room. Mel and I slinked off for breakfast at midnight to continue the conversation alone.

Mel was a theater and dance major at Yale, on a full scholarship. Not even twenty, she had already worked for Broadway productions, with plans to apply for the Fulbright Scholarship (which I know she'd get, since I can admit to drinking, every now and then, and looking her up on social media, charting her fabulous life).

That night, all we did was talk, endlessly, till we watched the sun come up on a West Hartford rooftop. I couldn't even remember how we got up there. I had to admit, listening to her array of accomplishments, I started to feel inferior and ineffectual, which was a weird, well, turn on. There was something sexy about a woman so young and self-assured, and not to mention gorgeous. Nineteen and she was killing it. I had my life together, knew where I planned to go—having already been accepted to UCSF for my master's in writing—but Mel? She was … special.

I saw a lot of Mel over that summer before I'd pack up and move three thousand miles west. I don't want to use the term "dated." It wasn't like that. But we got close.

It was a special summer. It didn't end there. Because this was me, and I had yet to blow it in a spectacular way.

Even after I went away to grad school, I often came back to visit my mom before she died. Major holidays. The sporadic long weekend. And when I was in town, I'd ring up Mel, who at the time was living in New York City, an hour or so from Berlin. Sometimes I'd fly into New York. Sometimes we'd get together. A lot of times she wasn't around. Mel was always off on some adventure. Paris. Africa. Trekking across South America, a pilgrimage on the Camino Santiago. Toward the end of grad school, Mel surprised me by showing up in San Francisco. She wasn't there to see me—she had some other magnificent opportunity—I can't remember what. They probably wanted her to run for president of the city, which wasn't a real job but for Mel they might as well have made an exception.

I'll never forget that three-day weekend. We didn't leave my apartment much. We didn't get out of bed much.

Yet I never got comfortable, unable to shake the notion I was punching out of my weight class. My being with Mel was like trying to force two incompatible magnets together. She couldn't be pinned down, would never commit to anything, even as I started to, as time went on, press harder.

My last semester in graduate school, we had a bad fight. I had too much to drink one night and called her, all pissy, saying, something to the effect, that I was tired of being her "fuck buddy and fallback option," and she called me "needy," which *really* pissed me off, and then we each said stuff we didn't mean, or maybe we did—that age is wrought with so much raw nerved emotion. Either way, we hadn't spoken since.

Mel had never been my girlfriend. We never defined what we were, but I can admit now, after all these years, I fell hard for her. And one thing was undeniable: Melissa McPhee was the first girl to break my heart since Annabelle Rodgers.

And according to Gary St. Jean she was at the mall in 1985 the afternoon Annabelle and Ava Rodgers went missing. All the times I'd seen Mel, she never told me she'd been there that day. We were from the same town, the Rodgers Twins' disappearance a big deal. Then again it's not like we *talked* about it. For such a devastating, defining event, it was strange how seldom the people of Berlin spoke about it.

I was making for the computer to look up Mel, when Tom Hazuka, my old professor responsible for my new job, called and invited me for lunch at his house.

Hazuka lived at the base of Lamentation Mountain, which any readers of mine would recognize. For my mystery series, I'd transplanted the relatively tame mountain range to the Canadian border, covering it in permafrost, adding all the hospitality of a gulag.

My former professor lived at the end of a delightful cul-de-sac, a charming blue two-story monument to small-town success. Hazuka was a great writer, his *In the City of the Disappeared* an unheralded masterpiece, a moving love story set against the savagery of the Pinochet regime. Tom was a role model, a mentor, and a good friend.

"Tom!" I said, perhaps too enthused when he opened the door. I couldn't explain how his invitation couldn't have been better timed, providing a needed reprieve from my own worst enemy: me. These last two days had left me trapped in thought. My head was like a rich chocolate cake: a couple bites were okay; too much of it made you sick.

Hazuka's forlorn expression broke the bad news before he said a word.

"The funding fell through."

"What do you mean?" A stupid response delivered via a question he'd already answered. I wasn't ready to accept an uncertain future. More than ever, I needed stability. After eons as an iconoclast and workforce renegade, I craved a place to go every day, a steady paycheck, for someone else to be in charge, healthcare. I'd been my own boss long enough to know, like the defendant who represents himself, I was working for an idiot.

Hazuka invited me in for coffee. I didn't want coffee. I also didn't want to make him feel worse. Whatever had gone south wasn't his fault. I knew he'd gone to bat for me.

"They're going with an adjunct for the position," he said, retrieving mugs from the cupboard. "Budget cuts. Soon as I got the news, I called you."

We had lunch. Sandwiches. Cold cuts from Stop & Shop. I couldn't eat more than a few bites. But there was one point where Hazuka was scraping every last dollop of mayonnaise out of an all-but-empty jar. I didn't know why watching that simple act of frugality depressed me so much.

After we said goodbye, I drove back to my place but didn't go inside. I stood on the front porch, overlooking Worthington Ridge, taking in the old houses and colonial artifacts that lined the town's historic section. Inhaling the changing of the seasons, chestnuts, saffrons, and mustards, I tried to will myself calm. Nothing was wrong. My life was as it was before. There were other colleges in the area, if I wanted to teach that badly. Though I knew, given my lack of actual teaching experience, my best shot was the hand-delivered gig. Instead of student teaching in grad school, I'd opted to edit the university literary magazine. Meaning I had the publications but no practical pedagogical application.

In my books, I often flirted with conspiracies. I didn't believe in them myself. I didn't have faith in people to pull off anything that elaborate, not when plans hinge on keeping mouths shut. The only way to keep a secret between three people is if two of you are dead. But earlier a detective had cautioned against writing this new book. Now I lose the job, a supposedly done deal? I tried to ignore the parallel of having employed this same plot device in another book I'd written, about an ex-baller who gets framed at his security job because he is poking his nose where it doesn't belong. The irony was, like in that particular book, I now had nothing preventing me from investigating, full time.

CHAPTER NINE

A quick social media check located Mel. In her current profile picture, she planked upside down, an impossible yoga pose, atop monkey bars at a beach. Santa Monica? Venice maybe? In the golden sunshine, Mel's long, lean torso, covered only by a sports top, displayed perfectly whittled abs from granite. I kept myself in decent shape. I worked out, tried to eat right (when I had an appetite). I hadn't let myself go like a lot of guys my age. But I'd never have two-percent body fat. The photo had been uploaded three months ago, as had her last generic post about loving life, hashtag gratitude. I wasn't sending another DM to go unanswered.

Back when the McPhees were our neighbors, not many people lived on Old Farms Place. In fact, there were three houses, total. And McPhees owned two of them, Mel's parents, Jeff and Nancy, in one, and her aunt and uncle in the other. I knew Jeff and Nancy had moved out of state, and that Mel's uncle, Ken, passed away long ago. Diabetes. A large man, he'd lost his foot when I was a kid. I never knew him before the wheelchair. He drank a lot. According to Google, his wife Barbara still lived there. The Ken and Barbie joke might've been funnier if their lives weren't so tragic. Forget Ken being footless and wheelchair bound, their adopted son Danny was a nightmare. He'd been locked up for good in 1986. Something to do with kidnapping and robbery?

I couldn't recall. Danny was ten years older than the rest of us. He did yard work for my family when I was younger. Mowing the lawn, whacking the weeds. Even then I could sense he was bad news.

After Mom passed, my uncle and I sold the house on Old Farms Place. Since then the street, like the rest of Berlin, had undergone a radical facelift. Turning down the hill, I had a hard time reconciling what I saw with the serene neighborhood of my childhood. Tall trees, high as redwoods, no longer speared the heavens lording over a boundless lake. Instead roads plowed through fields, connecting more plots and homes, endless sprawl rendering it indistinguishable from any other small town USA. And those huge trees and lake I recalled from my youth? They'd been relegated to unimpressive sticks around a dull, ordinary pond.

I parked on the street. When I was growing up here, a strange car would invite a visit from the local cops. We had driveways. Times change. Mine was another car among many, Old Farms a regular suburban hotbed, houses up and down hill and dale, former cow meadows turned tracts and subdivisions. I stared down the road, in the opposite direction of Barbara McPhee's house. Swede's Pond, which I'd used as the setting for my latest novel, shimmered beneath the high autumn sun. And like that, I was back in the summer of 1985, walking through tall stalks of rustling amber grains with Annabelle Rodgers. I'd have sold my soul just to hold her hand.

I was a forty-nine-year-old grown man; yet such a part of me still identified with that young boy. When I looked in the mirror, I didn't see my age; I saw that same kid. He was buried beneath the hard lines etched into weathered skin, behind the dark circles of black eyes that were losing their battle with time and whose shine had long since dulled.

Barbara McPhee's house was the first on the block at the top of the hill. She had to be eighty by now. I didn't remember much about Barb

McPhee or her late husband. I knew Mel's parents better. Ken and Barbara were reclusive by comparison. They'd adopted Danny. I didn't know more than that, like why they didn't have a child of their own. Maybe they preferred adoption because there were too many kids without homes in the world. Which would make them heroic. Except if that were the case Danny didn't reward their altruism.

Danny was a bad kid. You'd see him around town, outside liquor stores, leaning against brown brick, scowling and smoking cigarettes. My uncle's body was a mess and he couldn't do yard work, which is why he hired Danny. Iver could've been a hard ass and assigned me the job, but Iver wasn't like that. He'd let me and my friends kick it by the pool, enjoying summer vacation. I never liked Danny, who gave me the creeps. Sometimes he'd take a break from mowing the lawn, shirt off in the hot sun, staring down at us. On the lucky occasions we got girls to come over, like the summer of 1985, Danny acted even creepier, standing there, smoking, sweating, staring at girls ten years younger in their teeny bikinis.

I rang the bell, accepting Barb McPhee may've chosen to spend her golden, widowed years in Florida, and that a cherubic six-year-old might answer the door, followed by a confused mom. Unlike the city, where visits from a stranger elicited fear, here in my quaint hometown? I'd be invited in for a sandwich.

But Barbara McPhee did answer. Shorter, shriveled, and more seasoned, she looked otherwise the same.

"Hello, Mrs. McPhee. I don't know if you remember me—"

"*Of course* I remember you," she said, smiling. And then, with rail-thin shaky arms, she reached out and hugged me. I hadn't seen the woman in over three decades. In Berlin, you were always family.

I'd been in their house a few times over the years. Borrowing flour, a cup of sugar, an egg for my mom. The house hadn't changed. Which was both reassuring and unsettling, how time can stand still like that. The layout and decorations were unique. Knick-knacks and trinkets— Caribbean figurines and hand-painted totems—a curious detail, since folks in Berlin weren't known for being the adventurous type. Then again, Mel must've gotten the bug from somewhere. A framed photograph on the wall captured one of these tropical vacations, featuring much younger versions of Ken and Barbara. No Danny, who was easy to spot since he was darker. Puerto Rican, I thought. Which in lily-white Berlin made you stand out.

Barbara McPhee, with whom I couldn't recall ever having had a significant conversation, guided me into her living room and toward her bookcase, waving a hand like a game show hostess over all the fabulous prizes you could win. There, on the prime shelves, sat all my books, including the first press paperbacks that were hard to come by.

"Big, famous writer, you," she said, swelling with such pride you would've thought she was *my* aunt.

She asked if I wanted hot tea, coffee, water, juice, iced tea, soda, lemonade, and I knew if I didn't pick one, she wasn't going to relent until I did. I said tea was fine. Waiting in the living room, I followed the stream of sunbeams leading into a separate room, all four walls covered with nothing but photographs, positioned like an exhibit. Barbara McPhee had cataloged the entire town and its rich history, assembling a thorough retelling, highlighting Berlin's long incorporation. Old photos showcased farmhouses in black and white, on land like Old Farms Place before *any* houses were built. More modern pictures surrounded these, a lot from the mid '80s, a bittersweet spot for me, my recollection all pastel legwarmers and feathered haircuts. There were few people in the photos, or if there were they were not the focal point. Instead the camera's eye fixed on buildings, homes, gas stations, the progress charted.

The old woman returned with a pitcher of iced tea and glasses, setting them behind us on a tray next to a blocky old phone with a rotary dial. I pointed at the walls. "I didn't know you were a photographer."

"Not me," she said. "My son, Daniel." The name fell from her mouth like a rock sinking to depths irretrievable. "We thought he was going to have a real future at the paper."

"Paper?"

"*The Courant.*"

The Hartford Courant was Central Connecticut's biggest newspaper.

Barbara McPhee shook her head, somber. "My son never bounced back when the paper let him go."

"I didn't know Danny worked for a newspaper."

"He was older than you boys." She turned to the time capsule on the wall. "Danny loved to take his pictures. Loved to restore old ones, as well."

"Where is Danny now?" I regretted my lack of tact. For all I knew her son was still in prison. Or he could be dead, drug overdose or cancer, another victim of Berlin's underground burning dump. I hadn't thought much of the guy over the years.

Barbara McPhee didn't ignore my question. But she didn't rush to answer either. Her body language told me wherever Danny McPhee ended up it wasn't good.

"Danny's living in a motel on the Turnpike," she said. "We don't speak much unless he's asking for money."

Anyone living on the Berlin Turnpike has fallen on hard times, and the only people Danny's age asking their mother for money is a drug addict. How awful for a mother to be saddled with a son like that.

"I was wondering," I said, "if you knew where I could find your niece, Mel? Melissa." Facebook listed her home as "The World." Real helpful, Mel.

"You know my niece. Off on another adventure. Rio, I think."

"Rio de Janeiro?"

The old woman skittered out of the room, returning a moment later with a postcard. "Melissa knows I'm not much for computers so she always sends me postcards on her travels. This one is postmarked a month ago. Isn't that lovely?"

"What is she doing? For work?" When she's not doing inconceivable handstands at the beach, I wanted to add. I studied the postcard. South America. So not SoCal. I felt a little better, less shunned. No return address.

"My niece is always switching careers. I can't keep up! The last job she had she was doing stunts."

"Stunts?"

"For the movies." Barbara McPhee beamed. "One of those superhero ones. I can't remember the name. But it was very popular." Her expression turned troubled. "It's dangerous, that work. She injured her ankle."

Barbara McPhee ran down the long list of films Mel had been in, none of which she could name, but given context clues, if the old woman wasn't padding a resume, it was impressive, to say the least. Mel had doubled for several A-list actresses, a who's-who hit list. Hardly a shock. Mel had always been destined for greatness. Anything she attempted she'd conquer. I was happy for my … friend? Ex-girlfriend? Neighbor? Fuck buddy? It also saddened me too, because it meant she *had* been in California and never looked me up. Any success I enjoyed? Left in the dust.

I studied the postcard again. Mel didn't seem too hobbled.

"I think she may be receiving worker's comp." The old woman smiled. "Not that a stunt person earns as much as a famous writer like you!"

I winced a noncommittal grin.

"Do you have her number?"

"She *never* calls. But she does write from time to time." Barbara McPhee scribbled on a piece of paper. Given that the old woman belonged to a different generation, I expected her to pass along an international address. I was dreading having to schlep down to the post office to fill out a customs form for South America, and then wait for the six-week turnaround time. That was if Mel even wrote back, which was no guarantee.

Instead, Barbara McPhee gave me her niece's email.

CHAPTER TEN

Returning from Barbara McPhee's house, I crafted a short, tasteful (i.e., not at all needy) message to Mel. A writer, I had the tendency to (spoiler alert) over-share. I reeled back enthusiasm, quashing lingering romantics feelings and sticking to the mild, inquisitive satisfaction of reaching out to an old friend. I didn't mention the Twins or my books; however, my email signature did supply a link to my website, which listed my vast collection of published works, should one be so inclined.

After the email, I poured a glass of white wine, though I preferred red: it was all I had in the house. I wasn't up for a liquor store run.

I was hunkering down to do some serious writing.

Not many authors can admit to the hubristic allure of the job. It was an occupational hazard, playing god, making people do what you want them to, insulating yourself from the hurt and pain of the real world. Writing is a form of insanity.

Revisiting regional histories of violence, such as the Donna Lee Bakery Murders in neighboring New Britain circa 1974, I cribbed notes as I prepared to dive into the meat of the subject matter: the illusion of safety. Part of what allowed Berlin to survive the abduction: the Rodgers Twins weren't taken from our town; they went missing from Meriden. Meaning, the perpetrators could've come from anywhere. Believing this was a form of willful ignorance. Victims usually know their abductors. Random nabbings are, statistically, rare. My gut, which I trusted, also told me the Rodgers Twins knew their captor(s). Facts backed this up. No one had seen a struggle in the parking lot; no one heard a scream.

Without bodies recovered, no one could say whether sexual assault was a factor. I hated thinking anyone could be guilty of such atrocities, especially someone from my hometown. Just because I didn't like it didn't mean I couldn't—and shouldn't—allow for the possibility. That line from *Silence of the Lambs* echoed in my mind, how we covet what we see every day. A convicted criminal had been living on our block.

When I put Danny McPhee's name in the search engine, I was hopeful it would lead to an area of interest, a starting point, which would allow me to scribble down a few words.

I found so much more.

Evening gloam settled over the countryside, a comforting cloak of autumn and darkness.

The bell rang.

My friend Jim Case stood outside, eyeing me tiptoed through the transom. How did all these people find me?

"How'd you know where I was living?" I asked, opening the door.

"You told us that night at Sliders."

"No, I didn't."

"Yeah. You did." He twisted around me to get a better view. "You okay, buddy?"

"Of course. Why would you ask that?"

"One, you look drunk. Two, your place reeks of a college dorm. Where's the milk crate end table?"

"Funny. I'm not drunk. I had a couple glasses of wine." I didn't mention two was four, or the half a six-pack that followed, including the ill-advised trip to the liquor store down the road to pick up said six-pack. I wasn't drunk; I was engrossed. "I'm writing."

Pulling Jim inside, I checked up and down the street before closing the door and locking it. Any time I started a mystery, I began adopting the characteristics of my characters. Think method acting, but with writing. Like an actor, I had to inhabit the skins of my subjects. For instance, when I was writing my mystery series about the sad, alcoholic mountain man in the cold winter months, I'd start wearing a knit cap indoors, stop shaving, and drink a lot of small-batch, handcrafted IPAs. Now I was thinking like a murderer.

Jim continued scouring my place, shaking his head in disapproval. It *was* a mess. Printed-out sheets strewn, various tidbits culled from the internet. Add the empty bottles and overall disheveled-ness, the absence of décor—my house embraced a definite mad scientist aesthetic.

"Buddy," he said, "you need to shave. You look like a bum."

"Screw you. You want a beer?"

"Nah," Jim said, still treading tenuous for some reason.

"I'm glad you're here." I was anxious to share what I'd uncovered. "You remember Danny McPhee?"

"Nope."

"Sure you do. He was a few years older than us. Would've graduated high school before we were freshman."

"Buddy," Jim said. "You need to start unpacking. When you start teaching?"

"I don't." I waved him off. "No job. Adjunct. Funding. Sit down."

"Wait—what happened?"

"Sit," I repeated, more heated.

"Where?" Jim made a show of panning around. "There's nowhere *to* sit."

I pointed at the arm of the sofa, cushions cluttered with cardboard boxes vomiting clothes; I'd been using the space for a makeshift dresser. I scurried to collect my research notes at the computer, searching for one page in particular that I could not find.

"Buddy—"

"Got it!" I said. "Guess who was arrested for rape in 1986?"

"I don't know what you're—"

"It was something his mother said to me—"

"Whose mother?"

"Danny's. Danny McPhee. Melissa McPhee's cousin."

At mention of Mel's name, Jim's eyebrows twitched, and he was unable to hide the smirk. Every boy remembered Mel McPhee once she got to college.

"Danny did yard work for us the summer Annabelle and Ava went missing."

I filled Jim in on the recent turn of events, visiting Barbara McPhee, fleshing out the loss of a job I never had, my decision to follow my gut and ignore everyone's advice about not writing the new book.

"I'll take that beer," Jim said.

I headed to the kitchen, talking over my shoulder. "It was when his mom mentioned Danny working for the *Courant*. I started thinking. Newspaper? Who might be interviewing kids at a mall? Maybe a reporter?"

"I thought you'd decided not to write that book," Jim said, meeting me halfway to retrieve his beer.

"I never said that. You and Ron were upset."

Jim studied the label. "Ghost in the Machine? What the hell is this?"

"Handcrafted IPA. Small-batch."

"You're too good now for Michelob or Stella?" Jim popped the tab. "What happened with the teaching?"

"I told you. Job fell through. Hazuka called. CCSU is going the adjunct route."

"There's other schools."

"Yeah, there are, Jim. And there are hundreds of writers like me applying for those jobs. They have teaching experience. I don't. I haven't held a regular job since when? Sherri Cup in high school? I'm not getting a job in a factory."

"Can't you keep doing the writing thing?"

"I am! What do you think I'm talking about?"

"I don't mean the Rodgers Twins." Jim looked pained. "I'm talking mysteries."

"This *is* a mystery."

"I meant *fiction*. Write about that handyman on the mountain. What's his name?"

"The series ended."

"If you need money—"

"I have plenty of money. I need purpose."

Resigned, Jim downed a long swallow, waggling his fingers, an invitation to share. I tried to hand him my print out, but he shook me off. "Just tell me." So I laid my *Silence of the Lambs* theory on him. How we covet what we see.

"Danny was around a lot that summer," I said. "We were always at my house. You, me, Jack, Ron. Tracy Bartlett. The Twins."

"I don't remember the guy."

"There were three houses on the street, Jim. He lived in the first one. After I spoke with his mother, I started remembering more." That's how the brain works—it's a muscle like any other. Stretch it out and it works better, this begets that. "There was this one day in particular. We were all in my backyard pool. Annabelle, Tracy, Ava too." I paused. "In their bikinis. And they were beautiful."

"Dude, they were fifteen."

"That's my point. So were we! We were fifteen." With the September birthday, I wasn't quite as old. But close enough. "We can say they were beautiful. We were the same age! That is normal. Natural. Danny McPhee was, what? Twenty-three, -four?"

"I told you. I don't remember the guy—"

"Yes, you do! He was my neighbor. He mowed our lawn! There was one day that summer... The girls were sunbathing. Danny was trimming hedges. I remember looking up and seeing him there, smoking a cigarette, leering. It was predatory."

"Okay," Jim said, finishing his beer, heading into the kitchen for another without asking. "That's your big theory. Some old guy, who I don't know, saw fifteen-year-old girls in bikinis and abducted them." Jim tried to scoff but no sound came out. "And this Danny worked for the paper, so *obviously* he was the tape recorder man."

"Follow me." I headed to the computer. "The *Courant* ran a series later that summer about kids and the mall, how it was the new teenage hotspot, a suburban *Saturday Night Fever* exposé."

Jim peered past my shoulder, reading the byline. "I don't see Danny McPhee's name."

"He was an intern. Un-credited. Whatever."

"You talk to the paper?"

"And ask them what? If an intern, thirty-five years ago, was at the Meriden Square on a random weekday in July?"

I knew my pervy neighbor eyeing my fifteen-year-old crush carried little weight, regardless of temporary occupations. But I'd uncovered something far juicier and incriminating.

I pulled up the bookmark. "Read."

Didn't take long.

"Holy shit," Jim said.

"Kidnapping and rape. Girl was the same age as Annabelle and Ava."

"When was he arrested?"

"January following year. Here, look at this." I pulled up another, more detailed piece chronicling Danny McPhee's unfathomable crime, stepping away to let Jim absorb it. I didn't need to revisit the horrific details. The once was enough.

Shortly after the Twins disappeared, Danny McPhee, my former neighbor who bagged grass clippings the summer of '85, had been arrested for kidnapping and raping another teenage girl, a sixteen-year-old snatched from another Connecticut mall. Despite writing crime fiction, which covers all sorts of sordid material, I'd never been comfortable with graphic descriptions of sexual assaults. And when these crimes involve minors, I can't even summarize. The case is easy to find on the web. Look it up. I am not going to rehash it. Except to say, finding out about Danny's arrest and the horrific nature of his crime had taken me less than eight hours, with nothing but curiosity and working Wi-Fi. Why hadn't the police been able to do the same?

When Jim finished reading, the color drained from his face; he stood, pallid and wan. I thought he might throw up. Unlike me, the author of that particular piece had no such trepidation when it came to sharing gratuitous and graphic specifics.

"What did I just read?" Jim asked.

"The story of a monster."

"And he's walking free?"

"According to his mother, he's living somewhere on the Berlin Turnpike. No idea when they let him out."

Jim stared at the computer, before turning back to me, then out the window, nodding into the night. "Guy's an ex-con. Has a record. He'd be the first one they interrogate."

"Tell that to the two girls who went missing in Avon."

"You think Danny had something to do with that?"

"I don't know. I'm not a cop. But doesn't seem that far-fetched. Annabelle, Ava—this girl." To protect anonymity they obviously didn't divulge this girl's identity.

"You up for taking a ride?"

CHAPTER ELEVEN

When I was in grad school, I dabbled in poetry, a colossal waste of time. If fiction was a one-way ticket to disappointment, what did that say about poetry? The two saddest places on Earth: Greyhound bus stations and poetry readings. No one cares about poetry readings except other poets. Anyway, I once wrote a poem, "Ballad of a Waitress at the Olympia Diner," which won a prize in some literary contest. A couple hundred bucks. Which is more money than most poets see in a lifetime.

In the past thirty-odd years, I'd been to the Olympia Diner half a dozen times. When I used to fly back from San Francisco, I'd stop in, for old time's sake. I hadn't eaten there in ten years. Now I was making my second visit in as many days.

As we waited for one of Berlin's finest, Jim clouded his coffee, adding enough sugar to make the spoon stand up, while I reflected on the symbiotic relationship between life and art.

In my mystery series, my hero and his best buddy often met at the Olympia, albeit with the name tweaked. That's the fun of fiction. You get to make up stuff. In a way I was still playing make-believe, inserting characters into my drama. I could've picked another restaurant to meet Wayne Wright, who sounded less enthusiastic about getting together this time. In my books, it was always snowing when these Olympia

Diner meetings took place. I wanted teeth chattering subzero sinking to the marrow. Reality was Connecticut never got that cold.

The same highways I wrote about were alive tonight. Plenty of cheap motels on the Turnpike, too. But this scene wasn't artistic rendering. No hobos trudged through weeds with death in their eyes, even if Springsteen still provided the soundtrack—this was the East Coast after all; it's hard to be in a dinette and not imagine a few ghosts—but gone were the overtures of oppression. Tom Joad wasn't marching alongside a caravan, searching for aqueducts to bathe in; no one would die stoic in a factory tonight. If anything the picture out the window was downright pleasant.

As with most affluent towns, gentrification had taken over. Shinier shops, newer cars, more money, upscale chain franchises dedicated to appreciating property values. Berlin was by and large blue collar, but it was upper-crust blue collar, a town where hard work could still net a four-bed, three-bath McMansion in a charming community for a third of a million, which in modern-day America spelled a bargain.

A glossy black and white pulled in the lot, and soon Wayne Wright bulled through the front door. Noticing Jim and I right away, he charged down the aisle toward our corner booth. If I'd been entertaining notions his brusque demeanor on the phone was oversensitivity on my part—maybe he was busy?—the scowl told me I was right the first time: he looked pissed.

Wayne dropped beside Jim, grumbling something that may've passed for a quick hello as he stripped off his windbreaker, before turning to me.

"What you want?" he said. "I don't have a lot of time for lunch."

"It's ten p.m."

"Lunch for me."

Which I interpreted as hurry the fuck up. I would've preferred to ease into the conversation, the mood too tense. Jim shifted, uncomfortable. You'd think guys who'd gone to school together in a small town might first exchange a few pleasantries. "How's the family? Wife? Kids?" Then again, I had nothing to add to that conversation.

"I was poking around the web today," I said. "Research. For the book."

"The Rodgers Twins. Yeah, I remember. What about it?"

"Danny McPhee."

"Danny McPhee," Wayne repeated, as if I'd pointed out the difference between cumulous and stratus clouds or the benefit of using butter over margarine for certain types of cookies.

"For one," I started, perturbed to have to be spelling this out for a cop. "He was arrested for the kidnapping and rape of another girl, same age as Annabelle and Ava. Taken from another mall—"

"Aware—"

"And before that arrest he worked for the *Courant*. Perfect job for a guy seen by a dozen witnesses with a tape recorder at the Meriden Square."

A waitress came for Wayne's order. Given the odd hour, I was all set with coffee. Jim asked if I'd share a plate of fries. I said sure because I could tell he really wanted them but I still had no appetite. Wayne asked for a burger, to go.

"Not sure why you're telling me this," Wayne said after the waitress left. The other day he'd been gung-ho to be in a novel. Today? An inconvenience.

"Danny McPhee is out of prison," I said. "He has a prior conviction for an identical crime. Now two more girls from Avon have gone missing."

"Copycat?" Wayne shook his head, voice dripping incredulous. "You can't be serious—"

"Forget Avon." Although I failed to see how similar priors could be so easily dismissed. "Stick with Annabelle and Ava. Why wasn't Danny McPhee considered a suspect?"

Wayne panned between Jim and me. "This is for that book you plan on writing?"

"Yes. It's all research at this point—why doesn't any of this faze you?"

"McPhee? Because this isn't new information?" He rubbed a hand over his bald head. "Was Detective St. Jean able to help you?"

"No. To be honest, he seemed aggravated."

"You were smart not to bother him again," Wayne said. "You'd have ticked him off even more. If you're hoping to win favors from authorities, I wouldn't approach it like this."

"Like what?"

"Like you can solve a case the police couldn't."

"I didn't claim I could."

"St. Jean said you were aggressive, smug, acting like a big-city hotshot know-it-all." He waited. "I see his point."

I glanced at Jim, whose expression bordered between empathy and I-told-you-so. I tried to recall anything offensive I might've said to the Hartford detective. What had been interpreted as egotistical? Arrogant? Why didn't anyone share the same sense of urgency?

The waitress brought Jim's fries and Wayne's boxed burger.

I started ticking off all the reasons I was right and they, the police, were wrong. "A thirty-five-year-old cold case has been reopened. Danny McPhee, a known child molester and rapist—and *my neighbor* the summer of 1985—who frequently spied on Annabelle and Ava Rodgers sunbathing at my house—has been released from prison. That makes *five* girls, all the same age, each abducted from a mall."

Nothing.

I wished I'd saved one finger.

Wayne Wright leaned back with an irritated groan, dragging his burger closer, signaling he was done. "After the Rodgers Twins went missing—and remember I'm the same age as you—this all comes via archives available on the web—the police visited Danny. They grilled him. They ruled him out."

"How could they 'rule him out'?" This was 1985. DNA wasn't as prevalent, if it was used at all. I didn't have the greatest timeline on the scientific advancement but knew genetic testing was in its infancy.

"Guys," Wayne said, "this is a detective's job. Homicides, kidnapping, sexual assault. Leave it to the professionals."

I folded my arms and settled back.

Wayne rolled his eyes and groaned. "Danny McPhee had an alibi for the day the girls went missing. He was doing yard work for Ronald Martinelli, president of Webster Bank."

"It's easy enough to slip off," I said. Meriden Square wasn't *that* far away. "No one is sitting outside for hours watching someone ride a lawnmower."

"That day someone was," Wayne said. "Linda Martinelli, Ronald's wife. Who was interviewed. It was hot. She was lounging by the pool. She said Danny was there the whole time, going so far as to describe how he looked with his shirt off."

"Anyone been back to reinterview Linda Martinelli?" Jim asked.

"Died in 1998."

Wayne rose and slipped out a couple bills. "I'm trying to be nice here, guys." He caught me dead in the eye. "I know in your line of work, everything has to make sense. Motive, twists, red herrings—"

My eyes went wide.

"I took Mrs. Virostek's English class too. The real world isn't always so neat. Cases don't connect just because you want them to. Sometimes people go missing. Sometimes they don't get found." Wayne slid on his windbreaker. "If you want to make the details suit your vision, stick to fiction."

CHAPTER TWELVE

When we got out to the car, I sat behind the wheel, letting the engine idle while I stewed. Jim, who hadn't uttered a word in my defense, sat beside me in the passenger seat. Under a streetlamp, the bright light cast a white-hot accusation. Wayne Wright's response, like Gary St. Jean's, stung and disturbed. My ex-classmate had been so gracious and accommodating the other day. Why the about face? The mood swing was palpable. Despite his silence, Jim had witnessed the same hostile dismissal.

"That was weird, eh?" I said.

"What do you mean?"

"How Wayne brushed it all off? Danny's involvement?"

"Buddy," Jim said. "He told you Danny *wasn't* involved."

"Right. But that story—didn't it sound ... strange ... to you?"

"His explanation? If Danny had an alibi..." Jim trailed off. "I don't know why Linda Martinelli, wife of a bank president, is lying for some lowlife."

"I don't either. But Danny *is* a lowlife. And you read that article, the charges, the prison sentence. It's all too similar."

"Don't take this the wrong way, buddy. But I don't think you're seeing this for what it is. This isn't one of your stories. There doesn't have to be some angle or plot twist."

"You up for another ride?"

Jim made a show of staring at the clock. "It's almost eleven."

I knew what time it was. I hadn't been sleeping much.

"I have to work tomorrow," he said. "I don't get to make my own schedule."

I didn't respond to the dig. Even if it pissed me off. People always assumed being a writer meant sitting on my ass and squeezing out a book when I was bored. My annoyed expression must've caught his attention.

"Where you thinking of driving?"

"Up the Turnpike. Check out some motels."

Jim turned to face me, squirreling an eye. "Because Danny McPhee lives in one of them? You know how many seedy motels are on the Berlin Turnpike?"

I realized how stupid my suggestion was.

"You know I've read everything you've written," he said.

"Yes, thank you—"

"I'm not telling you that for a pat on the back. Buddy, this isn't one of your books. You can't go investigating anything. You don't have a license. In real life, you visit an ex-con like Danny McPhee—even if you *could* find him—and start asking questions about the Twins, he's liable to stab you."

"I think *you* might be the one caught up in fiction."

"Whatever, man, then he'll kick your ass."

"I can handle myself."

"In a fistfight? How old are you? No one gets in fistfights at our age."

"And Danny's even older. He'd be, what, fifty-seven, -eight?"

"So then he shoots you. Or cracks your skull with a blunt object. Or maybe he doesn't do any of those things. Maybe he just calls the cops on you for harassment." Jim panned over. "What's this really about?"

"I told you. My next book will be a true crime novel—"

"I'm not talking about your back-jacket blurb to your agent or whatever. I'm asking why you care so much. Because I'll tell you what I think. This isn't about a couple girls you knew thirty-five years ago for a few months. And it's not about this town."

"No? Okay, enlighten me. What's it about?"

"Jack."

Some shots fired in the dark can still hit their mark.

"I think you feel bad for what happened to him."

"He got cancer."

"And did you come to the funeral?"

"I lived three thousand miles away. I was hanging on to the threads of a failing marriage—"

"I'm not trying to make you feel bad. I'm trying to make you feel better."

"By reminding me I didn't attend my friend's funeral?"

"No," Jim said, "by reminding you that you didn't do anything wrong. Jack's hardships in life had nothing to do with you. He had it rough. You saw Jack and his stepfather at the mall. You told the police the truth."

"I was wrong. Jack was at baseball practice."

"An honest mistake. Jack's life was a hot mess long before the Meriden Square."

"Jack didn't need the aggravation. His reputation was already shit."

"Not your fault," Jim repeated. "His stepfather, Kurt, was an abusive asshole. And nothing you find out about those girls is changing that or bringing Jack back." Jim reached over and grabbed my shoulder in a show of brotherly affection that made me want to cry.

I turned away to look out the window. The lit-up nightscape of the Turnpike shone so bright my eyes started to water. "Can you do me a favor?"

"Of course, buddy."

"It involves your job. You're right. I don't know where Danny lives. But he's on this Turnpike. And I know he still calls his mom."

"I can't trace a cell phone."

"The woman is ancient. Old-fashioned landline, pea-green puke, rotary dial."

"You want me to look up records to get an address?" Jim shook his head. "If it's a landline… I can't do anything with cell phones. That's towers. Different ballgame."

"Danny calls asking for money. He doesn't own a cell. He's using the phone in his room. Or the motel office."

Jim chewed his lip. I knew he was trying to save me from myself. What was I going to do once I got the address? Follow Danny McPhee around in a trench coat until he let his confession slip during an elaborate monologue?

"Okay," Jim said. "Give me a few."

After dropping him back at his car, I drove around my hometown, radio on, observing all the changes, subtle and profound, wishing I had a son so I could tousle his hair and tell him to take a good look around. I had no heritage or history to share, no biological creation to carry my bloodline into the future. This ended with me. I had my books. Yeah, I was absolved all right.

The night remained warmed over, but you could feel the pull in the air, one season desperate to remain vital, the other kicking at the door to be let in. Change was inevitable. I couldn't bring myself to go home, where I'd be by myself, uninterrupted, alone. Normally I relished solitude. Thrived on it. Since coming home, I'd found my own company severely lacking. I couldn't deal with people. I didn't want to be alone. I tried to recall the last real meal I'd eaten. I was like a rabbit, subsisting on a fistful of nuts and seeds, the sporadic chalky sports bar. I could feel pounds melting off, and not in a good way. Unlike most, I enjoyed being on the bigger side. Not fat, sturdy. I'd grown up envying Uncle Iver, who was no slouch. I'd always felt small around him. Iver was six-four, two-forty, which rendered my three inches and twenty pounds fewer a personal shortcoming.

At that moment, I needed family. I hopped on the highway, driving toward New Britain to see my uncle. Though it was late, I knew he'd still be up. My uncle never married, no kids, outside of the surrogate one in me. He burned the midnight oil.

I hadn't visited him often enough to know his address off the top of my head. I knew the general vicinity and street. I was pulling up his contact information when my eyes settled on the Amber alert still frozen on my screen, the Avon kidnapping from a few days ago. And it depressed the hell out of me. Even though Gary St. Jean and Wayne Wright had insisted there was no connection between the two abductions, I knew as sure as I was still living and breathing Danny McPhee was somehow involved.

Unlocking the screen to scroll for my uncle's address, I saw I'd missed a text from Jim.

Danny McPhee was living at the America Inn.

CHAPTER THIRTEEN

The America Inn, a scuzzy single room occupancy motel, crowned the Berlin Turnpike before the major interstates diverted traffic to important cities like Hartford and Springfield. The complex sprawled grander than you'd think for a motel of its ilk, which housed the less desirable elements of society. From a distance, the layout made the place seem majestic, like a hunting lodge or gun superstore in Colorado.

I pulled up Danny's Facebook page—yes, the guy had a profile. I had five thousand friends—I was a public figure—Danny had sixty-seven. We had two friends in common. His cousin Melissa, however, was not one of them. And I didn't recognize the other two names. The account was private, no personal info. I wasn't sending a friend request to a convicted child molester. At least the thumbnail picture reminded me who I was looking for. Although time had exacted a heavy toll. Gaunt face like cracked old leather, Danny had those same intense eyes. What struck me most was how shaky the guy looked. Instead of a rabid Doberman frothing at the mouth, going in for the kill, which was my childhood recollection, this new version screamed old ex-con pervert, a pickled alcoholic, Harry Dean Stanton on a bad day.

Late at night, there weren't many cars in the expansive parking lot, which I cruised, checking for white sports utility vehicles with state license plates showcasing a B, 4, and 7 combo, the partial listed in the Amber alert. No vehicles fit the bill. No surprise. If you could afford higher end SUVs, you wouldn't be living at the America Inn. Furthermore, only an idiot would be driving around in the same car he'd used to abduct the girls. That voice kept chirping in my ear that I was the idiot for even being here. The police had already ruled the two cases, the Avon Sisters and the Rodgers Twins, weren't connected. They'd also said Danny didn't have anything to do with Annabelle and Ava going missing, period.

They were wrong.

If the police weren't going to avenge the Twins, I sure as fuck would.

And I felt a wave of dignity over that internal declaration. This was honorable. I should've been feeling some righteous indignation, right? Instead: a panic attack.

I got them all the time—I often saddled characters in my books with the affliction, because I knew the sensation so well. They'd come on without warning or reason, knocking at my door, an uninvited guest, eating all my food, making a mess of the place, showing no intention of leaving. You can't talk yourself out of a panic attack; and if I had a dime for every time someone would tell me to "breathe" during one of these attacks I'd have punched a lot of people in the face. One thing works: Valium.

I did not, however, have any Valium with me, which left the far less desirable option, Plan B: ride it out. There was a third option, alcohol. I'd gotten away with a bad decision the other night after Sliders. I didn't feel like tempting fate again.

It had been years—well over a decade—since I smoked cigarettes. Suddenly I found myself in dire need of one. I could taste that cool Laramie burn with the first inhale, thick tar coating my lungs and un-fogging my brain.

There was a gas station next door. I told myself it was fine, that a cigarette would quell the anxiety—all my detective heroes smoked.

Shocked at the price of a pack of Camels, I plunked down the ten spot, rushing outside to fire one up. I inhaled hard and waited for the calm to cascade.

Instead I almost vomited.

How had I smoked for twenty years? These things tasted like shit. If I'd eaten anything substantial of late, I would've spilled my guts all over the gravel. Instead my gag reflex evoked a dry heave as blood filled my face, capillaries overstuffed and about to burst. The coughing fit wouldn't abate. I was doubled over, mouth opened as wide as jaw bones would allow, a demon-like wail emanating from the bowels of my soul, which invited a disdainful stare from the housewife fueling up her hybrid. Given our proximity to the motel, she probably thought I was another bum with the delirium tremens.

The first raindrop plopped from the heavens, hitting the gasoline-saturated asphalt with a chemical sizzle, a pissed-off god casting judgment on my sins.

I was turning to rush back to my car when I saw him.

A man like Danny McPhee gives himself away by more than visage or countenance. I could tell it was him by the way his shoulders rounded, the slacked posture of a pedophile, forever scourged and shamed. I didn't know whether the rumors of inmate justice against his kind were true. One could only imagine the retribution he'd invite.

I was surprised to see Danny get into a car. There was no reason why Danny *wouldn't* be driving—it's not like voting; your right to operate a motor vehicle isn't stripped because you've been convicted of a crime. It wasn't a white car. It wasn't an SUV. It was a rusted gray '90s-era Civic, which last I checked was among the more popular cars to hotwire and steal.

He drove right by me, without giving me a second glance, before heading south on the Turnpike, toward Berlin.

The skies opened in earnest. I ran for my life, hacking up half a lung, hopping in my ride. Two days ago the last thing I thought I'd be doing was tailing Danny McPhee from a skid row motel at midnight. He was up to no good. Anyone out after midnight is up to no good. People don't change. I didn't expect him to lead me to the Avon Sisters, and I didn't think he'd head to a storage unit where he kept trophies of all the awful things he'd done to Annabelle and Ava. But I also didn't expect to be smoking again, let alone in my new car. Yet here we were. Because after that coughing fit subsided, I lit up another. It was good to have something to do with my hands, and bad habits are good friends when they return to roost.

The wipers were on full blast but did little to guide safe passage, the heavens dumping buckets as I tooled south on the Turnpike, past what they considered Mexican food on the East Coast, the old record shops turned spas, parts of my youth forever stripped and perverted.

Unlike the West Coast, where traffic halts to a standstill with the introduction of the slightest precipitation, East Coast drivers are more adept at navigating nastier conditions. Danny sped at a good clip. Half my life had been spent on the softer, gentler coast. Aggressive skills returned fast enough. Soon I was laying on the horn, flipping people off, and shouting profanity like the old days.

I kept a comfortable distance and a constant eye on my target. Back to chain-smoking, like a day hadn't passed, throat on fire, I felt like my amateur detective I'd spent years crafting, my hardscrabble, hard-luck antihero built on equal parts Rocky Balboa and Bruce Springsteen lyrics.

Given Danny McPhee's history and despicable nature, I wagered we were either headed for some lowlife bar where he'd sit alone trying to kill whatever brain cells remained, or we were on our way to a drug dealer. Same end, different means. Though if the latter, we'd be heading in the opposite direction; the North End of Hartford was where they sold that shit. Instead we continued south, past the new Stew Leonard's and Olympia Diner. For a moment I thought Danny was going to visit Mom.

Instead, he got off at my exit, heading toward my house.

The rain didn't let up, sheets slashing through the brake- and headlights, shimmering sheens of gasoline. Unhinged thoughts flashed in my head. Danny had heard I was looking for him and was coming to confront me. Then he drove by my house. I couldn't imagine where he was going. Unless he'd spotted the tail. Which I had a hard time believing—I wasn't riding his bumper, trailing a good quarter-mile behind. There weren't many routes around here, unless he planned to hop on the Turnpike, which wouldn't explain why he'd gotten off in the first place.

Where are you going, Danny?

Then he slowed down and hooked a hard right, and I realized his destination.

A small cemetery cropped a small hill. I'd forgotten it even existed because no one I knew was buried there, my mother cremated, her ashes in a silver heart I had yet to display. I debated whether to follow Danny into the courtyard in the rain, deciding it would be too conspicuous. I killed the lights, gliding to the side of the road.

The rain was relentless. I didn't have an umbrella with me. Rain is such a rarity in the Bay Area that it never crossed my mind to have one on hand now that I was back east. I slunk from my car, getting drenched from the downpour, keeping to the chain link, sticking to the shadows. I could just make out Danny's silhouette. He stood beside a small tombstone. What grief had struck so violently that

Danny needed to atone at this hour in the racing wind and pouring rain?

Taking a knee, he placed something at the foot of the tombstone, which he then hugged—he literally wrapped his arms around the cold, wet granite—before darting back to his car, zipping off. I walked up the small driveway, around the bend, trying to think of who might be buried here, hoping for the goldmine of a Rodgers relative. This was an offering of penance, some other clue that gave away his guilt… When I saw the pint of ochre liquid, I knew the alcohol wasn't left for any of Danny's victims.

Through the falling rain, I read the name and inscription.

On the modest headstone, etched below the birth and death dates, a simple missive:

Ken McPhee
Beloved Husband and Father
May the Road Rise Up to Meet You

CHAPTER FOURTEEN

Talk about depressing. If there was one consistent criticism about my books, and my mystery series in particular, it was that those books are depressing. And critics had a point. They *are* depressing. No, I wasn't as miserable as those books, and I didn't believe all the rants and rails I was capable of rendering through the mouth of a fictional, surly creation. Sure, I had some asshole tendencies (we're working on them in therapy). I can go from zero to sixty in point seven, screeching my brakes, careening toward the cliffs of despair in nothing flat. I didn't always have the firmest handle on reality when it came to making adjustments in real time; my worldview often got smacked upside the head. If this wasn't a true story, *no way* I write this scene. It was too goddamn pathetic.

Five minutes ago I'd watched Danny McPhee embrace his dead adoptive father's grave. Visiting a tombstone at midnight in the pouring rain didn't make him any less of a sociopath. But observing the way he'd stood there, shaky arms around the stone, the solemn reverence I felt, it moved me. Then again, it was stormy, ghastly, Danny a shadow—it's hard not to assign poetry to such moments.

The rain ebbed to showers, then drizzle, before skies wrung dry. Even as clouds parted to reveal pretty purple skies, I couldn't escape the malaise.

I started toward the side of the road, where my car sat, preparing to smoke cigarettes till my throat was raw and I was coughing again, searching for the asthma inhaler I did not have, before I drove to the liquor store to pick up another six-pack, maybe some good tequila, and go back home, where I could smoke and drink, poke around the web, and try to make sense of this crazy life.

Second sight, powers of observation—though too hippy dippy for my taste—had come through enough that I couldn't discount them entirely. There's a weird, inexplicable component to this life. If it turns out we've been living on the back of a turtle or in the Matrix all along, I won't be surprised.

I'm not sure that explains why I turned in the opposite direction of my car, up the pathway, away from the road. Maybe I was lost in thought, meandering. I don't think we need to cite the supernatural to explain how I ended up in front of my dead friend Jack Lotko's grave. For one, there weren't many cemeteries in town, and it's possible, even if I didn't consciously recall, that Jim or Ron mentioned Jack was buried here. But if Danny at his father's grave stretched the tenets of dreary metaphor, we were now standing knee deep in maudlin conceit.

As I explained to Jim, I had a lot of good reasons for not making Jack's funeral. Three thousand miles and a divorce get you a free pass for many things. But I'd been back a while, and I hadn't come to visit Jack once. When that bird chirped in my ear, I shut it up by saying I didn't know where the guy was buried. Obviously I did.

Seeing the tombstone of someone you love, knowing they are six feet in the dirt, worms crawling through eye sockets, their flesh eaten away, isn't as gruesome as it sounds. Not for me anyway. I didn't go for fairy tales or spiritualty. I wasn't going to see a robin perched on a telephone pole one afternoon, convinced my dear old friend was returning to say hi. But standing there, in the cold after-rain, I felt something. A presence. And it was warm, comforting, reassuring. I understood why Danny McPhee made the impromptu midnight trip. No one is ever really gone.

Of course I couldn't make that liquor store run—liquor stores in Connecticut closed at eight p.m. Unable to drown out the voices, I had more time to ponder. There were no similarities between Danny McPhee and me, and just because a guy stops by to see his deceased father in a wicked storm doesn't erase a lifetime of sin.

Over the years, Jack and I stayed in touch—email, text, the sporadic phone call—and I'd make a point of seeing him whenever I returned back east for a book tour. Jim and Ron always showed up at those events too, the four musketeers reuniting for cheap beer, Buffalo wings, and fried pickles at the Sliders after party. And it was always a blast. Of course I could admit part of that was I'd ascended to number one. We weren't kids anymore, Jack no longer de facto leader. My writing career had leapfrogged me to pole position. Total ego boost. Jack may not have enjoyed the financial status of Jim, Ron, or I, but he was special. Jack drank too much, fought too often, got married and divorced with the seasons, but he had that … thing. You *wanted* to be around him. Jack Lotko was a natural leader, and folks gravitated to him. Men wanted to be him, and women wanted to be with him. Beating a guy like that is near impossible, charisma a helluva drug, and that bitter, twisted, petty part of me was forever in competition. In the end I'd won. Which had me questioning whether my little fourteen-year-old brain had been conspiring all along. Nuts, I knew. And not true. I loved Jack. I would never try to hurt him. But my brain was a wormhole, and when it went dark, brother, saddle up your salamander, because we're digging deeper into the rich, pungent mulch.

Jack never held my Meriden Square accusation against me—it wasn't an accusation, just the honest testimony given by a mistaken young boy to the police. Jack provided an alibi, backed by baseball coaches and cleared by authorities. We never spoke of it. Didn't matter what I thought I saw, was *certain* I saw. The cops said he wasn't there, he wasn't there. Moreover, Jack would never hurt those girls, regardless of how big a bastard his stepdad was. I let it go. Or I thought I did.

Instead of alleviating guilt, I inherited it twofold. I'd let down Jack. I'd let down Annabelle and Ava.

I needed to see a familiar face, an ally, the one guy who'd been on my side my entire life, the only blood I had left. I'd been keeping a distance from Uncle Iver, for no reason other than fear of intimacy and a desire to isolate myself, defense mechanisms.

Darkness and despair greeted me as I set out on my quest. I hadn't been able to pick up reinforcements at the liquor store, which had closed hours ago, but I had enough alcohol sitting at home to keep me well lubricated. Add a couple of Valium to the equation and I might've been too sedated. Plus I was tired and underfed, which also messed with my equilibrium.

Uncle Iver never went to sleep before three a.m., rewatching Yankee highlights, chain-smoking; he'd get a kick out of my showing up to smoke a few with him—I'd been busting his balls since I kicked the habit. In the words of my former writing professor, Tom Hazuka: nothing rivals the glibness of the reformed smoker.

With my uncle's address now programmed in my phone, I bypassed the 9, opting for the scenic route through the charred after-hours of New Britain. The showers returned. Intermittent plinking and plunking, bursts of furious gale. Well into the witching hour, the cold autumn air pierced and penetrated the glass, taking sharper aim at my heart.

The entire drive on rain-slicked backstreets, running through this veritable cornucopia of regrets, fueled by hard liquor on an empty stomach, my brain wouldn't stop spinning, asking questions and *still* trying to solve a mystery because, ride or die, this was who I was.

The Avon Sisters—it had been four days. All they had to go on, according to the Amber alert, a generic description of a new white SUV and a partial license plate. B, 7 and 4. No one was looking at the most obvious suspect, Danny McPhee, a convicted rapist who knew both Annabelle and Ava Rodgers. No one was even *considering* the possibility the two cases were connected. Infuriating. And these numbers and letters were burned on my brain, B, 7, 4. Like a perverted game of bingo, I rearranged them as if they were a palindrome or anagram, a semordnilaps, a rebus.

I wasn't thinking well when I pulled in my uncle's driveway, thanking God for not getting pulled over. I didn't have an old high school acquaintance to give me a break this time. And I *was* wasted, shit-faced, blotto.

Rain fell harder, a light in the house switched on, my back teeth swimming as my brain fought against what my eyes saw, refusing to compute: Uncle Iver's brand new white Acura MDX, CT license plate B, 7 and 4, the SUV a spot-on match for the one suspected in the Avon Sisters abduction.

CHAPTER FIFTEEN

My entire life I could count the number of times I slept through the night on two fingers. Hair-trigger bladder. As soon as the slightest urge to urinate presented itself, I'd wake up. Almost every hour on the hour. Clockwork. I would've been more worried about prostate cancer had this condition not plagued me from my earliest memory. Plus, I drank an obscene amount of caffeine; I took my nighttime meds with a shot of espresso. Tonight, however, my delicate bladder was not a concern. For the first time since I could remember, I conked out for a full eight hours. Though this slumber, my first full REM cycle in God-knows-how-long, offered little solace. I had the strangest dreams, tormented by nightmares. In reality I knew dreams lasted a few seconds. They might *seem* like full-length feature films, but that is our perception. We experience snippets, newsreel highlights, what we are meant to see, like government propaganda from the 1940s. Given what I'd witnessed at my uncle's, the unwise alcohol mixing and barbiturate consumption, I shouldn't have been surprised the subject matter breached depressing, disturbing, distressing. I was shaken nevertheless.

There were no missing children in these dreams, nothing so obvious as jagged-toothed goblins. It should've been a carefree game of hide and seek. Instead I was lost in a forest, drawing on the old fairy tales my uncle read to me as a child. The impenetrable jungle moist with mulch, damp with decay, rot in the silt and fungi on pebbles. Indistinguishable tree branches swiped down to snatch me up. Knotted roots sought to ensnare, body-slam me to the ground, bury me forever. I was walking, carrying, dragging two large Army bags, blood stained and fetid, the burden I carried. A metaphor. My brain conflated harmless childhood games, manipulating them into persecution. Nothing chased me. But a presence lurked along the peripheral. Nameless, faceless, ominous. I knew if it caught me, it would eat me alive, feasting on innards, gorging on entrails, desert vultures descending on roadkill. I saw loved ones, past and present—my mother, Jack, Annabelle, even Melissa McPhee. I saw my ex-wife. I did not see Danny McPhee. I did not see my uncle. Which made whatever stalked me in the shadows all the more sinister.

I woke feeling hungover. I'd hightailed it out of my uncle's when the porch light switched on to race home, where I drained whatever dregs remained, beer, tequila, everything in between, ignoring the sacred tenets of order, beer before liquor, or after, or however the hell that adage went, popping pills before passing out, only to be tormented by those nightmares. Also we were going on several days (weeks?) of eating next to nothing. My body had begun revolting, self-preservation forcing itself to feed on reserves, muscle mass suckled dry for sustenance.

Choking down another protein bar, which tasted like talcum powder and dirt, I paced around my house, trying to convince myself that what I'd seen last night had also been a dream. The license plate number, make, model of the SUV in my uncle's driveway, another trick of the brain. When that didn't work, I attempted to employ logic. Why would my uncle be kidnapping young girls? Crazy! Outlandish and impossible! And that might've worked if my own brain didn't keep turning on itself, looping even crazier trivial pursuits, like how Uncle

Iver had never married, kept odd hours, spent so much time alone. Like me, Uncle Iver had his quirkier tendencies. I knew what was inside of me. Like Sherriff Lou Ford, I'd always felt a sickness, a darkness... *No that's the part where you go to create.* Quirky tendencies and sexual deviances are miles apart. *He was around that summer too.* Who wasn't? Everyone I knew was around the summer of '85, which was the problem, because the same logic I applied to assign guilt to Danny McPhee could also be slapped on my uncle or anyone else. *Except Iver never got arrested for an identical crime.* Right! Danny McPhee was a registered sex offender. My uncle's crime? He drove a white SUV, which half the people in this country did these days, and a few letters, numbers matched up. Random, rotten luck.

The knock on my door jolted my reverie, returning me to the moment. Uncle Iver stood on the porch. As he'd done last week, he was peeping in the window, beckoning me to let him in, wide smile planted on his friendly face. And I froze. My uncle had nothing to do with the disappearance of any young girls—the man was like a father to me, a man to whom I owed so much; a man I knew as well as I knew myself. But in moments like that, you aren't thinking straight. Yes, I was hungover, weakened by not eating enough. This was what happened when you deconstructed mysteries for a living: you forced imaginary pegs into fabricated squares that didn't exist. I invented narrative, adding obstacles and conflict, creating problems to solve. Good guys who do nothing wrong for boring characters make. All these swirling thoughts and images left me immobilized and looking like an idiot, as I stood there staring at my uncle, unmoved.

Iver threw up his arms, adopting an exaggerated expression of offended. I rushed to let him in, laughing it off, saying something about not having had my morning coffee.

My being a writer should've had no bearing or lasting impact on reality. I wrote about murder, kidnapping, shakedowns, sexual assault, crooked cops on the take, the deplorable behaviors of incorrigible people. These things, of course, existed in the real world too. Turn on the news, read a paper, which is where I plucked the majority of my plots. Real crimes, change the names. There was, however, no shut-off switch. When your work *is* your life, your imagination has free rein to run as wild and unhinged as it wants; and my twisted mind was sprinting to the darkest corners imaginable. I couldn't catch up and stop it.

"You okay?" Iver asked.

"I'm fine," I replied, slow and stilted.

Iver reached out to squeeze my shoulder, and I flinched. "Maybe you don't need any more coffee." And then he laughed because this was Uncle Iver.

Late-morning light lathered the living room full of white warmth, because that's the way glass responds to heat, even as the chill of autumn winds stabbed exterior walls with the knives of icy precision.

"Were you in my driveway late last night?" Iver asked.

There was no point denying. If he was asking, he knew I was.

"Yeah," I said. "Couldn't sleep."

"I came out but you were already racing off. Like a bat out of hell."

"It's rude to show up at someone's house unannounced," I said, and then realizing my uncle had done the same, added, "at that hour."

"You don't look so great," he said. "You sleeping all right?"

"Insomnia. The divorce. The move." When none of these things registered the reaction I wanted: "The job fell through." Which gave me the necessary time to get my head together while I recapped the college's decision to go with an adjunct, padding the impact it had on me, even though I'd already moved past it and was onto the next thing to worry about, namely whether my uncle was a rapist, murderer, or worse. I did not share these concerns.

Uncle Iver turned over his shoulder, glancing back out of the house. I was hoping he'd say he had to get going. I couldn't stop my rattrap brain from plotting another mystery, one where the culprit is both inevitable and a surprise, and how perfect Iver would fit the bill. His presence wasn't helping. I wanted him gone. Out of sight, out of mind—I didn't want to be thinking about any of this.

But he didn't leave. Instead Iver faced me with an expression I found impossible to read. "Without the teaching job, I guess you'll be heading back west." He winced a tight-lipped grin.

"I'm not sure of my plans."

"Gonna be hard to focus on this new book of yours, no?"

I struggled to recall whether I'd told Uncle Iver about my plans to write a true crime novel. Had I mentioned the Rodgers Twins the first morning he'd come by? I didn't think I had. I'd still been focused on the teaching job.

"Writing is *a lot* of planning," I said, keeping it noncommittal. "I have sixteen ideas about what to do next—"

"What are you going to do next? For a book? If you're not teaching, you'll go nuts sitting around, doing nothing. I know you. You need to keep busy." Iver smiled broad. "Talk to your uncle." He chuckled, mouth vacillating from smile to sneer.

He wouldn't take his eyes off me, an intense fixation that felt accusatory, although I knew that this was my perception, shaped by these little rodents in my skull, scraping with their sharp little nails.

After a quick outline, I said, "I have to get going," plucking a jacket from the floor, making a show of sliding it on and grabbing keys, wallet, moving toward the door.

Iver gripped my sleeve, face awash with parental concern. "What is going on?" He took a step closer. I froze. He slapped another hand on my shoulder, staring me in the eye, too intense, too concerned, too intimate. The last emotion I needed any more of, guilt, came flooding in.

I couldn't tell him a long stressful night had gotten the best of me. If I tried to explain my current headspace, I'd screw it up and do more harm. I had a tendency to blurt, say too much, be *too* forthright; and then I'd wake up in the middle of the night, bombarded by the embarrassment and humiliation of all the dumb things I'd ever said or done.

"Nothing," I said, slipping his grasp, moving toward the exit. "I have things to do."

Uncle Iver groaned, started to say something, then stopped.

"Don't worry about me," I said. "Go back to whatever you were doing. I'm fine."

When he didn't move, I did. But he caught me, throwing his arms around and pulling me in, hugging me tight, holding me in place and not letting me go. It was uncomfortable, but I didn't fight it, me a grown man, almost fifty years old, reduced to a small, feeble boy. I felt my body go limp, melting in my big uncle's presence. It was all I could do not to cry.

"It's okay," he said, squeezing me tight. "Life can overwhelm us all, kid."

When he released me, Uncle Iver backed away. "Let's grab lunch soon, okay? Want to talk to you about some stuff."

"Sure thing," I said.

Then he was out the door, and I bolted to close it before he had a chance to respond with obvious questions like if I meant to leave why was I staying inside and in such a rush to slam the door?

I watched him get in his white SUV and speed off.

Heading to the computer, I planned to pull up the latest on the Avon Sisters' abduction to see if there had been any movement, when I saw I had a new email.

Melissa McPhee had written back.

CHAPTER SIXTEEN

It wasn't long until the first snow of the season hit—white Christmases were rare enough, never mind white Thanksgivings. I'd arrived in the grips of a late-summer heat wave, and here we were little over a month later having to scrape off windshields and pour boiling water on sidewalks. Central Connecticut had always been a crapshoot when it comes to the severity of the seasons.

I was sitting at the Starbucks next door to Stew Leonard's, pawing at a scone out of obligation, watching flurries float. My cell buzzed. Uncle Iver. And like I'd done of late, I let the call go to voicemail. I'd been making myself scarce, focusing on writing, holed up in various coffee shops to work on my new book, suffering countless posers doing the same. If my uncle sprung a surprise visit, he was sure to just miss me. I wasn't keeping regular hours. Some nights I wouldn't even sleep at my house, driving out to the America Inn to sit in my car and chain-smoke cigarettes.

After that late night trip to Iver's when I saw his white SUV, I considered calling Wayne Wright, maybe dropping an anonymous tip on the police helpline. I wouldn't have to leave my name, just say I'd seen a car and license plate matching the vehicle used in the Avon Sisters' disappearance and supply my uncle's address in New Britain. Let the authorities take it from there. Except the first thing police do after an abduction is feed information through DMV. Any vehicles worth checking out had already been vetted. It wasn't easy but I had to put what I'd seen behind me and focus on the things I could control.

With coffee in hand and a spot in the corner secured, I got to work. Most of what I'd written was shit—first drafts always are. I'd long intended to tackle another memoir, one more sprawling and inclusive than the highly stylized first effort I'd penned about my wild years. This new memoir would encompass who I was *now*, the essence of what made me *me*. But after filling page after page with the mundane details of minutia, I realized, outside of that brief troublemaking stint, my life was duller than a suburban staycation in Boise. I didn't have the patience to describe barn houses, cow fields, or trickling criks. Likewise, stories of twelve-year-old twins arriving at McGee Middle School in the fall of 1982 failed to titillate. All that mattered was the summer of 1985.

Nothing beats the first time you fall in love. The heart is still whole, untarnished, like a pair of fresh lungs before you start inhaling acrid chemicals. You've seen the pictures. On the left, the healthy pink, nonsmoker's lungs, and on the right that monstrosity, the abomination of scarred black tissue, Darth Vader burning on the beaches of Mustafar. That's how I thought of my heart before Annabelle. Not that she was particularly cruel or mean. She didn't feel about me the same way I did about her. I was fourteen, lacking self-confidence, a weirdo artsy kid. She was a year older and beautiful, self-assured, mature, and wanted by every guy in high school. But for a few weeks in the summer of 1985, she gave me a chance. In a way, those few weeks we spent hanging out by my pool felt like an audition. I'd been given a shot. Like the Cure, if only I'd thought of the right words, I could've held onto her heart… But I didn't have those right words yet.

By the time I did she and her sister were missing, and my heart had been battered, burned like an after-lung.

That's where I cut off for the day, on the heart and lung simile. I stowed the laptop and grabbed my coffee to go, lighting a cigarette as I walked into the cold night.

I had a date to get ready for.

Due to Mel's fabulous lifestyle and hectic schedule, she said she'd only be on the East Coast "for a few days." I offered to drive down to NYC but she said she had "business" up here. I couldn't imagine what business anyone had in Berlin, especially a woman like Mel McPhee, but I was just happy she'd agreed to have dinner with me. We hadn't exactly parted on the greatest of terms.

Central Connecticut landed a long way from a culinary playground like New York City or Los Angeles. There's no shortage of pizza places and chain restaurants—Chili's, Applebee's, and TGI Fridays— but Berlin's a town where Olive Garden passes for fine dining and McDonald's is still considered food. One restaurant, however, was near and dear, the Great Taste in New Britain. I'd put it alongside the best Chinese food I ever had, including any in Chinatown. Even if I could admit some of that rating stemmed from nostalgia. I'd taken Mel there on our first date. (I'd taken a lot of girls there.)

Mel texted that her meeting in West Hartford was running late. I waited in the parking lot, less to be cordial and more because I knew the reception I'd get walking in.

Entering with Mel, the maître d' greeted me at the door with a warm, intimate handshake, as a team of waiters closed in to gladhand and ask about my latest book, a celebrity arriving on the red carpet.

This was the first time I'd seen Melissa McPhee since the '90s. Now in her forties Mel looked more radiant than ever. There's a meme going around about living one's "best life." Like most mantras based off "Live, laugh, love," I deplored it. But ten minutes into our conversation, I'd be hard pressed to find a better description.

When I talked to most folks from my hometown, I felt good about my publishing career. Next to Mel, I was relegated to junior league, a participant trophy runner-up for the Most Improved Swimmer Award. I would've said the only accomplishment lacking on Mel's resume was meeting the president. Until she dropped, with no great fanfare, a photo op with Obama, brushing it off by saying she'd "been with a group of people" and "didn't get to talk [to the former president] long."

For the past twenty-five years, Mel had traveled around the globe, stopping for extended layovers in Thailand, Bali, the Himalayas, and several other places that sounded equally awesome. After her Fulbright, Mel "did some international modeling." Most people tell you that and you roll your eyes. Except of course, who *wouldn't* want Mel to model? The woman was stunning. For a while she taught yoga, worked with Cirque du Soleil, did some acting ("nothing flashy"). There were assorted accommodations, fellowships, and residencies. After splitting a second Scorpion Bowl, I was pretty sure I was in love.

"And when I came back from Belize," Mel said, continuing a chunk of conversation I may've missed because I was stuck staring like a lovesick schoolboy, "I decided to get more into the stunt side of filmmaking." She waved a hand in front of my face. "Are you there?"

"Sorry. Thinking." Then, needing to say something, I added: "New book."

"Yes, I've read them all."

"All?"

Traditionally published, my work was readily available. But it's not like my books were stocked alongside Dan Brown and James Patterson in every Barnes and Noble around the globe.

"Hometown boy makes good," Mel said with a smile. "Why wouldn't I?"

I clamped up, biting my cheek not to ask what I wanted to.

"You want to know my favorite, don't you?" she said. "The depressing one in the snow." Mel laughed harder. It was a good joke. Most of my books were depressing and set in the snow. Mel poured us hot tea, a nice way to sober up for the drive home. For a snowy weekday night, the restaurant still bustled. "I liked your latest. The one by the lake. It reminded me of home."

"Where do you stay when you're in town," I asked, poking at fried dumplings and scallion pancakes, Capital Chicken, extra spicy with hot chilies and sautéed green beans. These exquisite foods and delectable aromas did nothing to induce hunger.

"My family has a fishing shack in Northwest Connecticut," she said.

"You stay in a fishing shack?"

"It's a bit bigger than a fishing shack, I suppose. Private lake access, cut off from civilization. Which is a nice thing to do from time to time."

"You're staying there now?" I wasn't, in any way, hinting it was getting late and the western mountains sounded like a really long drive on icy roads and, maybe, Mel would be more comfortable staying in town, at a place like, say, mine, which was just down the road…

Her wordless, blank expression put any hopes to bed.

"So tell me, Mr. Famous Author—"

"I'm far from famous—"

"What would make you move back to this little cow town? If I recall this wasn't high on your list growing up."

I explained about the job, its falling through, my decision to stick around. "Besides, I didn't hate this place as much as people keep reminding me."

"Wasn't your yearbook quote from 'Thunder Road'? 'It's a town full of losers'?"

"I wish." I wasn't going to admit what my actual quote was. Nothing says pretentious wannabe poet like obscure Pink Floyd lyrics.

"What are you working on?" she asked. "You must be knee deep in something. You creatives bounce off the wall without a direction."

"You date a lot of artists?"

"I *know* a lot of artists."

I wasn't wearing a wedding ring. "Dating" was the last thing on my mind, but I'd be lying if I said I wasn't flirting. Or trying to. Mel had been gorgeous when I knew her in college, and the years had been a friend to her.

Our waiter brought complimentary plum wine. I toasted to Dan Fogelberg and grocery stores on Christmas Eve, which might have been too obscure for most.

"Here's to hoping we don't run out of things to say," Mel said.

Tonight might work out after all...

"What is this about?" she asked, breaking the spell.

"The new book I'm working on," I said, pausing to sip the plum digestif, before casually divulging my true crime novel subject matter, as tactful as possible considering her cousin was a principal subject and the prime suspect.

Mel listened, stone-faced and unimpressed. I rooted around for details to spark curiosity and stoke flames.

"Here's an interesting fact," I said. "Sean St. Jean. Do you know who that is?" Nothing. "He's the nephew of Gary St. Jean," I added, answering myself. "He's a Hartford detective. Worked the Rodgers case, which they reopened, by the way. Anyway, Sean. He—"

"Pitched for the Phillies. A couple seasons. Long relief. Mid-'90s."

"Didn't know you were such a baseball fan."

"I'm not. He dated a friend of mine. He's from Berlin."

"That's my point. He grew up here. We always think of how no one leaves Berlin. But here we are. And there's a guy who pitched for a Major League Baseball team."

"What's with the Berlin history lessons?"

"We're talking—"

"My aunt wrote me."

"Barbara."

"I know my aunt's name. She said you were asking about Danny." Mel waited impatiently. "Why are you asking about my cousin?"

Mel McPhee had always been too smart. I could play this for a while, skirting issues, but I knew we'd only end up back here. So I told her about my meeting with Detective Gary St. Jean. Other than connecting the non sequitur about Sean playing for the Phillies, my pitch sailed high and wide. She was going to make me say it.

"Were you there that day?" I asked. "At the mall? Meriden Square? When Annabelle and Ava went missing?"

"You mean forty years ago?"

"Closer to thirty-five," I corrected.

"Why do you want to know?"

"I'm writing a book."

"Yes, you said that already. Rodgers Twins. Disappearance. Summer of '85. Let me help you out. Since you're having a tough time being upfront. Yes, Danny had driven me there that day. That's why you wanted to have dinner, right? Because of his record and arrest the next year?"

I tried to feign surprise.

"Everyone knows police questioned him. It was an embarrassment for my family. He was cleared. Please, don't drag my family through this anymore."

"That's not my intention."

"You've always had ulterior motives."

I didn't offer a defense. People always confuse knowing what you want and doing what you need to do to get it with being selfish and manipulative.

The waiter arrived to clear plates. The waft of exotic spices, sweet sauces, and MSG lingered even after he took away what was left. I hadn't made a dent in my plate, poking and nibbling to approximate a person dining. Maybe I should see a doctor.

"Did you hear what I said?" Mel asked.

"Of course." I realized I'd drifted off and missed something. Instead of asking her to repeat what she'd said, which was tantamount to admitting defeat, I held steady.

"Goddammit," she said. "You're still the same."

"Didn't realize that was such a bad thing, continuity, stability."

"It's not. Immaturity is."

Mel started to slide on her coat. I reached across the table and grabbed her wrist. Not the smartest move, given the irascible mood, forcing me to hold my hands up high in surrender as she yanked hers away, drawing attention and stares from other diners.

"Can you tell me about that day?"

"I was eight!"

"I think you were closer to nine."

"Whatever. My cousin drove me to the mall." She stopped, making sure I heard this next part, loud and clear. "Then he left. For his job at the pool. I ran into Annabelle and Ava. They let me tag along to a store or two. That's all I remember. And all I told police."

"What pool?" We had a few in town back then. "Memorial? Percival?"

"No. Gribbard. Danny handled landscaping. Mowed grass, trimmed weeds. He did yard work all over town." She tilted back her head. "He didn't have the easiest time finding work."

I remembered when they closed down the pool. "1985 was the last summer Gribbard Elementary was open." The school, pool, and baseball fields were all part of the same now-defunct complex.

"Danny was already screwing up," Mel said. "He cracked up a truck at the top of Orchard and Elton. High on drugs. Crashed through the farm field. His parents kicked him out after that. He was living at Gribbard Pool. In the shed."

"When was the last time you saw your cousin?"

"Jesus, you don't stop, do you? I don't know. Maybe seven, eight years ago? When he got out of prison."

I could see these questions touched raw nerves. I wanted to say, Forget it. Leave it be. I couldn't.

"Danny was like a big brother to me," she said. "I'm not defending him. But the story this town knows? Kidnapped a girl, held her hostage? That's not the case. It's more complicated than that."

I started to say something else, but by then Mel had gathered her jacket and purse. Before I could get out another word, she thanked me for dinner, saying it was lovely, or offering some equally empty platitude. Then she walked out of the restaurant.

After I paid the bill and collected the leftovers, I turned to make my way back home. And goddamn it, if the snow didn't turn into rain.

CHAPTER SEVENTEEN

Writing mysteries, you develop useful investigative skills. Mining assorted databases, accessing government-related social services, I confirmed Danny had been released from prison eight years ago. Meaning, he'd done close to the full twenty-five. I also learned Danny was receiving SSDI, Social Security Disability Income, a stipend unaffected by incarceration, which allowed him to work, though I couldn't imagine who would hire a degenerate like that. I wasn't sure what his "disability" was, unless being a rapist and a killer qualified as a bona fide medical condition under the new American Psychiatric Association guidelines.

The big discovery: my uncle had done more than hire Danny McPhee to mow our lawn—Iver had gotten Danny the jobs for Martinelli—and Gribbard. This was easy to confirm with a phone call to Ed Gentile Jr., who oversaw the ball fields. I went to school with Ed, whose dad Ed, Sr., was friends with Iver, and when I called to verify Danny's working there, Ed, Jr., told me about my uncle vouching for the guy. I couldn't believe it. Iver was kind and generous with his time and money, but he didn't suffer fools.

From there, local newspaper archives delivered me to one of Danny's old arrests, which put me in touch with Jill Penatore, a Berlin High alum and one of the few attorneys in town. Over coffee, I was able to coax how my uncle assisted with some of Danny's legal issues as well, including steep representation fees. Jill wasn't violating client/ attorney privilege; we were just old classmates catching up over coffee at Josie's Corner.

Uncle Iver's helping hand went above and beyond. Danny was our neighbor, not our blood. It was a minor detail. But it gnawed at me. Why go out on a limb for a stranger, a troublemaker, this hoodlum on the hill? Helping with jobs and legal costs, touting the character of a child molester?

With the connection between Danny and my uncle established, a clear line had been drawn tying the Avon Sisters to the Rodgers Twins. Still, I needed something more concrete, tangible, a piece of incontrovertible, ironclad evidence I could take to the cops. I wasn't going to solve anything in front of a computer screen. I knew I should get some sleep but my brain was firing on all cylinders. I needed to keep moving.

Firing up another cigarette, a nasty habit I'd resumed, hardcore— a dozen years without smoking, and there I was back to a pack a day—I refit my wool cap and scratched my graying beard and prepared to face the blistering, icy night. The wintery mix of December sleet and snow slanted hard. Maybe it was pointless, this needless, reckless adventure fueled by isolation, alcohol, and insomnia, the clock reading well past midnight.

The night was cold, black, windy and unforgivable, like a scene ripped straight from a thriller set in the northern New Hampshire mountains involving corrupt powers-that-be willing to go to all lengths to protect a deadly secret.

A mile into my journey, slipping and sliding on slick streets, I had to concede this wasn't my brightest idea. Sleet, wind, and brutal elements continued their assault. My lackluster appetite and heavy alcohol indulgence had left me woozy and lightheaded. I couldn't shut off my brain, couldn't stop thinking about what Mel had said that night at the restaurant.

"He was living at Gribbard Pool. In the shed."

They never demolished Gribbard Pool.

They'd shut down the elementary school, locked the gates and drained the swimming pool, happy childhood memories now a cement hole rivered with fungus. But that shed was still standing—I'd seen it the night Wayne Wright stopped me after Sliders. And tonight I was going to see what was inside.

Berlin is not a big town, with a small city center and shopping plazas linked by a couple main roads. Gribbard was isolated comparatively. Icy pellets and hail joined the sleet and snow. My tire treads struggled to gain traction. A ten-minute drive took thirty. Pulling off Chamberlin Highway, I spied the crumbling façade of the old elementary school, its adjacent weeded-over ball fields swallowed by untended blackberry bushes and thorny bramble. Then, there in the shadows: the shed.

Wheels rolling over sloppy gravel, I rang Jim but he didn't pick up. Voicemail.

"Hey, man," I said into the answering machine—which wasn't really a machine since those things died around 1985, but I was having a full-blown flashback—"I am going on a mission." I then explained my dinner with Mel, glossing over sexual tension and aggression, her throwaway detail about Danny's employment history, before telling him about my reconnaissance plans at the old Gribbard Pool.

I hung up and checked the clock. Two a.m. Of course Jim wouldn't be up—no one's up at two a.m.—he had to work in a few hours. Except he called right back.

I answered without first checking the caller ID.

"Where have you been?" my uncle demanded.

No one is up at two a.m. Except Uncle Iver.

"Oh yeah right," I said, stalling, adjusting. "Sorry about that. Been … mired in this new book…"

"I've stopped by your house several times. No one home. Call. Leave messages. You don't call back." Long pause. "I need to talk to you about something."

"Now's not the best time. I was … about to go to sleep."

"Sounds like you're driving."

"I am." I struggled to find a plausible excuse. "I'm … up … at … Gribbard Pool." I couldn't think of a suitable lie so my stupid brain blurted the truth.

"Why are you up there? At this hour? In this weather?"

The best way to lie—as a fiction writer, I lie for a living—is to infuse an element of the truth. Focus on that and you aren't lying.

I spun a plausible tale, about being back and nostalgia and not sleeping well and how sometimes when I had a new project and insomnia it helped to revisit familiar places, it soothed anxiety, quelled nerves, but I promised we'd get together soon and talk. Just not now. Because I was tired and had to go home and sleep.

"Call me tomorrow," I said.

"So you can't pick up? Nope. We're picking a time and place right now. Lunch. Noon. Great Taste."

"Sure. Sounds good."

"I know how much you love that place."

I promised I'd be there, ended the call, and parked by the bleachers of the old field, which was the spot closest to the shed. The closed school and pool were only outlines of a shadow. It was far colder out here than it had been at my house. I hadn't prepared well. Underdressed and antsy, I sat in my car a spell, smoking cigarettes and working up my nerve.

When my throat was nice and raw and my maudlin spirits manageable, I pulled my jacket collar and ducked into the blustery New England night. The nip and chill exposed body parts. With every howl and gale, my soft issue felt like it had been dipped in a bucket of dry ice, in danger of bumping against something hard and being lopped off. I considered packing up, turning around, abandoning my mission and going home. What did I think I'd find in an old concrete shed after some thirty-odd years? Decomposed bones? A map to a secret burial site? Surely, this defined a fool's errand.

The former tool shed had been incorporated into the earth, weeds wrapped around concrete, vines slithering up, intertwined in a villainous grip, a diabolical plot, dragging the structure back to the bowels of hell. Déjà vu smacked me hard. A padlock hung on the door. The shed was buried far enough in the woods that no one could see it from the road. No one was out at this hour anyway. Still, I gave a cursory glance. Then found a rock and smashed off the lock. The corroded metal cracked, rust splintering like an extra-dry red pistachio shell.

I patted down my coat, feeling for my phone. I needed a new wardrobe, my current one better suited for the chill months of autumn and not this deep freeze of winter. With my iPhone out, I pulled up the flashlight, panning the dirty floor to reveal a claustrophobic room clogged with castoff junk that hadn't been touched in ages—deflated soccer balls and old orange cones, chintzy flags for low stress relay races. Moving to the far corner, my light landed on what might have been, at one time, a cot. Walking closer, I saw that it was a bench covered with a blanket. Olive green, scratchy, military-issued. And there appeared to be a stain. Splotches of reddish brown...

Blood.

The blow rained down hard, starlight bursting behind my eyeballs, a searing flash of blazing white. Ambushed, I couldn't see who—or what—was responsible for attacking me. My phone flew out of my hand on impact, sent careening across the shed, smacking against the wall, its light extinguished. Blinded and disoriented, I spun around and instinctively put up my hands to cover my face. And not a second too soon. Something long, hard, and heavy—a metal rod or stick of lumber—found the knuckles that were cradling my ears and covering my eyes. The powerful smash left my ears ringing, rattling whatever bearings I had left. Stumbling backwards, I tripped over equipment on the floor, twisting me around, costing balance, sending me face first toward the hard ground.

Which should've cracked open my skull and spilt my brains all over the floor. But I bounced off one of those deflated soccer balls, which spared my life, even as I was left with a hell of a pounding headache. There I lay on my back, blinded, beaten, bloodied, frozen half to death. My fingers felt like grated cheese. Everything hurt and I was a dying. I couldn't think. I couldn't breathe. Every time I tried, a sharp pain seared through my abdomen, radiating shockwaves up my spinal column. My whole lumbar tightened and spasmed—throwing out my back was nothing new—but along with this gripping inability to breathe, this time I was paralyzed. In the dark, I waited for the fatal blow, knowing I'd be unable to lift my arms in defense. But it never came.

The whirring and wheezing infiltrated my mind and filled the space around me. Time ebbed. I drifted. I couldn't say whether I'd passed out or how much time elapsed before I saw the flashing police lights and a bright beam hit my eyes. I heard muttering, hollering, and then the panicked call for an ambulance.

CHAPTER EIGHTEEN

The symbiotic relationship between life and art is enigmatic, a word I don't like to use. Very little in this life, I've found, is unable to be explained. If you are smart enough and have the requisite tools, evidence, and time to examine, dissect, take apart to see how it works, you can figure it out. Yet, with art and life, such a tangled relationship can't be written off as random or happenstance. In one of the books I wrote, I had a character suffer a major injury to an obscure vein. I had never heard of this vein before writing this scene. Maybe it had come up in biology class, where it glommed onto some primordial part of my brain stem, hibernating for decades until needed, but I had no conscious awareness. I selected the vein at random after doing a Google search, trying to come up with a catastrophic injury that would be debilitating but not fatal. Random. Happenstance. Leaving it there wouldn't have been difficult. Except a year after writing that scene, my doctor told me I'd suffered an injury to that very same vein; it was back-flowing into my heart and might kill me without surgery.

Lying in the hospital bed at New Britain General Hospital following being assaulted in the dark at the Gribbard Pool shed, I couldn't help but reflect on the number of times I'd laid up my characters. I had people shot, stabbed, the living snot kicked out them. They took beatings and poundings, thrashings, and got up for more. I'd been cracked good once on the head and I'd lain there, a useless lump, gasping for air. If Wayne Wright and the Berlin PD hadn't shown up, I could've died. That's what the nurse said. The temperatures were in the high teens when they found me, and plummeting fast.

Besides the blunt head trauma, I'd also fractured a rib, which made sleeping difficult, despite the heavy dose of pain meds they pumped into my bloodstream. I'd done my share of illicit substances in my twenties. I wished I could say the Dilaudid and Fentanyl brought back happy pink clouds. I was in too much pain to relax or enjoy anything. Not that you get a moment's rest in a hospital. Every few minutes some nurse or orderly is coming by to take vitals and draw blood, measure this, reattach that. Hooked up to rows of machines, I had so many needles puncturing me, tubes and lines threading veins, draining blood, pushing assorted fluids, I felt like Neo being uploaded into the Matrix. The way the base of my skull throbbed, I was tempted to touch the back of my head to make sure no one had installed an industrial-sized bilge pump to siphon my humanity into a battery.

There was also the small matter of the police. Though a victim of assault, I had been trespassing, breaking and entering; the beating took place in the commission of a crime. When Wayne Wright closed the ambulance doors, he said to get some rest and that he would be by in the morning. Apparently, his superiors didn't share his compassion or well wishes for a good night's sleep.

Around four a.m. two men in sports coats came in. They flashed badges and introduced themselves. I nodded like I heard them or understood. But to be honest, I was borderline delirious, and I couldn't oversell the pain. No opiate is cutting through broken ribs. Worst of all, my recent smoking relapse had me coughing a fit. The only relief? A helpful tip from the nurse: whenever I had the urge to cough, I was told to grab a pillow and hug it as hard as I could to my chest to stabilize the rib. Still hurt like hell.

The two detectives, who in my head I kept referring to as Lotko and Ludko, a private joke about my high school friends Jack and Chris, who I'd once put in a book as homicide cops. Every time I thought about it, I'd giggle like a schoolgirl. I'm sure they knew I was hopped up on liquid opiates in their purest form. Still, the uncontrollable bursts of laughter made me feel like the Joker at Arkham.

They'd given me a nice room, high up, offering a clear, clean view of the frigid winter nightscape. The freezing rain and snow had stopped, Central Connecticut blanketed in fresh powder and shellacked in a shimmering sheen of ice. The high-powered hospital lights splashed down, lighting up the scene like a Christmas nativity.

I came back around to a pair of fingers snapping, recognizing I'd drifted off again. I made a promise, right there and then, vowing on my mother's grave that I would never write a novel that featured a writer as protagonist. We are only interesting to ourselves.

"Maybe we should come back later," a voice said, cutting through the haze.

A coughing fit took over. I scrambled for the pillow, squeezing it and burrowing my face.

The one detective slapped the other on the shoulder, nodding toward the door, where the night staff milled and scurried in the background.

"Get some sleep. We'll be back—"

"Before we go," the other voice said. "You take anything?"

"Huh?"

"Did. You. Take. Anything?"

"What do you mean?" I asked. "Like … drugs?"

"No, asshole. From the shed."

A new, more violent coughing fit gripped. I grabbed the pillow and clung to the inanimate object like a dying lover, coughing half a lung into the soft feathers. When I removed the pillow, it was covered in yellow splotches threaded with dark red blood.

I looked up and the detectives were gone.

I heard no footsteps beating a path down the hall, the interaction over so fast I wondered if anyone had been there at all or if I'd hallucinated it, slipping in a morphine dream.

I didn't feel like I slept much after that. I recalled closing my eyes for a second. Next thing I knew bright yellow sunlight shone, and an orderly was standing over me with my breakfast. If I wasn't hungry before, the warmed over, microwaved mush set in front of me wasn't whetting my appetite.

Still, I felt compelling to poke around, rearranging the bland, uninspiring fare, which as far as I could tell was some variation of egg. Poached, boiled? Rehydrated powder microwaved in a cup?

"Not hungry, buddy?"

I looked up to find Jim Case and Ron Lamontagne, matching bald heads glinting in the unflattering hospital overheads.

"Long time no see," Ron said.

"Busy." It's hard to explain to your oldest, dearest friends the need to isolate and duck phone calls. It happened, these times in my life where I knew I needed to be left alone. Not for my sake—for *theirs*. At times my presence could be unbearable; I had to remove myself from the situation because I could see I was irritating, grating, wearing on people's nerves. Doesn't take a psychotherapist or life coach to deduce the only consistent feature of all your dissatisfying relationships is you, a message so pertinent I had it framed and hanging over my writing desk. My ex-wife hated that picture.

"Breaking and entering?" Jim said.

"Did I make the paper?"

"*Herald* doesn't come out till the afternoon." Jim glanced out the window into the new day's light, white ice glinting in the dazzling sun. "Wayne Wright phoned this morning."

"I called you last night," I said.

"I was sleeping," Jim responded, like it was the dumbest thing he'd hear all day. "I have a job? Didn't get the message till Wayne phoned." Jim shook his head so sad and slow the pity practically dripped. "When are you going to drop this, buddy? Because I'll be honest. You look like shit."

"I got jumped and had the snot kicked out of me."

"You look like you're losing weight," Ron said. "And your skin is …"

"What?"

"Gray? Pale? Like a vampire?"

Jim tried to laugh. "You were always the best looking. Besides Jack. But you ain't winning any beauty pageants, buddy."

"Where have you been?" Ron asked.

Until last night, I hadn't called Jim or Ron in weeks, a month? They'd texted a few times, phoned once from Sliders to come down and join them for a drink. Like I'd done with my uncle, I avoided the call. I was on the hunt. I had so many pokers in the fire, questions burning my brain, story unfolding in real time; I didn't need distractions. The Rodgers Twins. The Avon Sisters. Danny. My uncle.

I wanted to confide in my friends, because I couldn't hold it in any longer. I didn't want to shoulder the burden. Why must the onus fall on me? And I was getting ready to unload it all, tell Jim and Ron about my uncle's connection to Danny McPhee, the license plate, summer jobs, legal fees, red bloody stains, what Mel had revealed on our date—date? I didn't know *what* that was—and I might have trusted my two oldest friends had my uncle not chosen to walk in at that exact moment with murder in his eyes.

CHAPTER NINETEEN

"What the hell has gotten into you?" Iver seethed. Last time I saw him this mad was when I was twelve and forgot to put the shower curtain inside the tub. Repairs to the water-damaged ceiling hadn't come cheap.

"We should get going," Jim muttered to Ron.

I tried to remember what day it was, if it was a weekend or weekday, if Jim and Ron had to beat the rat race. I did not want to be left alone with my uncle. Stupid, I knew. Not like the man would smother me with a pillow, even if he were guilty. Guilty of what? Driving a new white SUV with some common letters and numbers? We were in a hospital full of people. Still, I felt uneasy.

"No," I said to Jim. "Stay. I have to talk to you ... about something."

Jim glanced around. I could see he wanted to beat it and not get caught up in whatever this drama was between my uncle and me. But he said, "Sure, buddy." Then turning to Ron: "We'll grab a coffee and be back. Let you and your uncle have a minute."

The last thing I wanted. But knowing he was coming back soothed nerves.

After they left, the room fell silent, and that bustling ward didn't seem so bustling. Beeps and blips echoed far away down cavernous halls. I gripped my pillow.

"I'm gonna be honest," my uncle said. "You look awful."

"Rough night."

"Oh, I heard." He shook his head. That parental disapproval cuts to the bone, no matter how old you get. "I don't know what to say to you anymore. You didn't pull crap like this when you were a teenager."

"I'm writing a book—"

"Enough." Uncle Iver swished a hand through the air, dismissing my art like a passing phase.

"It's what I do."

"Writing about missing twins you had a boner for when you were twelve?" And before I could object to the crassness or insensitivity, Iver thrashed a hand again. "Save the sanctimonious commitment to your art. You're my blood, all I have left." He paused to inhale the deep regret. "Sorry for disparaging the dead—"

"Who said they were dead?"

"If they aren't, this will go down as the longest game of hide-and-seek in history." Uncle Iver ran his fingers through his still-thick hair, a good sign for me if male pattern baldness was hereditary. "I didn't mean to undermine your feelings. I know you cared about those girls. I remember them at the house, swimming, how happy you were when they'd stop by. You sure had eyes for that one—"

"Annabelle."

"If that was her name. Memory doesn't improve with age, kid."

"It was a vivid summer," I said, poking the bear. "Danny McPhee was around a lot, doing yard work, mowing the lawn, clipping the hedges. You remember Danny, right?"

"McPhee? Ken and Barbara's boy?"

The way he said it rankled, my uncle trying to pass off his involvement with a delinquent hoodrat like the paperboy he'd paid two dollars once. He'd helped get the guy out of jail. And now he was vaguely aware of his existence? But I knew better. As long as cards were on the table, I might as well play my best hand.

"You did a lot to help Danny," I said.

"Why do you care so much about Danny McPhee?"

"Because he was arrested. Not long after the Rodgers Twins went missing. Arrested and sentenced for kidnapping and raping a girl the same age."

"I don't think you have your facts straight."

"That's a curious thing to say. Like you're defending him."

"Danny wasn't a bad kid. He … had problems."

"You know he went to prison, right? That sounds like the very definition of a 'bad kid.'" A coughing fit took root again, inopportune timing as I felt I was getting on a roll. My fractured rib jostled, and it felt like a knife was being plunged into the most delicate parts of my body, the ones where all the nerve endings congregated.

When I finished, my uncle's expression had morphed from parental disapproval to one of grave concern. He wanted to say more, I could tell. But he backed off.

"Get some rest," Uncle Iver said, thumbing over his shoulder. "They're going to keep you for a couple days. Then *I'll* be coming to pick you up." The way his face now contorted and pinched made it clear I had no say in the matter. "We'll talk more then."

My uncle stepped toward me. I clutched the pillow. He planted a soft kiss on my forehead.

I managed to dab my eyes like I was satisfying an itch.

Iver turned to leave, walking out the door. Halfway to the elevators, he met Jim, who had returned without Ron. Down the hospital hall, I watched my uncle and Jim shake hands and exchange words. They took turns glancing my way, obviously talking about me. The gravitas on their faces grated on my nerves, if for different reasons. Then they broke off and my uncle headed for the elevators, Jim continuing toward me with coffee on a tray.

"Ron had to get to work," Jim said, reentering the room. I watched my uncle recede into the elevator's closing doors.

Jim grabbed a seat, spinning it around, a move reminiscent of the countless times I'd made characters do that, a show of intimacy, a means to establish confidence. Too familiar, too forward. I didn't like it. I felt like the critic in Tobias Wolff's "Bullet in the Brain"; my life and work so intertwined, objective analysis was no longer possible in this endless hall of mirrors reflecting back on itself infinitely.

"Quite the night, eh, buddy?" Jim brought the Starbucks to his mouth. I would've killed for a cup after this morning's woeful brew. As if on cue, Jim brought up another. "Figured you could use one too."

I snatched it up, overcome with a sense of appreciation for Jim. I hadn't seen much of the guy during the past thirty years, but he might've been the best friend I had left. Which was, granted, a low-hanging fruit. Despite wanting to position myself as a decent guy, I'd done a helluva job pushing everyone away. There was a Springsteen lyric in there somewhere, something about fools and turning hearts to stone and needing to risk getting hurt in order to be loved, but trying to pluck it from the vast, deep pool of endless pop culture trivia and obscure song lyrics only highlighted a useless skill that served as convenient distraction from the present, which in turn made me realize how I'd fucked up my marriage, how much I missed my wife, and, above all, how my reluctance to take on responsibility prevented my having children, thus exposing my biggest fear: being forgotten.

Jim leaned in. I braced for the heart-to-heart.

"I'm sorry," he said.

"For what?"

"For not seeing how important this is to you. Whatever *this* is."

"It's my work."

"Finding out who took the Rodgers Twins?" He scoffed. Not in a mean-spirited way, more a confused one, and I could empathize. The image I projected to the world wasn't accurate, my self-awareness as screwed up as the rest of this world I tried so hard to assimilate into, be a part of, and at the same time eschew.

"Talk to me, buddy," Jim said.

"Maybe my career isn't going as well as it seems."

"What are you talking about? How many books have you published?" He tried to laugh. "How many times you been on TV?"

"That's because Mike Piskorski works for a TV station." We'd gone to school with Mike, whose position at the local FOX affiliate landed me a couple primetime interviews.

"You're famous, buddy."

"No, Jim, I'm not."

"How many people can say they make their living as an author?"

"Not many." I waited. "And not me."

"I've seen the pictures of your place in San Francisco."

"My uncle's money. My ex-wife's money."

"Hey, no harm putting those good looks of yours—"

"You're not hearing me, man. My mother died and left me life insurance. My uncle had that bad accident, and got a huge settlement, and he helped set me up. I lose more money writing every year than I make. My contribution to the family budget existed in the tax write-offs."

"You're telling me you don't make *any* money from *all* those books? No six-figure advances? Ha!"

I didn't laugh.

"You serious?"

"No six-figure, no five, either. Try closer to four, and usually not the high fours. I publish with small houses, mid-size indie presses. Yeah, I've made some money, but I've put it all back into my own advertising, hiring my own publicist, attending conferences to get fawned over by a few fans who don't know better. I'm a fraud, man."

"I get it," Jim said. "Happens to me all the time. Crisis of faith. Like you don't deserve the good things in your life. I remember when Jack—"

"It's not Imposter Syndrome. And it's not an anecdote or teachable moment. I'm telling you the truth. I'm not D-list."

"So what's wrong with E-list?"

"More like F-list. If that's even a thing."

"I've read your books, buddy. And not just the ones with me in it. You're good." He winked, and I could see he was trying to add levity, but I was also being truthful for the first time in a long time and I needed to be heard. Maybe if I had done that with my wife she'd still be around. For whatever reason, I was ready to confess. And Jim was the one who was there to hear it.

"A lot of writers are good," I said. "I want to be special."

The nurse came in. "And how are we doing?"

"Can I get a minute?" I said.

"I think he needs more pain meds," Jim said.

The nurse laughed. "Any more pain meds and your friend here will be in a coma. We have enough painkillers pumping into his body to knock out a horse."

They both laughed. So I laughed too. Let the nurse do what she had to do, poke, prick, prod.

After a few seconds, Jim got up. "I have to get going, buddy. The phone company waits for no man. I'll stop by after work." Then to the nurse: "He'll still be here?"

"Until tomorrow afternoon at least," she said.

Jim raised his coffee in a toast and was gone.

While Nurse Ratchet—that's not fair, she was nice, but I was mad she'd interrupted what I was trying to say—tapped a fresh blood source, I stewed. I hadn't been able to broach the subject of my uncle, who was coming to pick me up. Despite common sense assuring me to ease up, I began panicking. Because in that instant I didn't know if I'd make it home alive, which caused my heart rate to spike.

"Well, that's not good," the nurse said, noticing the rapid pulse. "Maybe your friend was right."

She filled a new vial, pushing a thick knot of syrup, and like that I was out.

CHAPTER TWENTY

Our minds play tricks on us. I of all people knew that. A writer, I played with trope, illusion, the con. Smoke, mirrors. As my former graduate thesis advisor, Lynne Barrett, once told me, "All art is contrivance." As artists we are in the business of artifice. When a reader says a scene feels "contrived," it means we, the artist, did a lousy job hiding the puppet strings. Writers create something from nothing, pluck stories from the abyss and adventures from the ether, manufacturing meaning.

I was aware of this phenomena, dwelling on the minutia of my chosen profession because what the hell else are you going to do as freezing rain pelts the glass of your high-rise hospital room at three a.m. while skeleton crews and orderlies shuffle through the ward and you wait to be discharged into the custody of your uncle slash father who may be a murderer?

Maybe I was overselling the danger. But the wee, small hours are not the best time to think objectively after blunt head trauma. I was also pumped full of opiates, the pure, pharmaceutical grade that melted the fine line between life and death. Life is *supposed* to be pain. We are *meant* to ache. The rub, the irony, the big fat joke on all of us is that we spend most our lives trying to avoid what is natural and necessary. We seek out anything to blunt to the pain. Pot, pills, hard drugs, alcohol. We need the hurt to remind ourselves that we are still alive.

The bleak, sleeting night distorted any rational perspective. I couldn't see any further than the dim light shining through the fog, which didn't offer much lead-time. But like E.L. Doctorow maintains, "Writing a book is like driving a car at night. You don't need to see any further than your headlights. But you can make an entire trip cross-country that way." I may've been paraphrasing. I also may've been hallucinating. This was all part of the story now.

One thing was for sure: I wasn't lying around till daylight, waiting for my uncle to pick me up.

Gingerly, I swung my shaky legs over the edge of the bed. My ribs had been patched up, but any movement was agony. On a table in the corner sat a vial. I'd seen the nurse put it down along with a syringe. Like I mentioned, I'd had a few wilder years in my younger days. If I hadn't watched a careless night nurse leave the needle and vial there, maybe I don't do what I did next.

I unhooked myself from the Matrix, yanking wires, cords and plugs. I left the one hooked up to my vitals, the one reporting to the mainframe I was alive. Once that flat lined, the switchboard operator would send revival teams rushing.

At the table, I tipped the vial, inserted the syringe, filled a shot, and stuck it in my ass. Some liquid—not much—remained in the vial, which I held onto. Dragging machinery and rubber tubes behind me, I went to the locker, pulled my clothes, flecked with red from the attack, and dressed myself, dried blood cracking over sinew and bone. The morphine hit hard and fast, masking enough of the pain that I could slide on my jeans. Leaving the line attached, I grabbed my jacket and the rest of my belongings—cracked phone, keys, didn't have much. I turned and unplugged the machine from the wall, ripped the line from my arm, and seeing the coast clear, beelined for the exit.

A couple taxis waited by the ER entrance. I flagged one, and told them to bring me home. It's not a crime to leave a hospital. I hadn't been committed, wasn't under arrest. I was slipping out AMA, Against Medical Advice. Ill advised, but not against the law.

At my house I passed the driver my Amex—thankful cabs now took cards—and walked into my house of my own volition, if a little unsteady from the morphine, broken rib, and head wound.

Then I shut myself in, double locked all the doors and windows, and proceeded to pass out on the couch.

The simultaneous fury of a new day's shine and the violent shaking of my doorknob brought me back to life, a coma patient out of commission for forty years thrust back into a new world order he isn't prepared to face. I'd fallen asleep in my coat, still dressed, down to my socks and shoes. The knocking started back up and wouldn't relent. Disoriented, slackened and slowed from powerful sedatives, I didn't know where I was, didn't know who I was, didn't know *what* I was or what I wanted. If in that instant, the curtain were pulled back and it was revealed I were being filmed in front of a live studio audience on Mars, I wouldn't have batted a pretty little eyelash.

The banging continued, loud and hard. I knew the police were at the door—it was that kind of knocking—hard, bottom of the fist pounding. I often used the calling card in my novels to announce the arrival of authorities—no one knocks like the cops.

I felt in my pocket for the vial of morphine I'd stolen from the hospital. Technically, that was breaking the law. They aren't sending the cavalry for that. Still, I slipped off the couch ducking out of sight and feeling quite foolish. I wasn't thinking well. The sudden movement provoked a yelp of pain—I had to bite my tongue to stay silent, literally drawing blood (and as a writer I don't use "literally" lightly). My mouth tasted like a tin can.

"You in there?" a familiar voice shouted. "It's Wayne." Then he added, "Wright," as if I knew an abundance of "Waynes" in Berlin.

I popped out from behind the couch, doing my best to make it look as if I'd been sleeping and slipped off it, which wasn't at all weird. Not sure I pulled off the ruse but it was better than admitting I'd been ducking behind the cushions like a frightened rabbit. Of course, as soon as my feet hit the floor, the pain in my ribs sent lightning bolts through every nerve ending, up my spine, jiggling eyeballs loose in their sockets. The jolt reminded me of grabbing the electric cow fence as a kid.

"Your car is down at the Citgo," Wayne said, as I opened the door for him, trying not to wince. "Had it towed there. Terry Tatina's place? On Main? No charges for the tow." He followed me inside. "Would've towed it here but it was too nasty last night. All that freezing rain. Streets are a hockey rink this morning."

"Coffee?" I asked him, gritting teeth.

"I already had some at the station—"

"Great. Wait here."

I didn't care whether Wayne wanted coffee. Once I was in the kitchen, I hooked a left to the bathroom. The pain to my ribs unbearable, I retrieved the vial from my jacket pocket. I drew up what remained and jabbed the tip of the needle into my ass, then sat on the edge of the tub and waited.

After the pain subsided enough I could open my mouth to speak in complete sentences, I headed back to meet Wayne in the living room.

"Coffee brewing?" he asked.

"All out. Sorry. What's up?"

Wayne's incredulous look betrayed the stupid question. We both knew why he was here.

"I have coffee." I headed back into the kitchen, Wayne on my heels.

Of course I had coffee—it's the lifeblood of writers—and I was glad to be doing something with my hands, grinding beans, tamping down the basket. The noise from the espresso machine made conversation impossible, which was the point. I needed the medicine to hit harder. The extra time provided much-needed minutes to get my story straight. Wording is everything. At the fridge, I grabbed the milk, frothed some foam, and passed Wayne his tiny cup.

He stared at the miniature mug in his hands like it were an alien bug. "What's this?"

"A macchiato. Espresso. Frothed milk. You'll like it."

Wayne helped himself to a seat at my quaint kitchen table. I would've preferred to keep standing and maintain the distance between us, but my ribs wouldn't allow it.

"Why did you leave the hospital in the middle of the night?"

"I hate hospitals. Reminds me of my mom." Which *was* true. The orange-and-bleach smells of ointments and salves, balms and disinfectant, everything doused in sanitizer, stored in doublewide vats of propanol alcohol.

"You knew I needed to talk to you, right?"

"Yeah, I knew, Wayne. But I'd already talked to a couple detectives. And it's not like you don't know where to find me."

"Detectives?"

"Came by first night, four a.m. or so."

"Berlin cops?"

"I don't know. I assumed so."

"What were their names?"

"I didn't ask. I was out of it." I didn't want to admit I wasn't sure *any* detectives had been there or if I'd hallucinated the entire thing.

"They weren't Berlin cops, I can tell you that." Wayne's eyes went all thinking-man-squinty. "What they ask you?"

"I don't remember…" I took a sip of my espresso, fog clearing a bit. "They wanted to know if I took anything from the shed."

"Interesting." Wayne didn't say it as a statement. He didn't say it like a question either. More like he'd been stumped by an obscure bit of trivia.

My cell buzzed. Not wanting to be rude, I let it go to voicemail. The peculiar expression remained on Wayne's face. I took a peek and saw the call I'd missed was from New Britain General. I didn't need to listen to that one. I couldn't imagine my doctor and treatment team being too thrilled with my leaving before official discharge. Then again, the cops were here so how much more trouble could I be in?

I held up a finger. Not sure Wayne even noticed, so lost in thought. Cringing, I pushed myself out of the chair, took a couple steps, and checked the voicemail. It wasn't my doctor; it was a nurse. She didn't chastise me for leaving. She said there was a prescription for Percocet waiting for me at the local Walgreens.

Wayne was still chewing whatever fat he had on the brain, head tilted to the side, a regular Rodin, the only thing missing: fist propping up chin.

"Hey," I said. "You mind giving me a ride to get my car?" I didn't want the morphine to wear off while I waited on an Uber. I had no idea how reliable ride share was in Berlin, and I wasn't in any shape to walk downtown in the cold rain.

"Take a seat," Wayne said.

"If you can't give me a ride, let me call a taxi—"

"I'll give you a ride. No problem. But first I'm going to show you something. Maybe I shouldn't…" He was talking to himself. "This doesn't make any sense to me. I should've handed them over to my bosses when I found them the other night."

Now he had my attention.

My heart started beating faster in anticipation, the way certain moments predict the future. Wayne reached in his pocket and brought back … it looked like … old Polaroids?

I tried to make out the pictures. Another joy of closing in on fifty. My eyesight was going to shit—mornings were the worst, compositions a fuzzy smudge—and these were old, yellowed, fading. I almost said I needed my glasses. But I gave it a moment, let my eyeballs flit, flounder, redirect, and then the picture came into focus.

I couldn't believe what I was seeing.

It was Annabelle and Ava Rodgers.

They were alive.

CHAPTER TWENTY-ONE

The photos were from the '80s, a time before our phones captured every moment and meal, however mundane. Even if I didn't recognize the Twins, the hair, big and feathered, would've given away the time-frame. Rainbow sweatbands and tee shirts, teeny matching Adidas shorts. I also recognized the necklace I'd given to Annabelle. Which broke my heart. They were sitting on a couch, its faded brown indistinguishable from every other variation of taupe. Bland, flavorless. So conservative. So Berlin. The girls looked beautiful, young and vibrant, their smiles bright. Ava was laughing. Annabelle was happy too, even if there seemed to be a pensive quality to her expression. No, not pensive … blunted. Like when you've had too much to drink. Still pleasant but on the verge of getting sick. The room seemed familiar in a vague way, like how all your friends' houses looked alike when you're a kid. I pushed deeper into my subconscious but couldn't gain traction.

"Where'd you get these?" I asked Wayne, even though he'd already told me.

"We found them in the shed night you were attacked."

Is that Danny's living room in the photographs? No, I'd been to Barbara McPhee's. This wasn't their house. It wasn't the shed, either. It was a living room—a basement living room. Rich? Poor? Decorated in the style of the era. Whose basement was that? I'd *been* there.

"Why were you there?" Wayne asked.

"Huh?"

"At the shed?"

Right. No one can read your mind. I told Wayne about having dinner with Mel McPhee, who'd shared details of Danny's job at Gribbard, his getting kicked out of his folk's and living in the shed before he was arrested. I omitted the part about my uncle's helping him get the job.

"I thought he might've left behind a clue," I added.

"You could've brought this to the police."

"Yeah," I said. "I could have."

"Did you see these Polaroids that night?"

"It was dark. I couldn't see much of anything. Except … there was a cot. It was stained red—"

"Saw that too. Not blood. Paint."

"Where did you find those pictures?" I asked.

"In a corner, with some old soil and planting sod, gardening material fossilized at this point." Wayne jabbed a finger at the photos. "They were resting beneath a pot, on a plate." He hopped up, rubbing his chin, pensive. "Looking for evidence, eh? Well, if what you say is true, that Danny was living there—I think we may've found it."

Wayne drove me to the Citgo so I could pick up my car. On the way I told him where Danny McPhee was currently staying. Wayne said they'd be paying a visit to the America Inn, ASAP.

I got my prescription from the pharmacy, popping a couple Percs before I was out the door. Even though Wayne had said to sit tight and that he'd call me once he had anything, I couldn't do that.

I rang Jim, figuring he'd be at work. Planning to leave a message, I was surprised when my friend picked up on the first ring and told me he had the day off.

"Don't act so shocked," he said. "Even the phone company gives employees the occasional day off." He chuckled. "Don't worry. I'll be working double time after this ice storm is done with us. Half the power lines are going to be down."

Pulling out of the lot, I hooked a right onto Farmington Avenue.

"Where are you?" Jim asked. "Sounds like you're in a car."

"I am."

"I thought they were keeping you in the hospital a couple days? Wait. Are you supposed to be driving?"

"It's fine. Got some stuff to talk about. Mind if I swing by?"

After a pause: "I'll put on the coffee."

Even though Wayne was on his way to arrest Danny McPhee— even though a four-decade-old abduction was about to be solved—there was more to this story. I needed to tell the rest.

Jim sat, gobsmacked, unable to hide the disbelief. I'd completed the unabridged version of all I'd learned over this past month and a half, explaining about the license plate and how my uncle had helped Danny McPhee when we were kids; I told him about Iver's assisting Danny in finding work, vouching for his character, and paying good money to get him out of legal trouble. I hadn't buried the lede, either. I'd started with the photos of Annabelle and Ava Rodgers that Wayne recovered at the shed the night I was blindsided. That was only half the equation. I couldn't dismiss the connection to the Avon Sisters, snatched from West Farms Mall, which was less than a mile from Iver's house.

"Your uncle?" Jim asked, dazed by the news.

"I know. It's crazy."

"It's more than crazy, buddy."

"I can't shake these two crimes are tied together. My uncle drove me to the Meriden Square the day the Rodgers Twins vanished. He was there. Like Danny had been. And my uncle was at West Farms the day the Avon Sisters were taken. He and Danny McPhee were—are—a lot closer than I knew." I paced his kitchen. "Those photos? Of the Twins? I think they were taken around the time they went missing. Maybe even the same day. I recognize the room."

"Whose house you think it is?"

"Everyone had those basement living rooms back then. It's on the tip of my tongue. I can't place it though. The photos show a close-up of the girls. A couch. Total déjà vu. They are laughing. They might've been drunk."

"What makes you say that?"

"There was ... I don't know. Annabelle didn't look right. She looked . . . sedated."

"Drugged?"

"Possibly." I pinched my eyes.

"Could it have been your uncle or Danny's basement?"

"Iver lived with us at that point. Could've been Danny's? I'd have to see the space again. Mel asked me not to bother her aunt anymore. I don't know what excuse I'd need to see her basement anyway."

"Your uncle helping Danny doesn't mean much," Jim said. "Iver's a nice guy who likes to help people. Danny was your neighbor." He pointed a finger. "I think you could use a drink."

Jim went to the fridge and brought back beer. Small batch IPA. He was hooked. After that, we didn't talk, at least not about anything substantial, shooting the bull, laughing about shared memories, offering quiet ruminations on getting old. By the third beer, I knew I should eat something, but I couldn't, nerves gnawing my innards as I waited for Wayne to call. I didn't want to be alone. I was grateful for the company. But after a while, it started to get awkward. I grew tired, and I could sense Jim wanted back his space.

As I drove home on Worthington Ridge, my cell buzzed. Voicemail from a call I'd missed. I pulled over fast, expecting to hear Wayne telling me it was over, that they had the bastard in custody.

But it wasn't Wayne. It was New Britain General Hospital.

I quickly wished I had not played back that message.

CHAPTER TWENTY-TWO

The message had been left earlier in the day. I didn't know why it came through then, so much later. Cell service isn't always reliable, especially in a storm. Maybe God wanted to give me more time. Or maybe the Universe was waiting for the perfect time to drop the killer punchline.

My appointment with the doctor wasn't until the following morning, making that one of the longer afternoons and nights of my life. I couldn't relax. At least my lack of appetite was explained. Despite knowing better than to Google medical symptoms, it's hard to resist the urge when the doctor calls and says, "We've been looking at these numbers from your tests," and "We need you to come in right away."

Doesn't take a medical degree to know one and one add up to cancer.

Cancer killed my mother. It killed half this town. In my books I allude to the abnormal number of cancer cases in Berlin. Local lore blamed a burning underground dump, our own mouth to hell, an eternal flame of damnation never to be extinguished. That was the story anyway. I didn't know if it was true. I enjoyed the juxtaposition of a perpetual inferno set against the town's cloying religiosity. In some ways, a part of me must've known this would happen.

We start out invincible, are never going to die. When you are young, you can't imagine anything strong enough to strike you down; you defy God Himself to try. Of course you're also an idiot. Headstrong, stupid, stubborn, wrong—you end up fighting every battle, not just the ones you have to win, until exhausted, toll taken, it doesn't even require a solid shot to knock you out. I fought everyone and everything when I was younger. "What you rebelling against?" In the words of Marlon Brando, "What you got?"

At two in the morning, freezing rain plinking the glass, I sat at my desktop, several browsers open about the various types of cancer growing inside me. I looked at my pack of cigarettes beside me. Who picks up that filthy habit after a dozen years? I wanted to crush the box, throw it in the trash. What was the point? If I had the Big C, I was done for. Another cigarette wasn't going to kill me.

I was out of sorts, emotions pulling me six ways to Sunday. A middle-aged cliché. Divorced, drunk, depressed. Might as well start sleeping with my twenty-two-year-old student. Except I'd lost the job. Jesus. I glared at my bookshelf. This is what I was hanging my hat on? A bunch of books no one gave a shit about. A commitment to art that drove away everyone I loved or cared about. A mid-list talent stuck smack dab in the middle of over and done. I'd never sniff a *New York Times* bestseller list. I never missed my ex-wife more.

Walking across the cold tile to my fridge, I extracted raspberry jam and milk, found the bread and peanut butter and, despite not being at all hungry, choked down half a dozen sandwiches, finishing the job by pounding two percent out of spite. I felt the slop slosh around in my belly, unable to take root. My gut rejecting best efforts, I ran to the bathroom in time to throw up.

When I finished wiping the slime and snot from my graying whiskers, I plunked down on my throne, faced east, and waited for the day to break, even as the sun refused to shine.

✳ ✳

I arrived forty minutes early to my appointment. I tried to look non-plussed but the nurses knew why I was there, and I couldn't escape their condolence.

Soon as the doctor called me in and told me to take a seat, I said, "It's cancer, isn't it?" I'd never had patience.

Chart in hand, Dr. Phillips said, "We don't know." The universal "we." I hated that. "We need to run some more tests." *We* weren't doing anything. This affected *me*, and *I* had no say in the outcome.

He recapped what I already knew, how they'd drawn my blood the night I was jumped at Gribbard Pool, in all likelihood by Danny McPhee or my own uncle, maybe both, and how the results from those tests had come back … not good. The numbers were alarming, vacillating white blood cell counts, big problem with my lymph nodes, which now that he said it felt swollen, two soft-boiled eggs on each side of my neck, squishy and tender to the touch.

The doctor kept talking. I checked out. Given the life-or-death stakes, I should've paid attention. I tried but found myself distracted by the hum of heaters and bleating heart rate monitors down the hall. Like being back in high school and unable to focus on the War of 1812, my mind drifted away, eluding capture, big battle be damned.

Dr. Phillips droned on about next steps and treatment options, worst-case scenarios. He closed by telling me not to panic. How do you tell a man with an anxiety condition not to panic after dropping that bombshell? Treatment options? I'd seen *Breaking Bad*. I was lucky when a publisher paid me royalties on time. More than once, I'd *owed* a publisher after a bad quarter before earning out an advance. The infrastructure of the profession—having a literary agent, a foreign agent, a film agent, editor, outside publicist, web designer—meant that everyone got paid before I did. And as a writer, in effect an independent contractor, I didn't have employer health insurance.

Yeah, I was pissed, pissed that life had dealt me this lousy hand with no means to bet or bluff my way out. Pissed off for just being born. Childish, impetuous, bratty? Sure, I was holding my breath and stomping my feet. But I'd lost my mother at a young age to this disease. My good friend Jack had succumbed to it too. And despite my recent return to smoking—a lamentable, regrettable, stupid decision—that wasn't why I was in this mess now. Cancers take years to grow, and whether you get it comes down to luck of the draw: either your body is the type that produces cancerous cells or it doesn't. Uncle Iver smoked two packs a day his whole life. He didn't have cancer. Why me? Why now? When you grow up evangelical with a devout mother, you can never shake payback for wickedness, sin, a moral lapse. I soul-searched for what terrible thing I had done to deserve this. And the answers flooded too rapid to hold back the dam.

None of this was real, I reassured myself, clinging to belief that immunity hinged on inner resolve. Mentally weak equated to physically ill. Vengeful deities weren't out to smite me. And even if I knew, intellectually, that wasn't true—that I wasn't Cotton Mather in the Hands of an Angry God—my heart refused to cooperate with these simple facts. Enough therapists had gotten their hands on me that I knew the discrepancy between knowing something in your heart and knowing it in your head.

"Did you hear what I said?" Dr. Phillips stood staring at me.

I nodded like I'd been listening. We both knew I was lying.

What's the plan?

More tests. Try and relax. Drink plenty of fluids. Hope for the best. Results in a few days.

This was where you could find me if you needed me, ensconced in the tight, suffocating blind of worry's blanket as I investigated whether my own uncle was a kidnapper, pedophile, murderer, or something worse.

The nurses siphoned more blood, life force drained from a sprung spigot. Bagged, tagged, sent off to determine whether I'd live or die.

When they were done extracting everything they needed, they patched me up, and I returned to my car in the garage, already feeling dead inside. Yeah, there was the panic, anxiety, which was to be expected, the shock and fear. The other? I didn't give a shit, and a part of me shut down. If you've ever faced news like this before, the cancer kind, you know what I mean. Maybe it's because you can't accept it, are in denial; it's too much to take in. The living pieces of you, the flesh, bone, and cells, mutated or not, like the show, must go on. So it's autopilot, a system overridden; you deal with the requisite neurosis and uncertainty and craziness that comes with your own mortality, compartmentalize and file, another bill to be paid, stacked in the outgoing mail. Punch it in drive and go.

The last thing on my mind was writing. The problem with true crime, however, is truth doesn't care what you want. I was writing in real time. The story would unfold as it was meant to unfold. There was no pause button, no rewind, no fast forward. This was now part of the story. So when I turned on the radio and an update of the Avon Sisters came on, I laughed out loud, a high-pitched, caterwauling cackle. Because it *was* funny. Not ha-ha funny, but the timing of it all, how it coalesced, conspired to arrive at this precise moment in time. I couldn't put this scene in a novel, walking out of the hospital, running out of time, brought up to speed on the case at hand, because it was too convenient, too contrived, the manipulative strings showing. And yet here we were.

The Avon Sisters update didn't shed any new light. It had been two months now, and these periodic updates had grown less frequent, as close acquaintances and family members had been ruled out, and with it the hope that the Sisters would be found alive. The key, as anyone who has watched true-crime programs can attest, is the first few days, which are paramount to survival. After that, the likelihood of rescue plummets. It becomes about recovery.

Maybe if I had gone to Wayne Wright or Gary St. Jean and told them what I suspected about my uncle—maybe this story ends differently. But when was I supposed to have done that? When I saw the ordinary automobile Iver drove? When I uncovered any of the rest of the circumstantial evidence? A red-stained shirt, the location of a mall? Helping out the neighborhood ne'er-do-well? By the time it added up to anything—I wasn't even sure it added up to anything *now*—it was too late. I wasn't a cop, wasn't an investigator—I was a desperate writer making a last-ditch attempt to break through to the Big Five. Or to quote the Boss: on a last chance power drive. The pressure to make the next book be "the one" is crushing. My money was running out. I couldn't keep selling ten thousand copies and getting a handful of nominations, and earn a living. Great for the ego. Does nothing for the wallet. Bill collectors don't accept accolades in lieu of cash payment.

My cell rang. Wayne calling me back. At least I knew Danny McPhee was in custody. For a brief, shining second, I felt solace. Order had returned, justice restored. Only to see those hopes dashed too.

"Danny McPhee is on the run," Wayne said. "Someone must've tipped him off. Checked out of the America Inn. We've put out an APB."

CHAPTER TWENTY-THREE

The Berlin Turnpike had changed a lot through the years. Garden-variety upgrades. Inconsequential. Instead of Caldor, you got a Target. A few local staples, such as Bob's Furniture and the Olympia Diner, had been spared, blending in with the natural progression of amelioration. Yet, the sleazy motels remained, single room occupancy drug dens like the Kenilworth and rent-by-the-hour whorehouses ala the Grantmoor. And while I always played up these downtrodden elements in my work, social inequality and injustice a governing precept, I didn't have to play them up too much when it came to the Berlin Turnpike. Maybe it's the way some of us view the world. For me all Panera Breads and Home Depots look alike; each degenerate motel is unique, haunted by the specters of losing horses and blown sobriety dates, the missed birthday parties. And it was impossible to watch these hellholes whip by and not wonder what was going on inside these dismal spaces tonight. I'd never known poverty. Not real poverty anyway. During my down times, like San Francisco after college, I partied too hard, got a few too many tattoos. But I always had the option of coming back home. I imagined another version of me, one who partied harder and couldn't stop; who messed up so bad he ended up living in one of these wretched, roach-infested dumps; who knew firsthand of the horrors of which I wrote. True suffering, drug addiction, alcoholism, unfathomable losses and longing. I wondered if it were possible that another me existed somewhere. Was he as depressed and hopeless as the characters I wrote about? Could I be that man? Could he be me? And as I pulled tight my wool beanie and lit a cigarette, a chill shivered through my bones, silver oxide pushed to its freezing point.

There was one person I could talk to, the meeting place obvious. Lucky for me, I was catching Jim on his lunch hour.

"I hope I'm not getting you in trouble at work," I said, climbing from my car. Traffic roared along the Turnpike, making me have to shout across the Olympia Diner parking lot.

"You said it was important." Jim walked toward me, wrapping himself warm in his parka, and I caught the hint of a grin. "I get a lunch. Even if the phone company preferred I didn't. What's up? You sounded upset on the phone." He looked me over. "And no offense, buddy, I thought you looked like shit *last* time I saw you."

"Let me buy you lunch," I said, ignoring the dig, leading my old friend up the diner steps.

Where to start? Danny McPhee being on the run? The cancer? I opted for positivity, waiting till our coffees arrived at the back booth.

"What can you do at the phone company?" I asked, ripping open packets of fake sugar.

"What do you mean?"

"Legally." I paused long enough to be considerate. "And otherwise."

Jim's face washed blank before contorting perturbed. I couldn't blame him. I was asking him to threaten his job security, career, steady paycheck, health insurance, how he paid the bills. I recognized my approach was wrong. You can't ask a man to jeopardize his livelihood and not be one hundred percent honest.

"I have cancer, Jim."

The indignant blood that had been filling his face drained to pale. That word, cancer, can do that.

"When did you find out?"

"Yesterday," I said. "After I left your place. Checked a voicemail I missed."

"How do you know it's cancer?" he asked, searching for hope.

"The doctor is running more tests. It's not good." I parroted what Dr. Phillips said about the abnormal white blood cell count, lymph node numbers, glancing out the window to watch an icy, dystopian landscape that was a lot more fun to paint with words. "It is what it is." Tall poles and long wires dripped icicles, sharpened points poised to menace. I thought about my mom, my friends, my ex-wife, how I could've been a better friend, husband, son, human being, all of it for any of them, some of it for a few, just a couple better goddamn days.

"Shit, man," Jim said. "I'm sorry." He caught my eyes. "Even if it is, that doesn't mean…"

"I can feel it. It's inside me, eating away. I haven't had an appetite in weeks, months." We know these things. "My mother was my age when she was diagnosed. Jack died the same age."

"That's them. Not you. All I'm saying is it's not a death sentence. Even if the tests come back positive. You'll have options."

"I know all about those options." I watched my mother go through them, body blasted with radiation, face sucked gaunt, muscle mass wasting away till she resembled a cadaver, choking down twenty horse pills a day, puking in a bucket all night. Final hours spent like a marooned goldfish gulping for air. And recounting this, I cracked up, an unhinged shriek. A capped inhale escaped my lips, drawing peculiar stares from the other customers. Strange and disturbing thoughts continued to assault. I kept thinking how empty the church would be.

Who would organize the funeral? My uncle? Would he be conflicted, feel the need to lament, or would he rejoice over having gotten away with murder? Was I going out blazing, delivering justice by whatever means necessary to two families who deserved closure? Or was I a megalomaniac who needed to write one last story? That's the part that made me laugh and cry, the futility and pointlessness of any crusade. No one cared. I had no one in my life. My books didn't sell enough to justify this twist. I didn't even have a dog. I had wasted my years.

"Buddy?"

I knew I'd drifted off again. Coffees had been refilled, steam wafting, meaning the waitress had come and gone. I didn't remember seeing her. I hadn't planned on ordering food anyway.

"Why is this so important to you?" Jim asked.

"I think I wrote that exact line in a book once."

"You did. The one about the girl who got away. The *Cuckoo's Nest* mercy killing with that guy, what's his name, like George from *Mice and Men*."

"You really have read everything I've written."

"I'm proud of you, buddy." Jim pursed his lips, shook himself off. "You know what? Never mind 'why.' You say you need my help? What do you need me to do?"

"Wayne Wright called. They can't find Danny McPhee. He's running. I need to know what … accesses … you have. At the phone company."

"As a tech, I can listen from afar, look up the number to see addresses, install taps for the government. See billing, cut off their internet when I feel like it from my laptop, and put a tone on the line so it's unusable. Cells are trickier. Unless they connect to a landline. Though, I do install the fiber circuits that connect the e-towers to the world. In theory, I could take those down."

"I'm remembering that morning my uncle came to visit me. When I first got back to town. He stopped in out of the blue. He wasn't acting like himself, all disheveled, distracted. He kept staring out the window, like he was checking on something. And..."

"What?"

"He had a red stain on his shirt."

"Red stain."

"I thought it was ketchup, salsa. I don't know. I didn't think 'blood.' But then after he left, that Amber alert came in. The car. The license plate. He *told me* he'd come from West Farms Mall where the girls had just been taken. It's down the road from his house. I had, have this ... feeling ... in my gut."

"Have you talked to Wayne about your suspicions?"

"A stained shirt? A common car color and a few matching numbers from a license plate? A trip to buy some underwear and socks? I don't have proof of anything. It's a feeling, man. This is *what* I do. I dissect, take it apart to see how it works. There's a pattern, Jim. To everything. It's not random. My coming back for a teaching job that falls through? Annabelle, Ava, Avon? My idea for a true crime book. This ... diagnosis. It all adds up. It's a complete story, tragic arc and all."

"Have you tried talking to your uncle? About any of this? Buddy, this is the man who raised you."

"That's why it hurts. And, no, the last thing I'm planning on doing is talking to my uncle. I need more time. That's part of the reason I left the hospital. He was going to drive me home. I don't want to be alone with him."

"Has he been calling?"

"I haven't been picking up."

I waited for Jim to tell me I was nuts, to focus on my health, give up the ghost, but instead his face turned ashen gray.

"What's wrong?"

"I've always liked your uncle. He was like a second dad to me. I don't want—"

"Jim—"

"1985 was a long time ago. I can't be sure *I'm* remembering right. I don't want to plant something in your head, some false memory."

"Tell me."

Jim panned around the restaurant, before leaning in. "It was after the Twins went missing. I'd ridden my bike over your house. Your mom was at work. Your uncle was there, you weren't. Baseball practice." He exhaled a shameful gust. "He asked me to help him move something."

"Something."

"Two duffel bags." Jim stopped. "They were stained reddish brown. He said they were deer carcasses. He'd been hunting, chopping up steaks." Jim raised his brow, before narrowing his gaze. "They smelled like death."

"Why wouldn't you say anything?"

"Why would I? Your uncle hunted. A lot of people in Central Connecticut hunt. You *always* had venison in that big freezer in your garage."

It was true. Uncle Iver kept that deep freezer stuffed with all kinds of meat—venison, moose, filets he'd pick up from butcher friends—the man was always acquiring new meats. And what he couldn't buy in the store, he got the old fashioned way.

"Where did you bring them?" I said. "These bags." I was hoping Jim said somewhere convenient and accessible, like Swede's Pond behind our house, a body of water that could be dredged.

"*I* didn't bring them anywhere. He had me help him load them into the back of his truck. I don't know where he went after that."

"What color was the truck?" Back in those days my uncle got a new used truck every six months. Until he gave up fixing old engines and started enjoying his golden years with reliable automobiles that ran with regularity. Like this year's white Acura MDX.

"I don't know. Light blue?"

"I remember that truck." A truck like that must've changed hands a dozen times by now. Even if I could track it down—even if it was still in commission, which was doubtful—there'd be too much DNA and genetic contamination from countless other owners.

"It could be nothing," Jim said. "Your uncle moving deer carcasses after cutting steaks, like he said."

We both knew that wasn't true.

Jim leaned closer as the waitress passed by. "Come on. You don't really think your uncle is a … killer?"

"I don't know. But I don't believe in coincidences. You know how you can do all that stuff with the phone company? It's your superpower. Everyone has one. I do this for a living. Every character I write, I give them a superpower. Think about *Breaking Bad*."

"The TV show about the chemistry teacher turned drug dealer?"

"What was his superpower? Chemistry. When he needed to get out of a jam, he relied on it. Combustible explosions, magnets, whatever. Science. A character without a superpower is useless in a story."

"I'm not following."

"Your superpower is phones. Mine is understanding how storytelling works. There's a formula, a template to employ. When I teach classes, I tell students every mystery is two stories: the professional and the personal. It's a trick, a gimmick mystery writers use."

"Okay…"

"Once the Avon Sisters were taken, I knew."

"Knew what?"

"That two cases are one."

"Thirty-five years later?"

"I think it has something to do with Danny McPhee getting released from prison..." I cleared up and down the aisle. "I need to tie my uncle to Danny. Recent phone calls, records, any way to—" I rechecked to make sure the coast was clear—"tap, hack into their computers, whatever, man. If I can show they are still talking, we'll know something is up, right? There's no reason why the two of them should still be in touch."

"Okay," Jim said. "I'll do what I can. In the meanwhile, *you* avoid your uncle, and for the love of God stay the hell away from Danny McPhee."

After saying goodbye, I sat in the parking lot, scratching at the beard I should shave or at least trim, big game hunting and questioning the heavy stuff, the existential nature of existence, like why certain movies from the '80s held up (*The Breakfast Club*) while others didn't (*Heathers*). Icy pellets plunked the tin roof. I sat in my nice, new car, seat heaters warming my ass toasty, but I knew how cold it was out there, beyond these deceptive metal barriers, where monsters like Danny McPhee roamed free. I must've sat in that parking lot a good hour, wondering how long till the police found him. The thought of driving back to my lonely house filled me with dread. Where else could I go?

The whole way back, I sensed I was being followed, tailed. I told myself the anxiety, paranoia, the pressure was getting to me. But if Danny McPhee learned I'd been asking about him. Or my uncle wanted to keep an eye on me. Or ... I didn't know. Those two detectives who didn't work for Berlin PD, who may or may not have been real? Then again, I'd never had less of a grasp on what was or wasn't real.

Knocking myself out with a pint of tequila and fistful of Valium and Percocet, I rose to several red alerts on my phone. One was a missed text from Jim. Then four calls. The hospital. Great. Next, a number calling twice, blocked. And the last one? My uncle.

I headed to the kitchen for caffeine. For the first time in ages, I thought the sun was shining. The pathetic fallacy. The end was in sight, the clouds had cleared, the day bright. But I was mistaken; it was the glare from a light bulb refracting off the window, high-watt brilliance smack dab in the middle of my hungover forehead.

I decided to work backwards, pressed play, and hit speaker.

Hey, kiddo. You must be busy working on your next masterpiece. Wanted you to know I'm going on my trip north after all. Would've liked to say goodbye in person. But you were... The message garbled. I thought I caught the word "hospital." When it picked back up: *Won't have service where I'm going so don't bother.*

I called him back, straight to voicemail. I tried a couple more times, same outcome.

So don't bother.

That was it. As good as a confession.

CHAPTER TWENTY-FOUR

"Jim," I said over the speaker. "Iver's split. Gone. Out of town."

"Since when?"

"Yesterday? This morning? He made a point of telling me he'd have no cell service wherever he was headed."

"Convenient."

"Maybe it's not *that* weird. He also hates cell phones." Even after all this time I was trying to make excuses for the man.

"I did what you wanted," Jim said. "Got the phone records for your uncle and Danny." He paused. "You're right. Your uncle doesn't do much talking by cell. But a lot of calls from landlines. Danny to your uncle, your uncle to Danny."

"How far back did you go?"

"Far as I could. Couple months. Pretty consistent. When did your uncle say he'd be back?"

"He didn't. Made it sound like it might be a while."

"Shit," Jim said. "How's the book coming?"

The question caught me by surprise. Though it shouldn't have. It was all connected. "I'm writing it."

"Making good progress?"

"These things take a while, and…" I trailed off. It's hard to explain the magical moment of writing when you know you "got" it. Most of the craft leaves you feeling like a castoff, drifting on the deep, dark seas with no land in sight. Eventually you dive in, pick a direction, and start swimming, which requires a leap of faith that you'll reach land before drowning. More than a few books have sunk to irretrievable depths. Of course the lull in conversation only piqued Jim's curiosity.

"And what?"

"Writing this stuff—I don't know the answer. How it will unfold, resolve, end? Not in real time. Later I'll go back and reread and a … center … will emerge."

"What's a 'center'?"

"It what my old professor Tom Hazuka used to call it. A theme. Calling it a 'center' instead of a 'theme' reminds you less of high school." Feeling self-conscious, I stopped. "You really want to hear about this? How I write a book?" I couldn't imagine anything more boring than discussing process and métier with two killers on the loose.

"That's what we're doing this for, right? A book?"

Yes and no, I thought. The truth was I also enjoyed talking shop, which was part of why losing out on the job at CCSU stung.

"And you're my friend," Jim said. "Tell me."

"You start out in the dark, but as you write a pattern, a path will emerge. A passageway to take. I'll be able to *see* the truth clearer. Right now it's all jumbled—"

"Come to my house," Jim said. "Let's brainstorm."

"Now *that* brings back high school."

He courtesy chuckled.

"Aren't you working?" I asked.

"No. Day off. Come. Now. There's more I'm not telling you." The line got windier.

"Are you driving?"

"No," he said. "Grabbing something from my truck. I'll be honest. When you first told me you were going to write about this, I thought you were wasting your time."

"And now?"

"You've been jumped, beaten up, warned off by detectives. People are on the run. All I know: someone doesn't want you looking into this."

"You believe there's a connection between the Avon Sisters and Rodgers Twins?"

"Starting to look that way. How long before you get here?"

"Give me fifteen."

After I hung up on Jim, I checked my remaining messages from last night. A blocked number with heavy breathing. Twice. And one from Dr. Phillips. Not a nurse, the good doctor himself. The results were in. I needed to call. Immediately. The grave, somber tone told me all I needed to know.

I cracked the door, lit a cigarette, and gazed over Lamentation Mountain. Outside, the ice storm weighted withered branches like tattooed regrets on old men.

One lane was closed on Worthington Ridge, where a limb had snapped under the strain of too many storms. I thought it would be quicker to go around rather than wait for the line of cars to pass. The detour delivered me by our old high school. It's hard to drive by your old high school in a snowstorm as you approach your fiftieth birthday and not get wrapped up in nostalgia and bogged down by melancholy.

By the time I reached Jim's house, his truck was gone. Lights off. No one home. I checked the time on my phone. I wasn't *that* late. Five, ten minutes tops.

I hopped out of my ride and walked around, peeking in windows. I pulled my cell to use for a flashlight, studying prints in the snow, most of which had melted into a slurry of mud. I wasn't a tracker, couldn't get a read on anything. The heavy, gray sky hung ominous and foreboding as I fought the anxiety of my writerly mind.

What the—? He'd called me, told me to come over—after telling me he'd uncovered more dirt. And now … he'd disappeared. If Danny McPhee spotted that tail, maybe he'd turned tables and followed *me*. He could've seen where Jim lived...

I didn't return to the warmth of my cab, racking my brain over what to do. Call Wayne Wright and the Berlin PD? Even with my uncle gone, I didn't have enough evidence. Jim's proof of communication between my uncle and Danny McPhee bolstered claims of malfeasance. Except Jim had obtained that information illegally, rendering it inadmissible.

I started to search up Ron Lamontagne's number—Ron wasn't up to speed but if I supplied the CliffsNotes maybe we could save Jim from whatever trouble I'd gotten him into—when through the murk and drizzle I saw the headlights of Jim's truck come skidding into the driveway.

"Dammit," I said, walking up to greet him. "I was getting worried. I thought maybe Danny—"

"Forgot I had a prescription to pick up and they close for lunch. Thought I'd beat you back here. Took longer than I thought. My bad."

"It's fine." I nodded toward his house. "Want to talk inside?"

Jim studied the exterior of his charming cottage home. "Now you got me paranoid. I didn't tell you this, but earlier I got a couple calls. No caller ID. Heavy breathing."

"I got the same calls."

"How much of this new book have you actually written?"

"I'm making decent headway? I told you. I have notes, extensive files on my computer, charting timelines from when I saw Jack and his stepfather, filling in the blanks using what Mel told me. Some conjecture—Annabelle, Ava, Avon, where the tape recorder man fits in. Some more concrete details—dates, times, alibis."

"How much is actually written?"

"Half of it? Why?"

"Let's go to your place."

"I thought you said to avoid it?"

Jim laughed. "We aren't any safer here. Plus, I'd like to take a look at your notes. Maybe you're missing something. Two heads are better than one, right?"

"Six of one, I guess." I couldn't help but think how this mirrored the various obstacles and challenges I planted in my books. Jumped from behind, followed by mystery men, confronted by shady detectives. Was I a soothsayer, a visionary? Or was I playing out the predestined parts of a self-fulfilling prophecy?

"Follow me." I knew I had beer at home. And right then I could use a drink.

The traffic had cleared on Worthington Ridge. We were at my place within minutes.

And it didn't take more than seconds to see something was very wrong.

CHAPTER TWENTY-FIVE

You could see from the street that the door had been kicked in, frame splintered, top rail separated from the hinge. I didn't have the tightest security—this was Berlin; you didn't need chains or a deadbolt—one good boot stomp would do it.

I slammed the car in park, jumping out, Jim on my heels, as I bounded up the front steps.

"Jesus," Jim said, echoing my silent sentiments.

My problem of not having yet unpacked was taken care of, everything I owned kicked over, strewn about, table toppled, cushions tossed. What were they searching for? I didn't have anything worth stealing. I once put a hard drive in a book. Used it as a clue. Mysterious, tangible, a physical piece of evidence to be hunted. A McGuffin. Authors do it all the time to give the characters something to search for. It's a means to propel narrative. I didn't have any McGuffin. No stuffed falcon. No yellowed confession letter. No locked box key. Everything I had existed in clouds.

"Who would do this?" Jim said.

"My uncle?" Iver was too old to understand "clouds." Maybe he didn't go anywhere, sticking around, watching my every move.

"I triangulated Iver's last cell use. Northern New Hampshire. Toward the mountains."

"Canada?"

"Looks that way."

"Danny." Who else was there?

"What was he looking for? You said you don't have anything."

"I don't."

"Some notes and book on your … computer."

In the writing room, there was my computer, smashed to bits.

"All that work," Jim said. He sounded more devastated than I.

"Don't worry, man. Writers are paranoid. Everything I write is backed up in multiple places. Dropbox. I email myself. Losing a book because a computer crashes is every author's worst nightmare." I nodded toward the closet. "I own a laptop too. I don't drag a desktop into coffee shops. There are backups of backups."

Jim exhaled, relieved. "That's good, at least."

"When was the last time Danny and my uncle talked on the phone?"

"According to the phone records? This morning."

"Where was Danny calling from?"

"I couldn't get a ping. Strange. Like he was using software."

"Software? *That* guy?"

"He must still be in town." Jim brushed aside my concerns. "Don't worry, I'll crack it."

"I'm guessing this information wasn't obtained through lawful means?"

"If you're asking whether we can bring it to the cops? That would be a hard no. I cut serious corners and broke a lot of rules. FCC rules. Well-regulated rules that land regular people like me in hot water. This is for *your* eyes and ears only. You asked for the favor, remember?" Jim clasped a hand on my shoulder, motioning over the wreckage. "At least you know your hunch was right. Your uncle and Danny are up to something. You don't break into a house and destroy a computer if you don't have something to hide. And the timing of their last phone call is too weird to ignore."

"We can at least report the break-in."

"Sure. Then I'd say lay low for a couple. Back off any more questions." His hand remained on my shoulder. "Try and relax, get some rest."

"Not sure that's possible." I pulled my fingers through my hair. "The doctor called. Labs are in."

"Shit." Jim didn't want to follow up with the inevitable. If the news were good I'd have led with that.

He squeezed my shoulder tighter but didn't ask what stage the cancer was, which would've been crass. I wouldn't have been able to answer anyway. I didn't know. And I wasn't in a hurry to find out.

"Let me help you put this back together," he said.

"You don't have to do that."

"I know I don't. But I'd rather not leave you alone. And to tell the truth, I'm not looking forward to being alone either. This is spooking me out, buddy." He chuckled. "Remember when we were kids and I slept over? That *Twilight Zone?*"

My face washed emotionless, deadpanned and hobo-affected. I stuck out a dawdling thumb. "Goin' my way?"

Jim shuddered. "Knock it off! I still have nightmares about that shit."

We couldn't have been more than seven or eight when Jim slept over. And late at night, unable to sleep, we got the bright idea to watch *The Twilight Zone.* The episode featured a woman traveling west to see her mother. She starts out from the East Coast, from a town not unlike ours, aiming for California and the bright blue Pacific. Her tire blows out and she almost crashes. Soon afterward she sees a disheveled hitchhiker. When she slows, he says, hair-raising as hell, "Goin' my way?" So she speeds off, racing toward the West Coast. A couple hundred miles down the highway, she sees the same hitchhiker. A couple hundred more, there he is again. Feeling like she's cracking up, the woman stops at a diner, where she calls her mother from a payphone. The help answers and says her mom can't come to the phone because she's in shock—her only daughter died in a car accident a couple days ago. Jim was so scared he called his mom to pick him up. We often laughed about that one. Although right now the idea of the afterlife and spirits wreaking havoc with us mortals didn't seem so far-fetched.

Jim and I set about cleaning up, the break-in a blessing in disguise. Or at least a silver lining. It got us out of our heads, completing mindless tasks that occupied brain space, leaving scant time to contemplate the existential and deadly. It also forced me to unpack and make this house a home.

While we did it, Jim and I talked. He said, based on triangulation, Iver and Danny had gotten together frequently in recent weeks, lunches, coffee, random parking lots, details that painted my uncle in increasingly unflattering light. Still, I felt Jim was holding back.

I tore open a ten-pack of black tees. "What else aren't you telling me?"

"You know Scott Hartan?"

"Few years younger than us, right?"

"Works with ex-cons, parole officers, knows people in that … world. Anyway, I was talking to him because I know he was at Osborn Correctional, where Danny served time." Jim waited until he had my full attention. "Your uncle wrote a letter on Danny's behalf, helped him get paroled."

I dropped the box I'd been holding, folded linens wafting the fresh scent of detergent and sealed-in musk.

"Pretty passionate letter. Played a significant role in getting Danny out."

"I thought he did the full twenty-five?"

"Shaved a few months." Jim glanced at his phone, then around the room we'd made a serious dent in. "Can you handle it from here?"

"No problem."

I walked Jim to the door, my mind spinning with questions and throat burning from my recent smoking relapse.

I opened the door and there she was.

CHAPTER TWENTY-SIX

Jim's sidelong glance and raised eyebrow said, "I thought there was nothing going on with you and Melissa McPhee?" Which is a lot to convey with the wriggling of one's forehead but Jim had very expressive eyebrows. Made up for the lack of hair on his head.

It's hard to pretend there is nothing going on between you and a pretty woman when she shows up on your porch at noon instead of catching a flight to somewhere fabulous.

"Hey you," I said, nonchalant as I could. Part of me was forever stuck at twenty-three. I couldn't look at Mel McPhee and not wonder "what if?"—even as I'd grown more certain her cousin was a serial killer and rapist. We can't pick our family. We live in glass houses, which says less about throwing stones than it does the occasional profundity of Billy Joel. Sometimes it *is* all a fantasy.

Jim tried his best not to mumble or stutter but pretty women do funny things to a man, I don't care how old, and the harder he tried to play off the "Wazzup?" vibe he sought to project, the more he was left muttering and staring at his shoes, until he said he'd call me later, skittering down the walkway like a frenzied rodent.

Mel joined in my puzzled look, which I played up for effect. Mel must've evoked reactions like that over the years. Or maybe not. Modeling aside, Mel *was* indisputably beautiful. But part of her allure owed to how she looked to *me*. She held a special place in my heart. Uncle Iver always said certain women look better the more you get to know them. There were countless women in California who'd probably make Mel disappear in a crowd. Not to me though. It's like Arthur Lee sings, "You can be in love with almost anyone." I knew the lyric was "everyone," but I always sang "anyone." Felt more apropos.

"Do you know you do that?" Mel asked, while we still stood in the doorway and I remembered just how cold midday December in New England gets.

I hadn't invited her in off the porch, a mistake I now corrected, helping ease her in and shutting the door.

"It's like you disappear," she said.

"I'm right here."

"No," she said. "You're gone. Like checked out."

"Right. The present thing. Got that one a lot from the ex."

"It's not that," Mel said. "More like a trance. Do you sleepwalk?"

"Not that I know of." I smiled. "Then again if I walked in my sleep, I wouldn't know it, would I?"

"I don't remember you sleepwalking. What about your wife?"

"*Ex*-wife. And no. What are you trying to say?" What I thought was playful banter had turned into a serious discourse on consciousness and REM.

"A fugue state. You know what that is?"

I shrugged. I'd heard the term before but couldn't recall where.

"It's when you're awake but also not. Like the inverse of a lucid dream. That's what you look like sometimes. As if being remote controlled from far away."

"Brainwashed?" I chuckled.

She didn't. "Have you ever lost huge chunks of time you can't account for?"

"No," I said, now getting offended. "I thought you were … flying over water … somewhere."

"Yes."

That was it, all she offered, leaving me to wonder if she'd made up having to catch a flight to get away from me.

"Can I get you a drink?" Even though I was almost half a century old, saying that aloud made me feel like a pretender, a fraud playing grown-up. I wondered if everyone felt that way. When I glanced at Mel, everything about her so elegant and sophisticated, I had to think no. Several years younger, she was a woman. I still felt like a boy around her.

"I'm good," Mel said, getting on with business. "Are you following my cousin?"

"I thought you didn't talk to Danny?"

"I don't," Mel announced. "But I speak with my aunt. Barb said Danny called her, said he'd run into the town's 'famous author.'" She did the air quotes thing. God, I hated that. "Said you've been spying outside his motel room.'"

"Spying is a stretch." I didn't even know which room was his at the America Inn. But now that I knew Danny knew, it answered the question of who was hanging around, kicking in doors, and leaving obscene phone calls.

"Do you know where he is?" I asked.

"I told you the other day. I haven't talked to him in years." Mel stepped deeper into my world. "Nice to see you decorated."

"Have a seat. Sure I can't get you anything? An espresso? Americano? I'm a regular barista."

"Yes," Mel answered through a tight-lipped grin, "I'm sure."

"Mel, you know the police are looking for your cousin, right?"

She nodded.

"And you know that's partly because of what I uncovered research-ing this book?"

Again, recognition in the affirmative without a movement wasted.

"The police are involved now because I went to the Gribbard Pool shed, where your cousin possibly attacked me." I showed her the back of my head, strip shaved and stitched like a football. "Bludgeoned. In the dark. Left me for dead."

"Danny wouldn't do that."

"They found pictures."

"What kind of pictures?"

"Of Annabelle and Ava Rodgers. Old Polaroids. Can't say for sure, but they looked like they were taken close to the time the Twins went missing. And if they were in the shed where Danny was living—which according to you he was—that means, at some point, Danny had been with them."

"That doesn't mean he kidnapped and killed them."

"The Polaroids looked like the pictures on your aunt's wall. The ones Danny took. And when the police went to talk to him, he fled."

"Of course he did! He's an ex-con. A registered sex offender."

I threw up my arms. She was making my case for me.

"Julie."

"Excuse me?"

"That was the girl Danny was arrested for 'kidnapping.'" The air quotes again.

"You mean the fifteen-year-old girl he kept prisoner for three days? Raped? I'm sorry, I know it can't be easy having a guy like that in your family—"

Mel stood up. "It's not even noon…" She started for my kitchen. "I'll take you up on that drink."

I passed her, making for the fridge. I poured some OJ and

cranberry in a glass with ice and a splash of tequila. "Makeshift tequila sunrise."

"Julie was Danny's girlfriend. Sixteen, almost seventeen."

"Danny was twenty-three."

"Yes, which is statutory rape. And illegal. I'm not excusing what he did."

"Even if what you are saying is true." I held up a hand before she could take offense. "And I don't doubt it is. A twenty-three-year-old man 'dating' a fifteen-, sixteen-year-old is messed up."

"Yes, it is. Sixteen is too young to make consented decisions. That's why he was arrested. That's why he went to prison. But I think there is a difference between two people who'd been having a consensual relationship, even as screwed up as that relationship may've been. What I'm trying to say ... the story everyone knows, my cousin holding a little girl against her will, raping her—isn't accurate."

"Statutory rape is still rape."

"I'm not saying it isn't. Danny fucked up. Danny was, *is* a fuck up. He should've known better. But I know you can see the disparity between the two versions, can't you?"

I didn't want to consider that. "No man Danny's age should be 'dating' a sixteen-year-old, even if she's 'almost' seventeen. It's immature." I did the air quotes. *See how she likes it.*

"I'm not asking for you to have sympathy for Danny. I cut him out of my life long ago. I'm asking you to please leave my aunt alone."

"I talked to your aunt once."

"The police have been coming around. Harassing her. The further this goes, the more the press will too."

"What do you want from me? I told you. I'm researching a book."

"And what happens when this book comes out? Does well? Garners more attention? My family doesn't want that either."

I grabbed a beer from the fridge, returning to the living room to take a seat. She followed but chose to stand. Her right. "*And*," I added, showing I had as much to lose, "I think your cousin and *my* uncle may be working together."

"What on earth are you talking about?"

I explained the connection to the Avon Sisters. How Jim had … established … phone calls between my uncle and Danny. Now Mel took a seat, mouth agape, transfixed by a mesmerizing story, at least that was how I'd interpreted it. Like Capote, I wanted the new book to be literary enough to transcend genre and the purely procedural, espousing a commentary on the human condition. I felt on the right track.

"Danny fled," I said, answering my own questions. "So did my uncle."

"I don't care."

Her dismissal stung.

"How do you explain the photos?"

"Maybe the cops put them there. They've always hated Danny."

"After thirty-five years? They're trying to frame him. You don't believe that."

"No," Mel said, quieter. "I don't."

She looked troubled. I wanted to put my arms around her. And I might've if she didn't say what she said next, manipulating heartstrings.

"Did you know my uncle—Ken, Danny's father—died after he was arrested?"

"Suicide?"

"No!" she snapped. "Everything isn't so dramatic. My uncle wasn't healthy. But Danny's arrest didn't help. You write whatever you have to. But I'm asking, as a friend, to please consider the other people who will be affected."

I rose and moved toward Mel, but she slipped away before I could catch her. Any hope that this visit carried an ulterior motive abated. No one was going to be spending the afternoon together, never mind the night. What I'd thought was sexual tension was just … tension.

"What makes you so sure Danny and your uncle are that close?" she said.

"I told you. My friend Jim Case learned that my uncle helped with Danny's parole. Corrections officer confirmed that story." Since that information didn't come from Jim's telephone connections I didn't feel bad sharing sources.

"Your friend Jim is weird."

"You don't even know him."

"I remember him from when we were kids. Him and that other one, what's his name, Ron? You know they used to spy on me getting changed at the public pool?"

"What? When you were like ten?"

"This is stuff you don't have to worry about as a man."

"What are you talking about? That was thirty-five years ago."

"And yet I still remember it." She folded her arms. "Call it male privilege."

"You sound like my ex-wife."

"If I sound like another woman that's because at one time or another every woman's been sexually harassed."

Although I had a hard time chastising a couple teenage boys peeping in the girl's locker room, I knew enough to keep my mouth shut. I doubted they'd been looking for girls Mel's age. They were probably hoping to catch Karen Burger changing.

"I know what you're thinking," Mel said. "That's normal teenage boy behavior."

"Why do I feel like I am getting attacked?"

"Here's another fun one. When we girls were—this wasn't even high school, I'm talking McGee, middle school—you know what the boys would do?"

"Um…"

"They'd sneak up behind us girls with their fingers like this." Mel extended her pointer and middle fingers, fusing them together. "And creeping up behind us, they'd stick their fingers between our legs. Then laugh when we jumped, startled and scared. You think teachers did anything?"

"Sorry. That's messed up. For real, Mel. But, like, I didn't do—"

"But boys will be boys, right?"

"Not at all! I … I didn't … I wasn't …" I stopped.

I'd lost this conversation. Best course of action: exercising my right to remain silent. I wasn't sure how we'd gotten on the topic of gender inequality or male predatory behavior. This happened all the time out west in San Francisco. I'd hear all the horrible things men and boys did and feel the pressure to apologize. And what can you say? We *were* animals.

"Please," she said, walking toward the door. "Whatever you decide to do with this … book … try and remember it's not just about you, okay?"

I wanted to ask where she was staying, if she'd be around awhile, if maybe, at a later date, we could grab coffee or something? Given the context, I decided not to pursue that angle.

She opened the door but didn't leave right away, turning over her shoulder. "Danny deserved to go to prison. But keep something in mind. When you and I slept together for the first time? You were twenty-four. I was eighteen. Do the math."

I'd followed her to the door, her words rooting me the floor.

She leaned in and gave me sisterly peck on the cheek. "This time I won't be back."

Mel walked outside, into the cold, whipping wet rains. She hadn't even slid on her coat, bare armed in thirty degrees.

Why was I the one who felt exposed?

CHAPTER TWENTY-SEVEN

For several hours that night I lay awake in bed, unable to sleep. To say I had a great weight pressing on my mind undersold the tenets of gravity. Even after the cancer ate my mother's organs, stole her weight, smile and dignity, I convinced myself that there was something inside me, a stronger constitution, an indefatigable spirit that made me special, impervious to the wounds and ailments that brought down mortal men. I wrote a lot about Alcoholics Anonymous. I had a cousin in it. I can't say her name because of that whole anonymous part. But I was familiar with the organization, and my cousin, who also lived on the West Coast, visited often, car plastered with bumper stickers. I loved the AA slogans. My favorite: the piece of shit at the center of the universe. This was a common feature of the addicted, this feeling of both superiority and worthlessness.

I grabbed a cold moonlight beer, then fished a crumpled pack of cigarettes from the trash, finding the least bent butt, straightening it out, and lighting it off the stove. I stood at the side door, staring up at the moon. As often happens in Central Connecticut this time of year, the temperature vacillated. With the clearing clouds, glacial warmed to almost tolerable. Low forties, which for a conditioned California boy was still frigid. For a returned Connecticut native it proved a welcome respite. Maybe I was an alcoholic too. I didn't believe that. I'd started drinking beer because the characters I created drank the stuff. Lately, I'd been drinking harder liquor. Tequila, mezcal. Not the cheap swill. Top shelf. I was depressed, not a hobo.

There's something about standing in your boxer shorts, smoking a cigarette, and drinking an IPA at three a.m. in the cold winter months that offers harsher truths.

I told Alexa to shuffle songs and she couldn't have stuck a more savage landing. Bob Seger, the poor man's Springsteen. I'd always loved the blue-collar, working-class vibe, even if I'd never done much time in a factory.

Here's the thing with non-fiction—which this book is—you can't lie. And if the song that came on was "Hollywood Nights" or "Katmandu" or, heaven forbid, "Old Time Rock and Roll," then maybe I don't include this scene. But the random shuffle cued "Like a Rock." The misfortune of a Chevy commercial aside—I'd never been a truck guy—the line that always got me: "Twenty years where'd they go? Twenty years I don't know."

The longer we're here, the faster time goes because of percentages and math. A summer and season no longer make up one tenth of your life; they represent an infinitesimal bleep, a finger snap, one eye blinking.

By some standards, I'd accomplished a lot with my life. But was it enough? I once wrote a story about Da Vinci—brilliant writer, artist, philosopher—the man invented the first prototype for the helicopter—perhaps the single greatest human being ever to live. His last words: I've wasted my years.

And if he wasted *his* years, what had I done with mine?

I wasn't putting myself in the same league as Da Vinci. To misquote Samuel L. Jackson, I wasn't in the same league, wasn't even playing the same goddamn sport. But I thought about that Da Vinci quote a lot, about the drive and work ethic, the fire down below it takes to excel. Talent gets you through the door. Everyone has talent—this guy, that woman over there, Lou in Accounting who does hilarious impressions of English people. But ambition, drive, the ability to delay gratification and work your ass off is what separates the wheat from the chaff. I used to think I was driven, strong. In my younger days, I was ready to fight anyone, anytime. Piss and vinegar. You take a side, I'll take the other, and my endurance was unquestionable. My *real* superpower: I could bang my head against a wall longer than you. I didn't have that superpower anymore. I was beaten, broken, tired.

Of course it was middle of the night, I'd recently learned I had some form of cancer, I was divorced, out of a job, my uncle was a murderer, and the one that got away just told me I was a self-absorbed jerk. I didn't have anything. Except this book.

I didn't remember falling asleep. I didn't drink enough beer—there were only three left—to pass out. It was more exhaustion. And the cancer. I woke up feeling weaker than usual, slower, more apathetic. It was like the life inside me had seen the writing on the wall, and pieces of my soul were packing up and getting out of dodge.

With nothing on the agenda for the day, the plan was to grab some coffee, more cigarettes and alcohol, and get to work. I'd duck any calls from the hospital and Dr. Phillips—I wasn't up for that yet. Focus on stamping my indelible impression on immortality before they pulled the plug for good.

In contrast to the past few sludgy, sleet-riddled days, the morning that greeted me was downright pleasant. After that artic blast, forty-nine degrees rivaled the balmy tropics.

I needed coffee and alcohol. In the Stop & Shop parking lot, I locked up and started toward the entrance when I felt the hand on my shoulder, stopping me in place.

Wayne Wright.

"Still no luck finding Danny?" I said, bypassing hello.

"Not yet." Wayne checked me over. "You okay. You're not looking so hot."

"Ribs are killing me." Which was a lie. After the first couple days, I was patched up tight enough that the worst was over. Plus the Percocet helped. "Not sleeping well."

"Listen, my bosses need more of a statement." He pulled out his little pad. "The town isn't pressing charges for Gribbard—"

"Great."

"But the shed incident is still a B&E. And an assault. A pretty serious one. We'd like to catch who did it."

"I think we know who did it. Danny McPhee."

"I agree Danny is looking like a good bet. But we have to be thorough. Is there anyone else you can think of? Someone with an ax to grind?"

"Yeah," I said. The time had come for me to come clean. "My uncle."

Wayne listened as I told him the whole story, the Acura MDX, the license plate, the red stain on his white shirt, the mall, the constant contact between him and Danny, leaving out Jim's role in securing that last part. I couldn't mention the duffel bags Jim helped move, which would screw over my friend. So I stuck to my uncle's splitting town, cutting off all communication.

Saying this out loud felt good, a much-needed purge. I needed to unburden before I was gone. I wasn't fighting this cancer. I'd seen what it did to my mother. I never shied from a good boxing analogy, my love of Springsteen only rivaled by my deep appreciation of the Rocky mythology. Cancer is formidable, with a great win-loss record. Cancer, like any tenacious fighter, never stays down for long. Few go the distance, and in the end, it costs them everything.

When I caught Wayne's stare, he looked angry. "This doesn't look good for you."

"Huh?"

"You waiting to bring this up until after your uncle flees?" He panned around the sunshiny lot, dirty snow melting in oily pools. "You and I have a history. To others? You waiting this long to come forward? Looks like you were protecting him."

"That's not what happened."

Wayne scribbled down something in his notebook. "What you've told me isn't enough for a search warrant for Iver's place." He stopped. "What makes you think your uncle is 'fleeing'?"

"Every year he takes a trip up north to see the leaves change—"

"Hold on. He takes this trip *every year?*"

"In the fall. It's winter now."

"It's still fall. Winter starts December twenty-first."

"He's not going to see the leaves change. It's already snowing!"

Wayne tucked away the book.

I'd lost him.

"I wasn't withholding information," I said. "I was waiting till I had more." I choked down my frustration. "I told you everything I know—"

"Did you?" Wayne took a step forward, closing the distance between us. "Those photographs? The Polaroids."

"From the night I was attacked at Gribbard. What about them?"

"They weren't in the shed when you were attacked."

"You said you found them when you found me?"

"I did." He waited for me to catch on but I didn't know what he was getting at. "*After* you were attacked. They were left behind. They can test for that stuff. The decay wasn't consistent. If they were sealed up when Danny was living there, they'd have been more degraded."

"What are you getting at?"

"I'm not the boss. Right now, the B&E, coupled with the photographs... My higher-ups are questioning if somebody planted them there."

"Whoever attacked me! Danny! My ... uncle!"

Wayne returned a blank stare.

Or ... me.

"You think I'm making this whole thing up? Why? To sell books? You saw my broken ribs, my bashed-in skull! I did that to myself? That's insane."

"Like I said, I have bosses."

"What about the break-in at my house?"

"What break-in?"

"The other day, Jim and I showed up at my house. Door kicked in. Computer trashed. Ask Jim." I turned toward the sky. "I suppose I did that too?"

"I'll look into it," Wayne said. "But when people hear you're writing a book, looking into an ugly part of this town's history? You're not getting the benefit of any doubt. You're pissing people off."

"I get attacked, some asshole breaks into *my* house, and it's my fault?"

"I'm not saying that. But think how it looks to other people."

I got it. Given my timing, waiting to reveal my uncle's role, I'd implicated myself as well. If they couldn't get a warrant or find anything at Iver's, if they couldn't reach him, what's to say I wasn't the one trying to set *him* up?

CHAPTER TWENTY-EIGHT

That night I met Jim and Ron for drinks at Sliders. I'd asked Jim not to mention the cancer to Ron, who like any good friend would be concerned, and then I'd have to deal with his well-meaning questions about when treatment began, did I need anything, listen to reassurances how it was all going to be okay, and then drinks would be on him the rest of the night. He'd be worried. One of our good friends just passed away from cancer. I didn't want to do that to him. I didn't want to do that to me.

I also didn't plan on sticking around Sliders all night drinking cheap beer and smelling fried pickles.

When Ron went to the bathroom, I turned to Jim, who already knew tonight's real plan. I felt guilty for playing the cancer card but since Jim learned the news, he'd come around to my way of thinking, seeing the urgency. It wasn't difficult getting his help finding the address of the McPhees' vacation home, the one Mel told me about when we had dinner. Jim isolated it using his telephone company privileges, which had supplied more than coordinates on a map. Because of Jim, we knew Danny McPhee had been there recently. Jim pulled the phone records. Two months ago. Around the time the Avon Sisters were taken.

Mel's compassionate plea to spare her family didn't circumvent my wanting justice. It did, however, alter perspective on Danny. The story of a man who sexually assaulted a kidnapping victim wasn't the same as a stupid twenty-three-year-old having sex with his sixteen-year-old girlfriend. I wasn't judge or jury, and I wasn't the moral police. The law is the law and Danny had broken it. It wasn't up to me to decide a fair sentence. But a third of a man's life added up to no small price.

Could Danny be hiding out at the summer home? With Mel out of town, would anyone else be there in the winter? Worth the risk. There was also the possibility of hard evidence. If we didn't learn anything about the girls themselves, maybe we could locate clues tying Danny to my uncle. I'd considered telling Wayne Wright and the Berlin PD about the McPhee getaway house. But now that the police (at least some of them) suspected I planted those photos, any assistance from their end was out.

If the cops suspected I was involved in helping my uncle—or worse thought I was setting him up—I now needed Danny's help clearing my name as much as I needed the SOB brought to justice.

The problem started when Ron returned from the bathroom. I tried to call it a night, but he wouldn't go for it. The more insistent I became, the harder he dug in, and the more confrontational the conversation grew. The longer we argued, the more I had to divulge.

"Three are better than two," Ron said, defiantly. "If we find Danny you'll need me."

"He's almost sixty."

"No offense," Ron said. "But you look awful. I'm not sure you could handle an anorexic squirrel right now."

We piled in the front of Jim's truck, instead of taking my roomier ride, because we'd need the all-wheel drive. Ron's truck would've put us on one another's lap. We were close but not *that* close.

Mel hadn't actually called it a "vacation home"; she'd referred to it as a shack—although I had a hard time picturing Mel McPhee spending a minute in a shack. The residence was up near North Canaan, in the Western Connecticut highlands before the Massachusetts border, between the Adirondack and Berkshire Mountains.

Like three buddies on a late night ice-fishing expedition, we glided along cold asphalt. There were a lot of connections to make—84 to 8, then the 63 before the numbers all got prime and extra indivisible. Light disappeared deep in the heart of farm country.

For a moment, I forgot the severity of the situation. We were laughing, joking, remembering the old days, sharing a lot of stories about Jack. I started with the time Jack fought BHS's recently disgraced football coach, John Ratterson, back when they were in high school.

"Jack didn't fight John," Ron corrected. "Barry Dole did."

He was right. Both Jack and Barry were lanky. Unlike Jack, Barry wasn't one of the cool kids. He still handed Ratterson's ass to him. That fight was '86's version of Mike Tyson versus Buster Douglas, with Barry the heavy underdog that afternoon. We'd all gathered in the valley of Gribbard School to watch Barry Dole beat the living shit out of him. Barry peppered John with stiff jabs, keeping the favorite off balance, before unleashing a barrage of pinpoint, accurate rights and lefts that had John waving his hands in surrender. John Ratterson never picked on Barry after that. Couldn't believe I got the two confused, Barry and Jack, but both were tall, gangly, inelegant in their strides. Memory is like that. Physical traits, height, hair, hands, get conflated. Plus at fifteen, everyone looks the same. Being "tall" means having an extra inch or two—all teenagers look alike.

"How much longer?" Ron asked. The harsh glare of the cab's light shone off Jim and Ron's smooth pate, glistening, evoking sun smacking off slick ice.

I checked my phone. No point. No GPS in the cuts. "Your guess is as good as mine."

Ron started asking more questions. He didn't know what Jim and I did. I did my best to answer them. I wrestled with how much to share about my uncle. Iver wasn't a bad man. Except that if he did any of these things, then, yeah, he was. I started thinking about all the family members of the world's monsters—the Dahmers, the Ramirezes, the Gacys. What about the Dylan Klebolds and Eric Harrises, Starkweather, the kids caught doing unspeakable things? The twelve-year-old who stabs a college student in Central Park? These killers have mothers and fathers, sisters, brothers, who hold happy memories from better times. Days at the beach. Birthdays. First steps and developmental milestones, parents who recollect cradling little angels, desiring the best possible futures, only to watch their babies turn out to be monsters. Did they start hating them when they first heard the news? Or did it take time? Did all the good memories get washed away? Or was blood thicker than slaughter?

I was having a difficult time hating my uncle. I was confused, conflicted, compromised. He was still the man who taught me how to throw a baseball; the man who taught me to ride a bike; the father who talked me through my first brokenhearted night when young Annabelle ripped it out of my chest. I couldn't believe Uncle Iver took the Twins to avenge his nephew's puppy love. But the verifiable bond between him and Danny had grown impossible to ignore.

If it were proven he was a killer, I'd have to hate him. And I didn't know if I was strong enough to do that.

Most of this part of Connecticut was secluded wasteland, the western mountains and Berkshires, with their tortuous winding roads, canopies of trees, and gouging gravel pits twisting you up. In these hills, street signs ebbed fewer and further, most sprayed unintelligible from buckshot and bb guns, victims of hillbilly drive-bys. Of course, cell service was unreliable and bars disappeared faster than taverns in a dry town. I'd printed out directions before we left civilization.

The drive lasted forever, as we passed burnt stumps and lazy, one-legged hounds, collapsed red barns, roofs puckered and caved, beaten by the elements and economy. Majestic mountains rose to the edge of forever. Tall trees speared the skies, towering, twisty branches crooked around limb and rock, stabbing the stars. The air tasted like snow was on its way, extra clean and antiseptic. A winding, desolate road forked off into another less populous, more disparaging trail, shocks absorbing sinkholes. The heavy vegetation parted.

Mel had undersold the splendor. No, this wasn't the Hamptons. But it also landed a long way from "fishing shack." In the Bay Area, this much land and square feet nets millions.

Two stories overlooked a glistening lake in the early stages of freezing. A bright full moon reflected across the expansive sheen of ice. Flurries drifted like aimless angels, the ground covered with more snow than we had in the flats, night-songs echoing off valley walls.

We stepped from the cab, hugging ourselves and shivering. Up in these mountains, the temperature was at least twenty degrees colder. I often wrote about mountains. Like the life of a drifter, they seemed romantic, until you experienced them firsthand. I spent my late-twenties on the road. After my master's, I got sidetracked, years spent trekking across Nevada, Colorado, Minnesota, where I met my future wife. I read a lot of books when I was younger about the hobo life, Kerouac and the Beats, eating beans from a can, sleeping on hard ground, rocks for pillows. Once I realized I'd never play right field for the Yankees or be a rock star, I started a different dream, one where I roamed free in Europe, and wrote and loved and lost, contemplating the human condition on assorted precipices, gazing forlorn, smoking, smoldering with wanderlust. Each day would deliver me to another city and another beautiful woman, who'd be sitting alone in a bar at two in the afternoon and, miraculously, single, disease free, and not at all insane; and we'd have super intense conversations about love, life, death, and madness, before going to her villa or some luxurious hotel that somehow I'd have the money to pay for even though I didn't have a job funding any of these fantasies; and there we'd make love on satin sheets and eat rich, buttery breads slathered with delectable dark red jams. Like Ethan Hawke and Julie Delpy in the *Before Sunrise* movies. And then the next day, a new town, a new lover as I lived the stories I'd one day put in a book.

Until that Italy book tour, I never made it to Europe, and the closest I came to scrumptious cuisine and exotic lovers were late-night burritos at Taqueria Cancun and naked girls dancing in plexi-glass booths at the Lusty Lady.

It's funny the way we end up with a version of the life we want. It's never what we envision. Never as clean, sharp, poignant. We get a rendition, an interpretation, like viewing the sunset through the bottom of a cracked glass, a fractured kaleidoscope prismed.

I did become a writer, and the skies up here sure were pretty.

"He gets like that a lot," I heard a voice say.

I stopped stargazing to meet the stares of my two oldest friends, facial expressions resigned to the flighty headspace of their artsy pal.

Jim slapped the head of his flashlight, a stream of white extending across the terrain. "Okay, buddy. What are we looking for?" He turned to the house, which was battened down for the winter. I would've liked to get inside.

No one was getting inside.

While the rustic exterior was manufactured, a new design fashioned to look old, the house came with a security system. Crooks stumble upon this? Out in the wilderness, so far away from the mainland? They'd have it cleared in a couple hours.

"Jim," I said. "You know your way around a security system?"

"If it's hooked up to their internet."

"Okay, you try and see if you can disarm without tripping anything." I turned to Ron. "You and I spread out. Look for markers. Places where … a body or two … could fit." I panned the grounds, which were extensive, sprawling nooks, crevices and crannies. "See if anything looks disturbed."

"You think Annabelle and Ava are buried here?" Ron said.

"We're looking for more than the Twins."

We all set off in different directions. Stalking around the back of the home, I bumped into the yacht. That might be overselling it. But it was a big boat, covered up and hibernating until the thaw of spring. The McPhees had money—most people in Berlin did—but I hadn't anticipated their having *this* much money. I peeked in windows. Dark, vacant, undisturbed, red security lights blinking.

I scanned the grounds. Any usage of this vacation home meant Danny and/or my uncle couldn't risk burying bodies near it. The boat, the road to the beach, and surrounding landscape were out too. Which left deeper in the forest, higher in the hills. The nowhere lands.

I called after Ron, unsure which direction he'd taken. He didn't respond.

I'd been wandering for a while, using the moon skipping off the lake as my trail of breadcrumbs. The tops of tall pines and evergreens swallowed the moonlight as terrain pinched tighter. Jagged rock-face jutted at crooked, unnatural angles. The night smelled like bed sheets drenched in bleach, sterile with a hint of citrus. Echoes carried and bounced off boulders, each step fed back to me with a slight time delay. Footsteps crackled.

At the edge of a small drop-off, I wondered if I were alone.

I was turning around, when, for the second time in less than a month, I was bashed from behind.

CHAPTER TWENTY-NINE

Getting knocked out doesn't happen often in real life. It's a movie trope. Like fainting. But there are two worlds, the conscious and the un-, and a whole lot of gray space in between. Both subdued and aware, I was traveling in time while all these thoughts ran roughshod. There I was nineteen outside the Cool Moose with my band and buddies, then back to my late forties and fighting with my wife as she begged me to treat her nicer, be present, give more. But I knew how that worked. Part of why my wife loved me so much was because I withheld, didn't show the real me. Because who could possibly love the real me?

Weak and shaken, I tried to stand. My head rattled and my ears rang. I managed to stagger to my feet, feeling the back of my head, which was soft and warm, oozing with the heat of fresh blood. The gash was deep. I didn't know whether this was a new wound or if the sutures from the old one had ruptured. What had I been hit with? A sturdy limb? Hammer? Some other tool? I stopped probing because I couldn't find the end of the squishing and was worried I might be touching my brain.

I'd stumbled to a tree, wrapping arms around it like Rocky Balboa clinging to Apollo Creed in the late rounds. Man, was I a cliché—Springsteen, Rocky, and the New York Yankees. The only thing that would've made me *more* of a cliché was if my favorite book was *Catcher in the Rye*. (It is.)

"Holy shit!" Jim screamed, descending the slick hillside. "What the—?" I could feel his panic, which told me how bad this latest blindside was. "Ron! Ron!"

Footsteps clodded in the dark. I'd somehow managed to spin around, back to bark, sliding to the ground, my vision blurred and wonky; I couldn't focus on a coherent form, get two cogent thoughts to connect.

They kept asking what happened. The words in my head didn't make it to my mouth. What came out instead was a garbled, jumbled hodge-podge of unintelligible consonants and mountain goat bleating. I must've conveyed, "Attacked." I heard someone take off running. Time played with my perception of time. I didn't know how much of it had passed before I heard a voice, through heavy breathing, reporting, "Nothing."

I zoned out. I couldn't keep my eyes open.

I came to with Jim in front of my face, gripping my shoulders, eye to eye.

"That's it, buddy. This ends now!"

I woke in a hospital. Not New Britain General this time. I knew it was a hospital before I opened my eyes—I could tell by the blips and bleeps of machines doing God's work. Where had I heard that before? It was late, dark. I found the thick cord, working my way up to the call button.

A moment later a blonde woman appeared in the doorway. The nurse looked so familiar. I couldn't put a finger on where I'd seen her before. I knew I had.

"Where ... am ... I?"

"The hospital," she said.

Yeah, no shit. I meant which town. Did it matter?

She went about checking the wires coming out of my arms and skull. "Your friends brought you to the ER. You have a serious head wound."

"How bad?"

"You'll live," she said with a smile. I appreciated the levity. "But you sustained a concussion."

"Second one ... in ... two weeks."

"That's what I hear." She smiled with kind eyes. Familiar yet with a touch of sadness. It was killing me trying to remember where I'd seen this woman before. Thinking was only adding to the headache so I stopped.

The nurse adjusted my pillow. I realized I was hooked up to a catheter, not the greatest sensation to come to terms with. Its necessity told me I was in rough enough shape I shouldn't be walking to use the bathroom.

Freezing rain pelted the glass in a sudden fury, so hard and fast I startled.

"A little rain never killed anyone," the nurse said. "You get some sleep. It's all goin' to be okay."

After she left I listened to the pitter-patter of icy pellets, the raging storm strangely soothing.

Then I remembered where I'd seen that nurse before. She was a dead ringer for the actress in that old *Twilight Zone* that scared the hell out of Jim and me when we were kids.

Goin' my way?

CHAPTER THIRTY

There would be no stealth escapes this time.

When I opened my eyes Wayne Wright stood at my bedside, arms crossed, adopting an officious posture. Bright morning light gleamed off fluid bags and infusion pumps—forceps, hooks, and other things metal, the hospital room apparatuses I'd seen enough of to last a lifetime.

"This is twice," he said.

I didn't know if he was referring to my trespassing on private property, breaking and entering, or my getting the shit kicked out of me.

He peppered me with questions about last night's incident, framing any inquiry designed to help me. I considered Wayne a friend, but he'd admitted outside the Stop & Shop that several within the Berlin PD were viewing me with skepticism. This latest incident wasn't going to frame my involvement any better. I couldn't be sure whose side Wayne was on. Was he trying to gather information to help catch my assailant or was he asking questions to trip me up, get me to implicate myself for something I didn't do?

"This book you're writing," he said. "You're treating the recent abduction of Bethel and Brielle Paige as being connected to the Rodgers disappearance?"

I knew those were the names of the sisters from Avon, but it sounded strange hearing them aloud. To me, they were the Avon Sisters. Like Annabelle and Ava were the Rodgers Twins.

"I'm not treating anything like anything." Not the most eloquent response but I had severe head trauma, and I played that up. I gripped the side of my skull, groaning. "Talk to Jim and Ron." If this was a game of show and tell, Wayne had to go first.

"Jim and Ron already gave their statements. I'd like to hear it from you."

The breakfast I'd missed sat on the tray over my stomach. The lid remained closed. Whatever lay beneath smelled putrid, sweaty gym clothes left unwashed, the trapped-in tincture of body odor in a hot trunk.

"That detective you put me in touch with," I said, surprised by how raspy and weak my own voice sounded. "Gary St. Jean. He confirmed Danny was a suspect in the Rodgers Twins' disappearance."

Wayne Wright didn't answer. He didn't have to.

"And he was arrested for the same crime a few months later," I said.

"Not exactly the same crime."

"Now these sisters go missing. It doesn't take much to tie that together. Why haven't you caught him yet?"

"We'll get to Danny McPhee," Wayne said, now opening and reading from his little book. "Jim and Ron said you were standing on the edge of a cliff?"

"Not a cliff. More an overhang. Steep drop." I recapped best I could. The walk in the cold woods, stopping at the precipice, the blow from behind, and then waking up with the back of my skull split open.

"Is it possible you lost your footing and fell, hit your head on a rock?"

If I could've opened my mouth wide enough, I would have laughed. "I think it's obvious I didn't 'slip.' I was attacked."

"Not by Danny McPhee."

"I don't understand how you're defending—"

"Danny was picked up last night."

"Wha—where?"

"Outside another scummy motel on the Turnpike. Danny didn't do this."

"We were at his family's vacation house."

"Trespassing."

I couldn't argue with that.

"Tell me about your uncle," Wayne said. "You said the other day Danny and him had been in contact. Why do you think that?"

"Confidential sources." I couldn't share Jim had been abusing his powers at the phone company to tap telephone lines.

"And you still haven't heard from your uncle? Do you have any idea where he could be?"

I shook my head. Wayne slapped closed his little book, tapping it off his thigh.

"At least Danny is in jail," I said.

"He's already out."

"Out? How is that—"

"We had nothing to hold him on. He was interrogated about Gribbard. Claims he knew nothing about it. And like I said, he didn't do this to you last night. Because he was with us last night."

"You couldn't hold him longer? Figure out how to buy some time?"

"Not once he got his lawyer involved."

"Lawyer? Some public defender who—"

"No," Wayne said. "Paul Moskowitz."

He didn't have to tell me who that was. Only one of the best attorneys in the state.

"How could Danny afford someone like that?" Moskowitz was big time. The guy's ads were all over the radio. Not the type to take on pro bono or penny ante.

Wayne shrugged. "All I can tell you, Danny said he had to call his cousin. Next thing I know, we got a call from Moskowitz, who came down to the station. You can't push around Paul Moskowitz."

Cousin?

Mel?

I couldn't believe my uncle had been following me. The police said that with the new snowfall in North Canaan any tracks, tire or foot, had been covered up. What bothered me most—even more than not knowing the identity of my assailant—was why Mel would bail out a scumbag like Danny, even if he was her cousin. Addressing these questions made nothing clearer, and succeeded only in further muddying already murky waters.

I was released later that day, my insurance tired of paying for my repeated beatings. Jim picked me up. At least this time they sent me home with the pain pills. Jim and I didn't speak much on the way back to my house. I told him Danny had been picked up and let go, but he didn't bite. Fine. I wasn't in the mood to talk, and I knew he was fed up with all of this. His ire emanated in waves.

When Jim dropped me off, he said he was late to work. Clear in his tone: leave me alone.

For the next few days, I didn't do much. Didn't check social media, didn't read the news. Left my phone off. If someone wanted to reach me, they knew where to find me.

During this latest ER visit, surgeons had to re-suture the back of my skull, adding extra staples to cover new ground. I couldn't say whether the procedure was painful since they'd operated while I was sedated. Now that I was awake? My head sure hurt. Which is to be expected when you are clubbed senseless. By what? Whom? No blood-ied crow bar or ax handle had been found at the scene. Was it possible Wayne was right? Had I slipped on the ice and snow, hit my head on a stone? I hadn't seen anyone, no heavy weapon being swung. If it wasn't Danny, and my uncle was out of town—and they'd been trying to track him down, to no avail—who else would be following me in the snowy mountains? When I started wondering about Ron or Jim being part of this vast global conspiracy, I knew I was cracking.

To tell the truth, I didn't want Danny sent back to prison for jump-ing me. That would be like taking down Capone for tax evasion. The guy was guilty of so much more. I was happy to take the beating if it meant cold case detectives could continue their investigation and finally put away the bastard for good.

It was a miserable Thursday morning. Gray, dank, frigid, cold, misty, temperatures hovering at the freezing point. Saddest of all, when I finally got around to checking my phone, expecting to see at least a text or two from Jim or Ron, maybe Mel, there was nothing.

I called Jim, who didn't pick up. I left a message, then headed to the fridge to grab a beer. I tried to approach these loose threads like the plot points in a rough draft. The outline was there. What I needed now was cohesion, a workable order. What did I know for sure? I'd been attacked at least once. The police had Polaroids of the Twins found in Danny McPhee's shed at Gribbard. My house had been broken into, my computer trashed. The rest was circumstantial. The car, license plate, blood on the shirt? Danny talking to Iver, who was out of town on a scheduled yearly trip? Not enough to prosecute, not without a body, and especially not now that a hotshot lawyer was representing Danny. I didn't have a true crime novel. I had a writing prompt.

And yet that stubborn part of me clung to wanting more. I knew in my heart of hearts that the Rodgers case tied to the Avon abduction, and that inquisitive part of my brain, the one that connected A to B to C, couldn't let it go. There had to be more, a pattern I wasn't seeing.

I pulled out my laptop to write, which was how I did my best thinking.

I checked news on the internet first.

There was no point in writing today.

The Avon Sisters had been found.

CHAPTER THIRTY-ONE

It took me a moment to acclimate to the news. I'd developed an internal narrative, an arc with several different directions it might go. Where were their bodies found? Were there signs of sexual trauma? The big one, which I'd been struggling to answer: how would the Avon Sisters' disappearance and death tie to the Rodgers Twins? Because two cases *always* turn out to be one. It's *how* mysteries work. The personal and the professional are the *same* case. I conceived myriad possible endings. Except one where the girls returned home, safe and sound.

Cracking open a beer, I sat down to read the full story. And it was an odd one. I couldn't have dreamt up this twist if you gave me a thousand years.

In 2014, a man by the name of Trevor Hunter and his wife, Eloise, took their two daughters, Carly and Cate, ages nine and ten, on a trip to the Catskills. Trevor had grown up in Upstate New York before moving to Southington, Connecticut, a few towns over from Berlin. Then again most every town in Connecticut is "a few towns" over. Trevor was a country boy, raised on fishing in cricks and camping beneath bright, wide-open skies. Eloise, reared in the city, didn't comprehend the allure of that life, so it took some persuading on Trevor's part, but in the summer of 2014, he convinced Eloise to take their two young daughters to rent a cabin near Kings Falls, New York, outside of Copenhagen.

Taking a break from the drudgery of sales, where he spent most of his adult life, barricaded in his undersized cubicle while he tried to convince strangers to buy things they didn't really need, Trevor felt revitalized in his natural environment. He hunted. The girls fished. His wife worked the loom. They lived like pioneers. It wouldn't last. The sun went down sooner each day. Trevor began to sense his wife and two young daughters growing weary of the lack of running water and electricity, having no internet, not being able to talk to friends. Trevor didn't mind cutting their time short, time he'd secured by quitting his job, a minor detail he hadn't shared with Eloise (telling her he'd negotiated a three-month sabbatical). He wasn't worried. He had money saved. The experiment was, to him, a success. Now Trevor could go back to the rat race and day-to-day grind, a new man refreshed. Those couple months in the Upstate wilds recharged him.

So they contacted the cabin's owner. Trevor didn't expect a refund, and the property owner didn't offer one.

On their last day, Trevor wanted to take his wife and two girls on a hike to the waterfall, Kings Falls, from which the region drew its name. Eloise begged off. Neither girl, according to their mother's statement, wanted to go, but Trevor convinced them to make the most of their last day together in the country.

The walk there was tricky, since the area was closed to the public. Carly and Cate complained, wanting to turn around, go back, head home, anxious to return to their normal lives.

Kings Falls connects to the Deer River, which drains into the Black River, a larger body of water that empties into Lake Ontario and bigger bays. That particular year had seen a lot of rain, far more than usual. Trevor hadn't accounted for that. The accident happened when they reached the top.

No one charged Trevor with a crime. He hadn't done anything wrong other than wanting to share part of his childhood with his children. But the way it happened—Trevor's momentary distraction, the girls slipping, falling, knocked unconscious, pulled under by the riptide and swept away—was the nightmare every parent fears. The marriage couldn't withstand the strain—the media attention, the constant, communal judgment. Eloise left. At first the media glommed onto the Chris McCandless angle, man versus nature, the romance of leaving behind this city grime. Then reporters grew tired of writing that story. There were new tragedies to take its place. And everyone forgot about Trevor Hunter.

The years between 2014 and 2019 don't account for all Trevor's movements. It was clear he blamed himself for the death of his daughters, which ate away at him. Trevor couldn't find work. He suffered a psychotic break, landing on disability. That much was known. But there were huge gaps. Drug use was hinted at. By all accounts, he was barely surviving. Sometimes he was homeless. The few residences secured, single room occupancy motels, broke up the stays in shelters.

Then sometime in the summer of 2019, something inside Trevor Hunter broke for good. Or maybe it was already broken and the patchwork couldn't hold any longer.

How Trevor Hunter managed to convince Bethel and Brielle Paige to get into his stolen car wasn't addressed, at least not to my writerly sensibilities. By all accounts the two sisters were ordinary middle-class, fifteen-year-old girls. I wondered if the paper was withholding certain details out of respect for the family.

The most captivating part of the story was how Trevor Hunter drove the girls back to King Falls, attempting to repair the past. The cabin he'd rented in 2014 had gone under and was now abandoned.

Again the paper didn't make it clear whether Trevor knew that before-hand or if it was sheer luck. One would have to believe the latter, since Trevor Hunter didn't come across as a man with ability for planning. Yet people surprise us all the time.

Bethel and Brielle Paige were abducted from the West Farms Mall in West Hartford in October. They were found two months later in December, when one of the girls left the cabin and made it to town, where she spoke with police.

Though they were kidnapped, a criminal charge that would send Trevor Hunter away for a long time, both girls were adamant that he never touched them in a way that was inappropriate. Trevor slept in his own bed, and the girls in theirs. Although terrified at first, the girls came to trust, even care for their captor. They said he was kind. He was often seen smiling, laughing warmly. The girls said sometimes he'd call one of them Cate or Carly, which was confusing. Bethel and Brielle didn't know the whole story, but they felt sorry for him. When asked by police if they were restrained or locked up, the girls said no, making it clear they'd had ample opportunities to run away. At first they said they were scared to run, certain there was a security system set up to prevent them from doing so. They soon learned there was no such system. When asked why then they remained captive so long the girls didn't have an answer other than pity and confusion, and which came first was hard to say.

I read several articles on the web. All shared the same details, only the writing differed. Sometimes Trevor Hunter came across as a grieving father. Other times more deranged, a man who lost his mind watching his two children fall from great heights to their deaths.

Divorcing myself from the human tragedy of it all, the story itself was fascinating. It reminded me, in some ways, of Mary Kubica's masterful *The Good Girl*, another exploration on Stockholm syndrome.

But as interesting as all that was, there were two details that stood out above the rest.

Or rather it was the two omissions, the names that didn't appear anywhere in the story.

This had nothing to do with Danny McPhee.

And this had nothing to do with my uncle.

CHAPTER THIRTY-TWO

My go-to mystery-writing philosophy—two cases turning out to be one—was out the window. How had I forgotten this was reality and not fiction? The real world offers no pattern, no order, no rhyme, no reason. The good news was two girls, presumed dead, beat the odds. They were returned home, alive and well. And that was to be celebrated. I wasn't disappointed my "theory" didn't pan out in exchange for that happy ending. I didn't hold out hope Annabelle and Ava would be so fortunate. But I could still solve the mystery of what happened to them. The glue of my theory, an allegiance between Danny McPhee and my uncle, still held. Phone calls. Meet-ups. Going on the run. Polaroids. But the neat package I'd been banking on—the Avon Sisters tying to the Rodgers Twins' abduction—to complete the arc, govern literary trajectory, and help sell books was wrong. And if I was wrong about that, what else had I been wrong about?

I thought like a killer. Because I wrote about killers. I roved the bedlam of madmen and lunatics, of deviants and monsters. I ascribed the worst of intentions. I believed in that darkness, and thought it resided inside everyone because it lived inside me.

Reaching for the phone, I started to call Wayne Wright but stopped. What was I going to do? Recant? I *had* been attacked. It must've been Danny because no one else made sense. But Wayne already casted doubt on a second attack...

Wayne, who went to school with Annabelle and Ava...

Wayne, from whom I got almost all my information...

Wayne, the existence of another player in this game...

How did I know Wayne was on the level? I never spoke to any of these "higher-ups." All my news about this case came via Wayne Wright. How did I know he was feeding me the truth?

I was losing my goddamn mind.

With the wintery mix of sleet, snow, and ice, December misery returned. I couldn't escape the cancer coming for me. Anxiety and nerves made me smoke more. I sat in that house all day speculating how far the malignancy had spread. Stage Three? Four? After plowing through a pack and a half and drinking more than I should, I coughed up blood. Not a lot. But definitely blood. A fat, slick, dark reddish brown blob of it. Abominations were feasting on living tissue, tumors transmogrifying, turning into something ravenous, lustful, eating up the organ meat it found desirable, spitting out the rest.

I tried to write. Pointless. You need your head in the right place to do that. Tonight, it was anywhere but. After a fruitless search on the web, being sucked down holes of assorted serial killer cases, which brought me to more twisted, perverted stories, the horrors of horrors (do yourself a favor. Never look up "Albert Fish needles"). I was ready to give up this inane mission, call it a day, even though it was barely six p.m.

Behind me, the trash bin had filled up like last call at Sliders. Empty liquor bottles and beer cans toppled over the edge, spilling fuzzy navels. Gathering and stuffing down my sins, I tied off the bag, and headed toward the side door, half hoping an icicle fell at the right time and pierced my carotid so I could call it quits, for good. It wasn't impossible. Falling icicles kill a couple dozen people every year. But if I died, the story died too.

And I knew the only way this story ends was if I wrote it.

I opened the side door.

And there stood Danny McPhee.

CHAPTER THIRTY-THREE

Shrouded in the frigid elements, Danny hugged himself, staring at me to let him in. A polite request to enter my home, an odd display of manners from a convicted pedophile, ex-con, and thug who may've tried to brain me.

The night was dark, there wasn't a soul in sight, and I was stinking drunk.

Sure, Danny, why not?

I stepped aside.

"Goddamn," Danny said, slipping inside and shivering, his lips blue. "Can you turn up the heat in here?"

"I like the cold," I said. Which wasn't true. I'd been out of it, neglecting to check the heater all day. When I did, I saw it was fifty degrees. If I fell asleep like this, the pipes freeze or I die, maybe both.

I blasted it as high as it would go, waiting for my adrenal gland to do its job. A killer was in my house. Why wasn't I afraid? Maybe that was where the cancer had set up camp, flanking my kidneys, awaiting final orders to strike. Whatever the reason, the fight or flight wasn't kicking in, no nervous energy flowing.

I asked Danny if he wanted a beer. He said no thanks, he didn't drink.

I grabbed one, and we sat at the kitchen table, casual and civilized, like his cousin Mel and I had done the other day. Only now it was I, the dying author, and Danny, the rapist, in the quaint confines of my rented house as we tried to warm our frozen bones.

"I got dropped off," Danny said. "After work. Saw your car. Figured what the hell? Maybe I talk to the guy and we work this out. Whatever beef you got with me."

"You work?" I didn't know why the thought surprised me so much.

"How else do you get money?" He rubbed his hands, trying to spark enough friction to stimulate veins and get the blood to flow faster. "Construction. Sucks in the winter. Most of the companies close down. Not much work. But my parole officer pulled a few strings, did me a solid, outfit up in Enfield. Bitch of a commute. One of my co-workers lives in Newington and picks me up each morning since I'm not supposed to drive."

"You don't have a driver's license?" Who doesn't have a driver's license at his age? "How old are you?"

"What the fuck is your problem? What do you care how old I am? Why do you keep sitting outside my hotel room? Harassing me? You told the cops I … attacked … you? I never attacked you. I ain't seen you in forty fucking years. What you care about my life so much for?"

"I'm writing—"

"And, no, I don't have a license. I don't drive."

"I saw you driving the other day."

"When you were following me? Yeah, sometimes I borrow this guy I know's Civic. But I'm not supposed to. My license was suspended, and after all the years inside, I don't have the money to pay the fines, which accrued. And, yes, I know what the word 'accrued' means. And for the record, I'm not much older than you."

"I remember you being a lot older than us."

"Well, you remember wrong. What are you? Forty-seven?"

"Around there." I felt a slight tinge of pride that he underestimated, though I wasn't sure why other than vanity's sake.

"I'm fifty-seven."

"You look older than fifty-seven."

"Yeah, fuck you, too." Danny McPhee nodded at my cigarettes on the table.

"Help yourself."

He lit up. "I was going to quit. But why?"

"I stopped for twelve years."

"Why the fuck would you start again? Are you a moron?"

I'd anticipated hostility. I'd braced for it. My left hand had been cued for a fist since he walked in. This wasn't a cordial conversation. Danny acted rude, abrasive, confrontational, and didn't hold back how little he liked me. I refused to let him intimidate me even as Danny played the heavy, casting stink eyes and puffing up, employing the techniques he'd picked up in prison when he felt disrespected. Danny McPhee wasn't a nice guy. Despite the animosity, I didn't get the impression he was a thug either. To survive that many years on the inside, you have to develop a front, a presentation, construct a harder veneer.

I studied the lines on his face, craggy and cracked, his cheekbones sunken and gutted, which added an aura of toughness and rigidity.

Outside the storm picked up, bombarding my roof with icy bullets. The bitter winds roared and raced along the pavement outside.

"I ain't looking forward to tonight," Danny said, motioning toward the Berlin Turnpike, in the general vicinity of whatever rattrap he called home. "Goddamn heater never works in those places. You got a heater, you got the money to pay your bills? Use your heater, man." Then, as if just remembering why he was here: "Why you keep following me?

Bugging me? Feeding bullshit to the cops? You know if I so much as fart at the wrong time, they can send me back to prison? My life is shit. Those Turnpike motels are hellholes. But they beat the inside of a cage." Before I could respond, he held up a hand. "And save the 'writing a book' crap."

"I'm working on a true crime novel." I paused. "About the Rodgers' disappearance."

"Jesus!" Danny slapped the table, laughing. "Man, if they could've hung that one on me too, I'm sure they would've. I was cleared, bruh. Got fifteen people—pictures—proving I was nowhere near the mall that day."

The absence of fear was replaced with a sense of security. Danny McPhee wasn't menacing in any way. I went right for it.

"I saw you there. And you were arrested, sentenced for the same crime, Danny. Different girl, maybe. But the same crime."

"I dropped off my cousin. I didn't go in." Danny McPhee smiled. Or maybe it was more of a sneer.

"There's nothing funny about rape."

If there was a time for Danny to take exception and reach for my throat, that would've been it. Instead, the accusation seemed to sadden him, cause pensive reflection, a turtle retreating inside its shell.

He crushed the spent butt. "I have another?"

I passed the pack and told him to keep it.

"You read up on all this, eh?" Danny asked. "My case. Conviction. Sentencing." He almost sang out these words.

"I know about what happened, yes. I know she was your 'girlfriend.' But she was sixteen."

"Julie was seventeen." His eyes filled with sorrow at the mention of her name. "I loved her. Yeah, I was twenty-three. She was underage. But I didn't rape or kidnap nobody."

We sat still a moment. Like with the heat, I'd left the lights off, and darkness enveloped us both. My eyes adjusted to the interior gloaming. The glowing ember from Danny's cigarette pierced the black space, a red-hot fire, spotted briefly, then extinguished.

"Okay, Danny," I said. "Guess you're one more innocent guy sent to prison. I've seen that movie before. I think it was called *Shaw*—"

"Julie was my girlfriend," Danny said again. "Julie St. Jean. The cop that busted me, made sure I went away for a long, long time. Her uncle."

Gary St. Jean.

Julie St. Jean. I remembered a girl by that name. She was a junior when I was a freshman. Pretty, popular, unattainable. All girls that age are. I didn't know her.

"I loved her," Danny said. "And she loved me." He jumped up to the side door, opening it; a burst of subzero rushed in. He flicked his cigarette into the swirling winds and snow, sealing us back inside.

I had a good idea where this story was going. I let Danny tell me the rest anyway.

"We wanted to get married," he said. "Our age difference didn't seem like a big deal to us."

"Gary St. Jean's her uncle?" I never put the two together. Gary and Julie. Gary St. Jean, the Hartford detective I'd met with.

"I just told you that, dipshit. I knew her uncle was a cop. Half the family's in law enforcement. Her cousin Sean was hot shit. Good ballplayer. Drafted by the Reds. Ended up playing a couple seasons for the Phillies or some shit. The family didn't want a guy like me around."

"What are you telling me, Danny?"

"Gary St. Jean and his cop buddies, his judge pal. Threw the book at me." Hard stop, period, nothing dragged out.

"They can't give you twenty-five years because they don't like you." My words came out less as a statement and more like a question.

"*They* can do whatever the fuck they want. Julie and I hadn't planned on running away. We were up at the Enfield Mall and just decided fuck it. We crossed state lines, which tacked on a bunch of charges."

"You were from Berlin. Your parents had money. Don't tell me they rolled over."

"Bunch of charges tacked on," he repeated. "They offered me a plea. Would've been out in five. But I loved Julie, and she loved me, and we didn't want to wait five years. We didn't think we were doing anything wrong. I decided to fight the charges. Cops got pissed when I wouldn't take the deal, went at me twice as hard. Case dragged on. My shit lawyer acted like he couldn't be bothered. My dad had lost half his leg by then. Diabetes. It was a bad year. Those girls going missing. My father dying. Attorney not giving a shit. Then they started trying to say I took those twins, fed the press bullshit, and everyone turned against me. It worked. The truth never came out. Twenty-five years. And I did damn near every one of them."

"If what you're telling me is true," I said, having a hard time defending the man who, up until a few minutes ago, was my tormentor, a convicted rapist and possible killer.

"Facts is facts." The way Danny said it, the words didn't come out bitter or weighted down by regret. More like a man who'd bet his life savings on black, leaving it up to the gods, and the wheel landed on red. The odds spin in your favor, you're set for life. And if they don't? Wasn't meant to be. It wasn't meant to be for Danny McPhee.

"Julie must've told them the truth." It had to be easy enough to verify.

"You mean that we were dating? It was consensual? Of course." Danny glanced over. "You know I'm adopted, right?"

"Yeah, I know."

"My skin's darker because my real parents were Puerto Rican. At least one of them. I think. I never met them. But I looked different. It was easy."

Danny was darker. Not much. You wouldn't think a thing like that mattered. In a town like Berlin, it matters.

Danny saved the bombshell for last. "She was pregnant. Couple months. Pretty white girl. Me. Half-breed baby. In this town? With her family?"

He looked like he wanted to cry. A funny look for a tough guy. Danny shook his head, which I took to mean the baby was the first problem to be fixed. "For the first few months Julie sent me letters, saying she'd wait. But she was a kid. I wasn't getting out. The letters stopped." Danny turned toward the Turnpike, at all the cars speeding somewhere in the night. "Heard she got married, had kids, big house, all of it. Some guy named Galas. Plainville. I don't know. I never bothered her again."

"What about the Rodgers Twins?"

"The girls that went missing that summer, Meriden Square. What about them? I already told you I had nothing to do with it."

"You interned one summer at the *Hartford Courant*."

"*New Britain Herald*."

"Thought it was the *Courant*—"

"*Herald*. Getting coffee and shit. I wanted to be a photographer." He cast a sidelong glance. "An artist." I wanted to tell him that there was nothing romantic about the gig. Although writer's block and thin skin had nothing on three decades of hard time.

"What about my uncle?"

"What about him?"

"You guys are friends?"

"You could say that. Your uncle's good people. You're lucky to have him."

"Did my uncle write a letter to the parole board for you?"

Danny nodded, one head bob. "And I'm grateful."

"You talk a lot?"

"What's with all the questions about Iver? Once in a while? He's my friend. I did a lot of work for him back in the day. We stayed in touch." Danny's face washed angry, lean, mean. "That enough for your little book? Can you stop busting my balls like a fucking weirdo?"

He stood up. I did too, groggy and unsteady. I had more questions, but I couldn't think of any right then. He wasn't on the witness stand and I'd hadn't had time to prepare a sufficient cross-examination.

"I'll give you a ride to your motel," I said.

"Fuck that, man. You're drunk as shit. I'll Uber."

CHAPTER THIRTY-FOUR

After Danny left, I poured three fingers of mezcal, grabbed the last beer, and lit a cigarette. Might as well enjoy the final few butts before the firing line. A coughing fit took hold. I dragged myself to the sink, straining to breathe. I hawked up and spit out another wet, metallic glob, washing away the sick.

On my laptop, I went to Facebook and typed in "Julie Galas." Easy to find. Several friends in common. I searched her profile, which was public. Lots of pictures of her from the same specific distance, taken at the same high angle women seem to favor these days, three-quarters, lit from above, the good side. There was a science to it. According to her profile, Julie, who went by Jules, was a divorced single mom. One of the kids looked old enough for college. Several pictures featured Jules with her current life. She didn't appear to be suffering—McMansion, Berlin money, the finer things.

I scrolled her timeline. She seemed to get on okay with her ex-husband. There were several family pictures, child on each side, the pose affected by amicably divorced couples, apart but together.

What would've happened if she'd married Danny McPhee? Would she have the same big house on the hill? Danny had always been a loser. And losers tend to drag you down.

I didn't feel bad for Danny McPhee. Still, thinking about the different courses lives can take, it wasn't hard to imagine another life for Jules, one where she and Danny stayed together, where he didn't get sent away. I was twelve years older than my ex-wife. If I'd been Danny's age when we met, she'd have been eleven. A terrifying thought. But when you meet at thirty-six, and she's in her mid-twenties, no one cares. Women mature faster than men. I wasn't defending Danny. Or maybe I was. Life, like most sports, is a game of inches.

Pouring another shot, I called Jim, repeating everything I knew, all Danny had told me.

"I don't know, man," Jim said. "A six-year age difference gets him locked up for twenty-five years? That story sounds like bullshit. Why are he and your uncle still talking?"

"He said they're friends."

"And you need to be resting, not dealing with this bullshit. Did you call the hospital like I told you to?"

"I wish my uncle would answer his phone."

"You're *calling* him?" Jim asked, incredulous.

"He's my uncle." I didn't want to admit it, but, yeah, I'd reached out a few times. Straight to voicemail. I'm not sure what I would've said if he answered.

"Yesterday you thought he was a kidnapper and a murderer." Jim paused. "Did you ask Danny about the duffel bags? Stained with red?"

"You didn't say anything about Danny being around that day—"

"He wasn't. Doesn't mean your uncle didn't fill him in." I heard Jim exhale, a heavy, disgusted groan that spoke volumes. "I wish you'd leave this alone. Let Danny McPhee rot at the Kenilworth Motel. I can see it wearing on you. Every time I see you, you look worse. And where's it gotten you? Have you talked to the doctors? You can't keep avoiding this cancer because it's inconvenient—"

"You saw my text about the Avon Sisters?" I said, ignoring his concern.

"Yeah. Read the article, too. Nothing to do with the Twins. You need to call the doctor. Cancer doesn't go away on its own."

"Something Danny said is bugging me."

"Everything bugs you. Call the doctor."

"You said the other day that someone doesn't want me looking into this."

"Are you drunk? Buddy, you are slurring your words."

I lit a cigarette off the stove.

"And … are you smoking? Have you lost your fucking mind?"

"Sean St. Jean is Gary St. Jean's nephew. I mean Julie St. Jean was his niece. Remember him?"

"Remember who?"

"Sean. St. Jean. No. Danny's girlfriend. Her. Julie St. Jean. Sean, Gary. Gary's the cop."

"I don't understand what—"

"Sean had a shot at a big league career. They didn't want Danny around. Not with Sean fast-tracked for the pros, all the press and publicity—teams aren't signing a guy related to someone like Danny. Too much baggage."

"Huh?"

"Did you know they were planning on getting married? She was pregnant. Aborted the baby."

"I can't follow a thing you are saying. Listen, stop drinking. Go to sleep, you need to rest, and first thing in the morning you're going to see the doctor."

"It makes sense. Cold case? There was no cold case! Soon as I start poking around, Wayne tells his guy, who makes up some bullshit story about the case being reopened, like that is going to satisfy me."

"What guy?"

"Gary St. Jean. The Hartford detective! He jams up Danny, sends him away. If I look into this, try writing a book, it exposes how they all conspired to ship Danny off. You know he's Puerto Rican?"

"Who's Puerto Rican?"

"Danny!"

I could hear Jim collecting himself. Part of me sympathized with how hard it must be dealing with me. This was the danger of being a writer with an anxiety disorder. Once I got started, I couldn't be reeled in. I *had* to put this together, solve the puzzle. I'd never rest. I was too drunk to communicate the new version, the one where a disgruntled Hartford detective had been behind the scenes pulling the strings the entire time.

"Buddy," Jim said, calm as could be. "I'll be honest with you. I've understood about half of what you've said. And *what* I've understood sounds fucking crazy."

"Danny said—"

"Danny said! Danny said! Danny? The guy who until half an hour ago was clubbing you senseless, working in conjunction with your uncle to cover up how many murders? Do you know what you sound like?"

"The family doesn't want a baby," I said, reworking the draft in real time. "Not as big a deal. Now. But you remember Berlin growing up. A half-Puerto Rican baby, when your brother's about to go pro? Cousin. I can't believe I missed that. The scandal."

"Man, you are reaching. Nobody is hatching some elaborate plot to set up Danny McPhee. Jesus, buddy. She was a fucking minor. He was fucking a minor. Her parents found out. He got arrested."

"I bet he's the one who attacked me."

"Danny—"

"Gary St. Jean! Or he hired a gangbanger to do it for him. Aren't you listening?"

"I'm listening. But nothing you're saying is making sense!" I heard Jim take a deep breath. If we were on the West Coast I might've accused him of employing meditative techniques. But they don't do that back east. "We. Are. Done."

"Where's that leave the Rodgers Twins?"

"Still dead? It's like I've been telling you all along. No story, no book, no mystery."

"I need more than that, Jim. I accused Jack and his stepfather—" I started coughing, a hacking, lung-butter cough.

"I'm taking tomorrow off," he said. "First thing, we see the doctor."

I started to object but Jim shut that down.

"I don't want to fucking hear it. Not another word! You are sick and you need to know your treatment options. That is step one. We see the doctor. After that, you want to run off and play cops and robbers, have at it. But I'm finished feeding this crap. It's killing you, buddy. I already watched Jack die. I'm not losing you too."

That one got me, right in the heart.

"You hear me?" he said.

"Sure."

"No, no, don't 'sure' me. You're going to go to bed. Promise."

"I promise."

"You're going to need all the strength you got."

"I can't forget about this."

"Fine," Jim said. "You win. You agree to come with me to the doctor … I'll see who Danny called, because I guaran-fucking-tee you as soon as he left your place, he made some nervous, panicky phone calls."

"What about Gary St. Jean?"

"I doubt a distinguished Hartford detective is clocking and knocking you senseless in the snow. But I'll run a line on him too. Okay? Happy? Now, go to sleep."

I hung up and lay in bed, like Jim said. The mezcal shots hit me hard and I couldn't power down. I tried thinking of solid blocks of color, muted grays, charcoal, navy blue, midnight blue, black, but I couldn't shut off my brain, alcohol festering in my belly, this massive influx of new information overloading my system. The story was there, waiting for me to connect the dots. Tie the threads. This is what I did for a living. It's who I was. It's what I did…

Jim's knocking on the door woke me. Bright buttery sunshine slathered across azure skies. For a moment I thought I was back home in California.

❁　❁

The waiting room at the Oncology Department is a horrible place for self-reflection. You get to rehash, replay, and reimagine every lousy decision that brought you here. Maybe if I hadn't clung to the misguided idea I could play professional baseball, despite lacking any discernable skill (if scouts covet five-tool players, I was about six short). The sooner you accept the majority of life's platitudes are bedtime stories you tell children—you can be anything you want to be; it's what's on the inside that counts; money doesn't buy happiness—the faster you can move on with the disappointment. No one gets what they want. The world doesn't need more poets.

I sat alone, insisting Jim drop me off—I'd taxi home. I didn't know how I was going to respond when I heard specifics. And if I broke down in tears or had a panic attack, I wasn't adding embarrassment or humiliation to my burden.

I wanted to believe I'd take whatever news in stride but it's hard to stay positive in situations such as these. Waiting for Dr. Phillips to arrive, I was prepared for what was coming. Accepting what I was leaving behind was tougher to stomach. When you are approaching the finish line, with so much left undone, it's hard to accept it's over. My friend, Micah, a singer out of Ohio, one of the greatest songwriters I've met, has this song where he's interviewing himself. And I started thinking about that song. Playing both reporter and subject, he asks a series of questions: "What's your biggest fear?" ("Dying before my work is done.") "And when will your work be done?" To which Micah, answering himself, responds, "Never."

Gave me chills thinking about that line. My work would never be done. Despite earning a minor cult following with my first book, a memoir about a rebellious rock-and-roll wannabe, I hadn't written my best book yet, not even close. I still had more to do here, and being denied that opportunity made me furious. I was biting and grinding my teeth so hard, I could smell the enamel dust, a cavity hole ground dry to the root.

I decided to flip the switch, force myself to find the sunny side as they were bringing out the dead. I was once on a panel at a writers' conference and an attendee asked, "What's the best cure for writer's block?" "Having a deadline," I answered, to the thunderous applause and laughter of about eighteen people.

It was true, though. I never believed in writer's block. There were plenty of times when I couldn't think of what to write—didn't *want* to write—still, that's a prison we put ourselves in. And the key to getting out? Writing. And nothing motivates or inspires writing like a deadline. When you do this for a living, you are given an advance and a due date, and when that due date comes around, you've already spent the advance. It's amazing how easily having a due date fixes that problem.

Death was the ultimate due date. I *had* to be finished with this new book before I bit it because there could be no extensions. And better yet, staying with this upbeat bent, this final effort would have to be my best. Because there could be no other opportunity to ascend the mountain and claim the mantle. Death was life's final draft.

I heard my name called, and a young nurse ushered me into a small office. She said to have a seat and that the doctor would be in soon. Perusing outdated gardening and homemaker magazines, I felt a strange, soothing calm wash over me. What happened next was no longer up to me. Freed, I had been released from my bonds. All my willpower, fire, and desire couldn't change fate.

A few minutes later, Dr. Phillips entered, looking haggard and disheveled, salted head rumpled like he'd been woken from a power nap on a couch in a closet, clipboard in hand. Took him a moment to acclimate, as he patted pockets and felt around for pens, pads, pills, or whatever he was looking for. Perhaps, he'd already taken the time to fill out the death certificate.

"I've been trying to get in touch with you for several days," he said.

"I know. I've been busy."

The doctor looked baffled. The excuse was generic, textbook, and above all stupid. Procrastination can't change a diagnosis.

The doctor opened a file, pursing lips, furrowing brow, no doubt working through the best ways to tell a man he is dying. I braced—not for the worst, that had been established—but for the bartering, the part where I begged God for time. That's all I wanted. More time. My friend Tom Pitts, another writer I knew out west, once sang with his band, Short Dogs Grow, "I don't want the money back, I want the time." I'd never wanted anything more. *Give me a couple more years, please. Six months, like gold in my hands...* For as dark as days could get, and this life delivers plenty, a strange thing happens when you find out you are about to run out of them. You plead for a second chance. *Dear God, I'll do anything…*

"You don't have cancer," Dr. Phillips said.

I waited for the rest, the other part, the thing that was worse, the real disease that had taken away my appetite, made the mere sight of food nauseating; the real reason my white blood cell count was off; why I was losing weight and coughing up blood.

But he didn't add anything else.

We sat like that, at opposite ends of some perverted standoff.

"I don't understand," I said.

Like he was describing it to a ten-year-old, he repeated, slower this time. "You don't have cancer. The tests came back. Negative. If you returned my call, you could've saved yourself some anxiety."

"You could've left a message?"

"You could've called back?"

Touché. But that still didn't answer what was wrong with me.

"What do I have then? You said the original blood work came back irregular."

"It did. Which is why we tested for cancer. A man your age, that's the first thing we rule out."

"What did you rule in?"

"If you're waiting for me to tell you you're dying? You're not."

"I'm coughing up blood."

"Coughing?" he asked. "Or spitting up?"

"What's the difference?"

"One would be coming from the lungs, stomach. Like with cancer. Or a serious case of bronchitis." He paused. "How are your sinuses?"

"My sinuses?"

"Are they dry? You relocated from the West Coast? Might not be used to the indoor artificial heat. That happens a lot in the winter.

235

Sinuses dry, crack, bleed. You swallow the blood during the night, comes up when you wake. Not uncommon."

"I started smoking again," I admitted.

"Well, that's stupid."

"I thought maybe…"

"That it's stupid? It is. But cancer takes a while to grow. You want it that bad, keep on smoking. It's no doubt irritating your throat—and sinuses—but you don't have cancer. Not yet."

"I have no appetite."

"For how long?"

"Months it seems."

"Anything stressful in your life?"

"Besides life?"

The doctor returned a condescending grin. "I meant anything traumatic, worrisome that happened within that time frame?"

"I moved cross country for a new job I didn't land after my wife and I got divorced."

"I suggest you talk to a therapist." The doctor stood up, ready to move on to the next patient. I wasn't as eager to let him go.

"I don't understand. How does a blood test—why did it look like I had cancer?"

He pointed beyond the bunched-up coat on my lap, to my tee shirt and the colorful ink running up and down my arm. "Tattoos."

"What about them?"

"How many do you have?"

"Tattoos? A few. Several." I paused to add them up. "A dozen."

"Calcified tattooed pigment in your lymph nodes can mimic cancer." He shrugged. "We'd have to run more tests, but that'd be my guess. It happens."

Dr. Phillips walked to the door and stopped, turning over his shoulder.

"Don't look so glum," he said. "Seems you're going to be with us a while longer." He gestured over my person. "I suggest you ease up on the drinking—I can smell it from here—and stop the smoking. And for the love of God, son, eat a cheeseburger."

CHAPTER THIRTY-FIVE

Sitting on the curb of New Britain General Hospital waiting for an Uber, I felt my relief hindered by an untenable strain. The dying part was unchartered territory, fear of the unknown fueling uncertainty, but there was an allure to staring into the void. It would be over. No more waking up, no more trying, no more falling short. It took me a moment to navigate around that, to accept that, yes, I was going to be here a while longer, and that I could do a better job with all of it. And when I came around to thinking this, accepted there was no easy way out, that I *would* do a better job with this second chance, a wave of euphoria washed over me. I felt every cell tingle and spark, and when the tears came I didn't stop them. I wanted to live. My work here wasn't done.

My cell buzzed. I figured the Uber driver needed directions, which happens a lot with ride sharing. It wasn't Uber. It was the Berlin Police Department.

"Hello, Wayne," I said. "What's up?"

"I'm calling about the break-in."

My head was in a different space, questions of mortality taking precedent over property damages. I didn't know which break-in he was referring to. There had been a few. The McPhee vacation cottage, Gribbard Pool.

"Your house?" Wayne said.

I'd forgotten I told him about that in the Stop & Shop parking lot, where I confessed my suspicions about my uncle. Only last week but it felt like a lifetime ago.

"The town has a website," Wayne said. "A helpline, hotline. Tip line. We post nonurgent crimes there, and eager citizens, often older folks, will check out the blotter. It takes time."

"Okay…"

"Put it online when you told me. Got a hit today. A neighbor reported seeing a man pushing hard on the door, and then kicking at the base. Didn't think it urgent—those houses on Worthington Ridge are so old—doors get stuck."

"Wayne, what are you trying to say?"

"This woman wrote down the license plate." Wayne stopped. I could hear the regretful cadence of his breathing. "Not sure you're gonna want to hear this."

"Say it."

"It was Ron Lamontagne's car."

"Are you sure?" Why would Ron break into my house?

"The way she described the perp, sure sounds like Ron. Bald, fifty-ish … white."

Wayne didn't need to add that last marker. That applied to ninety-nine percent of the town.

"I know Ron is your friend," Wayne said. "Figured you might want to air this out? Maybe talk? The two of you. I *can* send a squad car by…"

"No, no, that's fine," I said. "I'll give him a call. I'm sure it's a misunderstanding."

A call came in. Uber driver. I ignored it. Let them charge my account the five bucks. I needed to clear this up. There must be a mistake.

I rang Ron, who picked up on the first ring. After a quick hello, I explained the reason for my call, and waited for a reasonable explanation, or at least plausible denial, which was all I needed. Plausible deniability, a governing precept of my profession. You don't need an ironclad defense. Just enough doubt to cast suspicion. Like a trial. Reasonable doubt. The defendant is likable enough, case dismissed. The old woman was probably another busybody with nothing better to do. Recording license plates over suspicious activity was nothing new around here.

Except Ron said, "Yeah, I did it." He didn't say it nice either. "You should've left this stuff with the Rodgers Twins alone. You don't know what you did."

In that split second I tried to wrap my head around myriad conflicting facts and fates.

"Jack's dead!" Ron said. "His stepfather is dead! Who you trying to help? It's over, man! Over!"

"Ron, what the hell—"

By then he'd hung up.

I'd been sitting beneath the porte-cochere, feeling my world growing darker, a trick of the subterranean lightlessness, where slivers of silver crept through the cracks in the concrete, slicing up the hard and impenetrable, creating the illusion of a catacomb.

The signal must've cut out. I was underground. Of course it cut out. I took a deeper breath, tried to remember this was real life and not make-believe. *You are not a god plotting a goddamn book.*

Back out in the natural light of the day, I tried Ron again, but the call went straight to voicemail. Once more, same result. As if the phone had been shut off. I texted a simple, non-panicky, "Call me." Then I rang Jim.

"Hey, buddy," he said. "What's up?"

I led with the big news.

"Ha! How great is that? Cancer-free!" He let go a terrific blurted laugh. "Hey," he said. "You'll never believe what happened this morning. After I dropped you off. My *first* call of the day, I walk into this woman's house to fix her phone, and she's standing there, wearing a robe. Thing falls half open, she's staring at me like I'm a piece of meat. Felt like I was in a porno—"

"Jim," I said, cutting him off. "Something's wrong with Ron."

"Huh?"

"Wayne Wright called. Ron's the one who broke into my house the other day and smashed the computer."

"Hold on." I could hear him stepping away, leaving me to wonder if I really was interrupting every telephone man's once-in-a-lifetime fantasy.

New Britain General sits atop a hill. From the right spot, toward the park, where I'd been walking, you could gaze out over the whole of a tiny town's empire. There was a time when New Britain was a major industrial player in this state—Stanley Tools was born here—but those days were long gone. Now it was just another East Coast smokestack of brown brick and closed factories. When emotions overwhelm, as they were hitting me now, you feel so separated from it all, like you've been removed from the playing field, relegated to sideline observer. The longer you watch this crazy game, the more you wonder if you're going mad. Only thing missing was my fiddle and the column of flames.

"Buddy," Jim said, coming back on the line. I could hear the wind whipping outside. "What's up with Ron?"

I explained the phone call, what Ron said, which when repeated sounded less menacing and more just plain weird.

"Where are you?" Jim asked.

"Still at the hospital. Should I head to his house?"

"I doubt he's there. He'd be at work—guy never misses a day—but that call sounds freaking bizarre, who knows? I'll run the GPS on Ron's location and call you back. Sit tight."

I sat tight all right. I thought about my dead friend Jack Lotko, asking why I'd been spared the same disease that ate him alive. I thought about his rough childhood and his bastard stepfather. I compared that to the blessed start guys like Jim and I had. I thought about Ron, too, realizing I didn't know as much about his family, which didn't mean anything. Or maybe it did. He could've had it rough like Jack, been abused, neglected. Jim, Ron, Jack, and I were like a little gang as kids—and until you're twenty, you're a kid. But we were all the same back then. You don't talk about your homelife or share your burdens. At twelve, fourteen no one had hit puberty hard enough to shoot up. Jack wasn't yet the towering, lanky guy he'd later become. Jim and Ron had the same mop-top hair, before they joined the ranks of male patterns. I didn't have a dad, but I had an uncle who fulfilled the same role. Thinking about Iver made me feel bad because I'd thought the worst of him. And of course, I reflected on Annabelle and Ava, who were kids like we were, only they never got the chance to grow old. Half a century later, our quiet idyllic town had yielded so many distinct fates—and yet … was ours any different than any other small town? Win, lose, draw, no one gets out of here alive. It's not how many times you get hit or how long you last in the fight. In the end, we all go down for good. *Rocky* was a lie.

My cell buzzed. Jim. I held off saying anything. I could feel something wrong, a sixth sense, a premonition, a logical conclusion, or the natural crash course to the story, which was never going to end happily.

"Buddy," Jim said. "I was able to get the GPS location on Ron's phone. Oh, shit, man. It's bad…"

"What?"

"He was calling you from the McPhee house in the mountains."

"Why on Earth would Ron be there?"

"I don't know what's going on, but let's you and me handle this, okay? There's gotta be an explanation, right? This is Ron we're talking about."

"I'm not planning on calling the cops. Not with what I know about Gary St. Jean and that whole shitshow."

"Good. I'm on the other side of the state," Jim said. "You catch a taxi home. Grab your car. I'll meet you at the McPhee vacation house. Wait for me. One more thing."

Somehow I knew what he was going to say before he said it.

"I got a hit on your uncle's cell too."

He didn't need to finish. But he did anyway.

"Iver is at the house with him."

CHAPTER THIRTY-SIX

The drive from Central Connecticut to the fringes of the Adirondacks is a scenic trip with wonderful views. Under different circumstances, I might've enjoyed myself, instead of tugging my wool hat over my head harder because I couldn't shake the stakes, chilled to the bone, no matter how high I turned my heat—I knew it had to be eighty degrees inside the car but I was shivering, popping pills like Skittles, hitting a pint, and speeding. Add to that, the roads were a slick deathtrap. I was endangering families, innocent people, moms, dads, kids, racing to get from here to there, an asshole freaking out behind the wheel, grappling with a panic attack. What else was new? I had excuses for the panic attack. I didn't have any for driving as fucked up as I was. I kept watching the rearview, hoping a cop *would* pull me over. But as so often is the case, where are the cops when you need them?

A miracle I didn't kill anyone, and not to excuse driving under the influence, but I never would've completed the journey without the chemical sedation. As far as panic attacks go, this was a twelve out of ten. Substances hit in a variety of ways. That many benzos should've knocked me out. On this murky, miserable, misty afternoon in the mountains, however, they produced the opposite effect. Not saying I wasn't fucked up—I was—but with the adrenaline I'd also developed a tunnel-like clarity, which despite the anxiety produced a steady, determined hand on the wheel. I maintained composure. I know that sounds contradictory. Then again so is the human condition. Or, as Walt Whitman writes, "Do I contradict myself? Very well, then I contradict myself. I contain multitudes."

I didn't know if I contained multitudes. What I did contain was a lifetime of questions and sorrows. I phoned Mel, relieved when she didn't pick up. *Please, Mel, don't be mixed up in this...* I ran through the possible combinations. Ron knew something big enough that Iver ran when Ron rang. I couldn't pin down what that "something" was. Now they were together? Weeks after my uncle disappeared? If Jim helped my uncle move that duffel bag, and those *weren't* deer carcasses—and there I was again, assuming the worst of my own flesh and blood—that left one other possibility. The red-brown blotches. The smell of death. The lifeless bodies of two young girls...

Relying on my sense of direction—a good thing since I didn't have printed directions this time—I retraced the nameless streets and forgettable routes, holding on hard to the night Jim, Ron, and I drove up here.

Twisting around tall pines draped in fresh snows, I convinced myself that the gnarly stump was the same gnarly stump, that the speed-limit sign with bullet holes was the same redneck target practice.

I came upon a big boulder, which I definitely recognized. I remembered thinking it looked like the head of a bull moose. I swung a hard right, fishtailing through the icy sludge, the long, gravel drive shrouded pristine from an overnight snowfall.

When I saw Jim's truck my brain was slow to catch up. There were no fresh tire tracks. None of this was clear. I didn't see Ron's ride. I didn't see my uncle's white Acura MDX either. Just Jim's truck.

How had he gotten here so fast? Had they overpowered him, taken him hostage? Was he hurt? Why weren't there any tracks?

I ran around the side and pushed open the door. Of all the possibilities I'd considered waiting for me, this was the last one I expected.

CHAPTER THIRTY-SEVEN

The first eyes I met were Danny McPhee's, stretched wide as an anime character. Last week those same eyes had been whittled mean, cynical and bitter. Now they were screaming for help. What other option did he have? He couldn't talk with the rag stuffed in his mouth. And he wasn't going anywhere, not with his wrists duct taped to the arm of the chair.

The one face I expected—and dreaded—to see, Uncle Iver's, was nowhere to be found.

Ron Lamontagne was there. And so was my friend Jim Case.

"Hey, buddy," Jim said. "Want a drink?" He pointed at a couple liquor bottles on the counter. "Got some beer in the fridge."

I couldn't process. Though, later on, I'd see it plenty clear. Sometimes our mind won't let us go to places we are not ready to go.

"Got some good IPAs," Jim said. "I know you like those."

Ron said nothing, looking paler than an Irishman sunbathing in winter.

Danny McPhee trembled in his chair.

"Where's my uncle?" I asked.

Jim walked to the fridge, and plucked a couple beers, holding one up for me. I shook him off but he set both on the counter anyway. Then he measured out two fingers of scotch. He motioned to hold on.

He pounded one shot and shot-gunned the beer like we were back in college.

Jim shivered and laughed. "Goddamn," was all he said, before turning around. "Have a seat, buddy."

"I'll stand. What's going on, Jim?"

"Every fall your uncle goes to see the leaves change. Takes a drive up to Vermont and New Hampshire."

I knew that. It had been a while since I'd lived back east but I knew that. My uncle liked the changing foliage. He'd told me over the phone he was taking the trip. I didn't believe him.

"That last time at the hospital," Jim said. "When he was walking out. He said he'd be taking that trip and wanted me to keep an eye on you. And I've tried. But he's coming back. And pretty soon you guys will be talking, and I'm sorry to have to do it this way. But…" Jim faux groaned. "You are so hardheaded."

I turned to Ron, hoping for a clue. Shell-shocked, he remained rooted and silent, averting my eyes.

"Sure you don't want to take a seat?" Jim asked, pointing at the couch in the open living room. "We have a lot to talk about." When I didn't move, Jim plunked down in a kitchen chair with the extra beer, which he cracked open. "For weeks I've been trying to think how to resolve this, and this is the best I've come up with. I'm going to need you onboard, okay?"

I took him up on the offer this time. The seat, not the beer—I needed to be clearheaded as possible, willing myself sober. Ron made no move to join us, standing behind me, looming. Danny McPhee fixated on the action with his popped cartoon eyes. I had a feeling he already knew more than I did. Whatever this plan was, it wasn't working out in Danny's favor.

"What's going on, Jim?" I asked.

"We have a problem, buddy." He held up his hands. "But it's not insurmountable. In fact, it is easily fixed. So easily fixed—" Here his words slurred as the rapid intake of alcohol started to take hold, assaulting various receptors. "Timing isn't ideal." Jim burst out laughing. At what I had no idea, since nothing he'd said was funny. "Don't get me wrong," he continued, picking up the conversation the way drunk people do. "I am grateful you don't have cancer. Really, buddy, I couldn't take losing another friend." He clasped his hands. "But, man, if you did? It would've been *so* much easier. You'd be too preoccupied." He stopped, stumped. "By the way, what *is* wrong with you?"

I pointed at my tattooed sleeve. "Ink pigment in my lymph nodes. False positive."

"I'm glad, buddy. I really am. You know I love you, right? You, Ron, and Jack were the best friends I ever had."

"Why is Danny here?" I said. "Why is he tied up?"

"Because he's a piece of shit pedophile." The matter-of-fact statement confirmed basic mathematics. This plus that equals problem solved.

"You know it's not that simple," I said.

I could see Jim had gone from sober to hammered in a matter of minutes. I didn't know how much he'd had to drink before I got here, but a few facts were undeniable, starting with the lack of tracks and the fresh snow on Jim's truck. There was no other vehicle. Whatever Jim was about to propose required a great deal of liquid confidence, and he'd been here a while.

He hopped up and grabbed the whiskey, forgoing the glass this time, trading shots from the bottle with beer chasers.

"You were here when I called Ron," I said to him.

"Sorry about lying to you," Jim said. "After I contacted Berlin PD with the anonymous tip about seeing Ron's car outside your place when I broke into your house—"

"Wait. *You* broke in? Why?" Jim had been with me when we discovered my place ransacked. Which meant he'd headed over, trashed my computer, raced back to meet me at his place, *then* returned with me to help look for the thief. That was some crackheaded shit.

"I wanted to see what you found about the Rodgers Twins. If you had substance. For your … book." The way he said "book" he might as well have been using the word "turd." "But then you told me about all the backups, emailed copies, laptops … clouds. I had to come up with a better way. And you wouldn't listen. No matter what I said or did. Blame Danny, exonerate your uncle, implicate both. I feel sorry for your ex-wife. You're impossible to work with."

A hard wind smacked the outside of the vacation house, rattling the windows. I listened for wheels speeding up the drive, a rescue I knew wasn't coming.

"Why did you have to come back?" Jim said. "Why couldn't the college hire you and then you write another book about another sad sack, self-destructive alcoholic? Sell a few copies, make like you're a superstar on Facebook to feed your fucking ego, and then none of this would have to happen."

"What has to happen, Jim?" I turned to Ron: "Say something."

Ron said nothing. Jim, however, tongue loosened by liquor, let it all spill. Even if I was forced to piecemeal some of it together, assembling the random, tangential thought processes of a drunk.

"You knew the Rodgers Twins for a few years," Jim said. "Why the fuck do you care?"

"About what happened to them?"

"Don't!" Jim snapped. "Don't tell me for thirty-five fucking years you've been beside yourself over the fate of two girls you barely knew. So you crushed on one of them. Big deal. What pretty girl *didn't* you crush on in high school? Lisa Blake. Tracy Bartlett. Heather Richotte. It's fucking high school! All we did was crush on the pretty girls who wanted nothing to do with us!"

I casted a sidelong glance at Ron, wishing he'd find the courage to speak up, stand up to Jim, who was so far down the road to self-righteousness I wouldn't be able to catch him before he crossed the finish line to full-fledged zealotry.

"I'll tell you why," Jim said, pushing himself up. "Because you're a drama queen. Always have been. You're like the fucking Texas of human beings. Everything has to be bigger with you. Every story, every emotion has to carry this profound weight. But you know what, buddy? Sometimes there is no revelation. Most of the time there is no reason. Shit happens. We deal. We move on. Mid-life crisis because you got divorced? Who hasn't? I'm divorced. Ron's divorced. The only fifty-year-olds still married are the boring assholes."

"Why is Danny here?" I repeated.

"I fucking told you! He's a rapist piece of shit pedophile."

"And he went to prison for that."

"What about the Rodgers Twins?" Jim sneered.

I turned to Danny, desperate for an admission of guilt. Admit you took the girls, be the patsy, play the fall guy, let us get on with our lives. But a man's eyes don't lie.

Jim plunked back in his chair, loose and limber, kicking out his feet, resigned to the fact I wasn't moving a muscle until I learned the truth about the summer of 1985.

"I'd gone by Jack's that day," Jim said. "Jack wasn't home. His step-father was." Jim shook his head. "Kurt Shaw. Guy was an asshole. I was fifteen. He offered me a beer, like I was a regular man. I thought that was the coolest thing ever. Jack wasn't going to be back for a while. I don't know where you were." He flashed at Ron. "*He* was at swimming class. After a couple beers, Jack's stepdad says he has to run to the mall, pick something up, asks do I want to come along. Sure, I say. I'm on my third Miller Lite and I'm feeling flush and warm. How was I supposed to know?"

"Know what?" I said.

But Jim wasn't listening to me. "There was a guy there. Brown suit. Maybe thirties, could've been forties. Who the hell knows? Young look-ing, but at the same time kinda old. Weirdo. He had a tape recorder. He was going around asking questions. Stupid questions. Like what's mod-ern teenage life like? Dumbass shit like that. He pulled me aside to ask me the same shit." Jim laughed. "You know I figured, years later? Like you, I bet he was a writer. Some asshole trying to write a stupid book. One of those dumb fucking faces." Jim stared at me, oozing contempt. "But tape recorder man, he was the perfect alibi. Everyone looking for him. If the guy had come forward…" Jim stopped there. "Who knows? Maybe he was riding across country, hitting various malls, before holing up in some cabin to write the Great American Novel."

"I'm not following…"

"Shut the fuck up and listen." Jim took a swig of whiskey.

Ron still wouldn't meet my eyes. Danny's wouldn't leave them. I had no choice but to let Jim retrace his steps in his own time. Dealer sets the price.

"Kurt said to meet him back at his truck in a couple hours. I often wonder what if I'd lost track of time? Got distracted, wandered off…

But I kept track of it, and I get back to the truck at two, sharp. And there they are."

"Who?" I had to ask, had to hear him say it.

"The Twins, sitting in the front seat of the truck, next to Jack's stepdad. They were drinking beer and smoking pot and giggling. I'll never know what that old piece of shit said to those two pretty girls to get them in that crappy truck."

"You never say their names," I said. "Annabelle and Ava. You always call them 'the Twins.'"

"They were twins. So fucking what?"

"So say their name."

"Fuck you."

"Say their names, Jim."

"Fuck. You!"

"I was there," I said. "I saw Jack's stepfather that day." I caught on. "It wasn't Jack I saw. It was you."

"Yeah, I remember seeing you, too. Afterward, when you said it was Jack with his stepdad I can't tell you how relieved…"

"Jack always said he wasn't there," I said, answering myself in a whisper. "People didn't believe him."

"No," Jim corrected. "*You* said you saw him. No one else. No *people*. You—*you* didn't believe him."

"What happened next?"

"I don't know," Jim said, grabbing a beer.

"That's a lie." Until this point Ron had been little more than a statue. It was the first time he'd spoken. "That's a lie, Jim, and you know it."

"Shut up, Ron." Jim swiped a drunk, dismissive hand. "I'm sure the hotshot writer has figured it out."

"I haven't."

"I told you all I know."

"That's not true," Ron said.

I appealed to Ron now, as Jim must've known I would. Strangely, he didn't seem to mind, like he needed Ron to tell this next part.

"I'm going to get some air," Jim said, leaving me alone with Ron and a tied-up Danny McPhee.

"Jim called me later," Ron said. "He told me to come over to Jack's. It was like five in the afternoon, but summer and bright. I rode my bike there. Jack wasn't home. Jim called me down to the basement."

I stared, troubled and pressed, desperate for an explanation to exonerate my friends and knowing one wasn't coming.

"Annabelle and Ava were downstairs," he said. "They were drunk. Fucked up. Kurt Shaw and Jim were drinking beer too. And Jack's stepdad, he was ... taking pictures."

"What kind of pictures?"

"The girls were *really* drunk, being flirty. Kinda undressed. Not all the way. Their shirts were off but bras still on. You know how pretty the Rodgers were."

Jim opened the door, apprehensive to return to the scene, a clue that he didn't have the stomach to hear these confessions aloud. Now he was back for the big reveal.

"Pretty?" Jim scoffed. "Goddamn teases."

"They weren't doing anything wrong," Ron said. "They were dancing. In their bras. Their pants were still on. Jack's stepdad was laughing with them. Everyone was laughing. It seemed like a good time."

"Were you having a good time, Ron?" I asked.

"I work with girls that age," was all he said.

"Then what?" I asked.

"Nothing," Jim said.

I turned to Ron.

"After that we left," he said. "That's the truth."

"Did Annabelle and Ava leave?"

Jim shrugged. Ron looked more distressed.

"They were wasted," Ron said. "Like passing out drunk."

"You left them there like that?"

"I had to get home!" Ron said. "I had a curfew." He turned to Jim. "He did too. We were fifteen."

"So you left two girls, in their bras, passed out in the basement of Jack Lotko's sleazy stepfather's house?"

"He said he'd wait for them to sober up and then drive them home," Ron said. I could hear how much he wanted to believe that, how all these years later everything would be fine, like rewatching a sad movie and wishing it ends better this time.

"Yeah," Jim said, as if admitting the obvious were an affront. "They were smashed. But they were conscious. Before we left Jack's stepdad went on a liquor run. What did you expect?"

"What did you guys do?"

Jim shook his head. "We didn't rape them or anything if that's what you're implying."

"I'm not implying anything."

"They were drunk!" Jim said. "We were all drunk. We fooled around. We were kids. Jesus, man, guys like Ron and me were never getting a crack at girls like that."

"What did you do?" I repeated.

Jim wouldn't answer, bored with the line of questioning. But Ron had to get his confession off his chest, the lapsed Catholic in need of absolution.

"They weren't unconscious, I swear," Ron said. "They were a little out of it, yeah, and we maybe did ... stuff ... we shouldn't have."

"Like what?"

He shrugged. "We touched them. Regular touching."

"What's 'regular touching,' Ron?"

"Regular touching. How you touch girls, the parts of their bodies you want to touch. They were the prettiest girls in school. They didn't stop us."

"They were too drunk to stop you. Did Jack's stepdad put anything in their drinks?"

"How the hell were we supposed to know?"

"Because you were there?"

"What do you want to hear?" Jim said. "That we felt them up? Finger banged? Sure. Whatever. But we didn't rape them." He stopped, as if this next point were the coup de grâce in an ironclad defense. "And they were *alive* when we left."

I stood there, speechless, Danny McPhee's bug eyes boring a hole because we both knew what had to happen next.

Too much had been exposed.

A scapegoat had to take the fall.

CHAPTER THIRTY-EIGHT

So there it was, the rest easy to piece together. While Jim finished
the whiskey, Ron rubbed worrisome hands, and Danny McPhee's
eyes stuck like glue, I completed the story. There's always truth in lies.
Peppering honesty between deceptions is how the best liars live with
themselves. And as a writer, I was the best goddamn liar I knew.

Jim did help move a duffel bag, stained and smelling like death.
Except he didn't help my uncle. He'd helped Jack's stepfather. My uncle
comes back early and I question him? Jim would've backtracked, said
it was Jack's stepdad, he'd been confused, concoct some other lie, buy
himself more time. And I'd believe him. I trusted the guy. He was my
friend.

As for the rest of it, sure, there were holes. But holes are meant to
be filled. There would be plenty of time to do that when I told Wayne
Wright and Gary St. Jean the truth. They could handle the justice. I
had no idea how that part would play out. But with Jack's stepfather
Kurt Shaw dead, Jim would be able to manipulate facts to paint Ron
and himself in the most favorable light, with no one to refute his version of events. What would happen to them? I didn't know. I'd like to
say I didn't care. But of course I did. I wondered where Jack had been
during all of this. Now that he, too, was dead, I'd never know. He was
one of those holes. But Jack's home life back then was awful. It wasn't

uncommon for him to take off and spend a night or two in the woods. The summers in Central Connecticut are paradise. Maybe Jack came home and discovered what had happened. Maybe Jack helped harbor this horrible secret too. Except the Jack I knew had more integrity than Jim, Ron, and I combined. No, Jack was better than that. He had nothing to do with any of this, cursed to carry the burden of my misplaced accusation.

"Cut him loose," I said to Jim, nodding at our tied-up prisoner. I had no idea what Jim thought was going to happen, bringing Danny along. But no one here was a killer.

Jim spun around, wielding the empty whiskey bottle like a machete.

I wasn't scared. Even with the weight loss, I was still as big as he was.

"We're not in a shed, Jim. You can't club me in the dark in the back of the head."

"That was Danny," he said, incensed.

"And the other time? When my skull was split open in the snow, I'm guessing that was Danny too. Even though he was in a Berlin jail?"

"Yup." Jim shook the hoisted bottle.

"So this was all ... Danny?" I had to laugh. I felt bad laughing at the poor guy. Jim thought this plan was going to work? That I'd go along with it?

I tried to convey a look to Danny, duct-taped to a chair, gagged and terrified: he'd be all right. He'd paid his price according to the law. Good enough for me.

There was a knife block beneath the cupboard. "Ron," I said, appealing to the more sensible of the two, "grab a knife and cut the guy loose. We can figure out what we do next. But nothing is happening to Danny."

"The fuck it's not," Jim said, pulling a knife from behind his back.

I now noticed that block was one blade short.

"What are you going to do? Stab me? I've known you since we were kids. Put that down."

Even though he was drunk and angry, I felt confident I could reason with Jim, who I knew, at heart, was a good guy. Wasn't he? Then again, what did I know about "good"? I'd hurt people, screwed up, fucked around, and done awful things I was ashamed of too. Was it as bad as what Jim and Ron, Danny had done? Depends on whom you ask and whose heart I broke. When I looked at Jim again and saw how far gone he was, I stopped feeling confident. Had he been more involved in the Rodgers Twins' disappearance than I'd been led to believe? Maybe Ron went home. Maybe Jim stayed behind. Maybe Jim hadn't been content with copping a feel. He clutched the handle of the knife, knuckles turning white, prepared to slash his way to freedom.

"Jim," I said. "Think about it. If you got the GPS from Ron's phone and could access all the calls Danny made, so can the police."

"How stupid are you?" he said. "I didn't get GPS or tap any phones! There's no service up here." He pointed at his cell. "Wi-Fi calling. And I work for the phone company. I'm not some rogue superspy. Cells are towers! I told you that at the Olympia Diner. I don't have access to them. You didn't hear anything except what you wanted to hear. So I fed you what you wanted to hear—about your uncle, Danny, hoping to get you to drop it if Iver was involved. Left the pictures in the shed. You couldn't even recognize Jack's basement! How many times had you been there? I pointed you in every direction. Just leave Ron and me out of it. But, no, you had to go and play hero." Jim lifted the knife high above his head and plunged it straight into the countertop. "You fucking couldn't leave this alone! For some stupid book? No one gives a shit! No one cares about reading books. No one cares how you *write* one! Not that you ever shut up about it, you boring fuck. Now Hartford *will* reopen the case unless *we* fix this."

"Tell the cops what you told me. How much trouble—"

"Why should I get in *any* trouble? I was fifteen, horny, and drunk. I did some stupid shit I shouldn't have. Okay? It was wrong. I know that. I have to live with it. I knew Jack's stepfather put something in their drinks. I was drunk too. You want me associated with this forever? A registered sex offender like that piece of shit." Jim jabbed a finger in Danny's face. "Almost forty years have passed. What good is coming from confessing now? I'll lose my job, friends, never get a date let alone remarried—everything! And they will still be dead."

"Jack's stepfather killed the girls?"

"I don't know. I guess." Jim grew more flustered. "He asked me to put some bags in his truck when he told me to come over the next day. At that point, I didn't even know the girls were missing."

"What did you think was in the bags? You said they smelled 'like death.'"

"Buddy," Jim said, pleading. "Hear me out." He held up his hands.

Freezing rain whipped against the roof and windows, icy winds gusting across ravine walls and smacking stone, adding to the claustrophobic feeling of being trapped in a tomb.

"He"—Jim pointed at Danny McPhee—"*did* rape a girl, he *did* kidnap a girl. Girlfriend? Ha! He wasn't a fifteen-year-old kid trying blackberry brandy and beer for the first time. He was a grown-ass adult."

"What do you think we're going to do?" I asked.

Calm as day, Jim pointed over my shoulder. "The lake out there isn't frozen yet. Not all the way. The center will not hold."

"That's the plan? We drag Danny out to the lake, tied up, and drop in him in the water, call it a suicide? How did he tie himself up?"

"We get him to write a confession. Then we knock him out. Smash him in the back of the head."

"Like you did me?"

"I never meant to hurt you." Jim clasped hands. "We're friends. You know me, buddy."

"Yes, we are friends, Jim. And if I need to speak to authorities and testify to all your wonderful qualities, I will. But I'm not helping you kill a man."

"You write about this shit all the time."

"Yeah. Write about. In a book. Are you crazy? I'm not participating in a murder! Besides," I said, "I called Mel on my way up." I made a show of looking out the window. "Are you planning on convincing her to kill her cousin too? This is a *horrible* plan."

"He's a rapist!"

I reached for the knife stuck in the board to cut Danny loose. Jim wasted no time jumping on me. He was screaming and swearing, swinging his fists. How much rage was from the alcohol or deeper-seated hatred, desperation, I didn't know. I hadn't been in a fistfight since I was a kid. Not that we were exactly engaged in one now. We rolled around on the floor, wrestling like little boys. Sometimes I got the better, sometimes Jim did. It's not bravado to say if I didn't have a sutured skull and tender ribs, operating under my normal fighting weight, I would've won.

Wrangling free, I scrambled to my feet, moving toward Danny. Jim got up and dove, a shoestring tackle, knocking me to the floor. Then he kicked me as hard as he could in my fractured rib. I curled in agony as Jim ran out the door.

A powerful engine rumbled and horsepower roared, followed by big truck tires burning rubber as they peeled out. I managed to crawl to the counter and drag myself up, watching Jim's red taillights disappear in the sleet and snow that was really starting to come down.

Ron helped steady me on my feet. Then he went and cut Danny loose. Hunched over the tabletop, I could see Danny wanted to lash out at something, someone, but it wasn't going to be me—I'd been defending him—and when he looked at Ron, the fury faded from his eyes. Spent and exhausted, he bent at the knees, resigned it was over.

"Help me to my car," I said. "Ron, you'll have to drive."

Out into the squall, which was fast turning into a mountain blizzard, I staggered, Danny and Ron supporting each side. When we arrived at my car, we saw what Jim had been doing when he took that break outside to let Ron confess.

All four tires were slashed.

Dragging me back inside, they laid me on the couch. I asked them to pass me my phone that had fallen out during the fight. No service. I knew that.

"There's a landline," Danny said. "Upstairs."

"Don't bother," Ron said. "First thing Jim did after calling you was cut phone lines and internet. At least Mel's on the way."

"No. She's not. I couldn't get through. I don't even know where she is. Paris, Prague, remote tropical island—your guess is as good as mine."

"So what do we do?" Danny asked.

"The only thing we can do," I said. "We wait out the storm."

The storm lasted three days and nights.

By the time we were able to get out of there, make it to town and get help, it was too late.

The police put out an APB for Jim. They found his truck in the White Mountains of New Hampshire. It was abandoned. The snowy terrain up there is the badlands. Maybe Jim Case had thought this through far enough to stash another ride, though no evidence existed of that. A man trying to escape by foot could die a million and one ways in the mountains.

My guess is I'll never see him again.

And neither will you.

POSTSCRIPT

Bluebirds chirp from budding branches, pink and white flowers, crisp apple scents drifting in with the tart tang of new-mown grass. The ice hasn't been melted long, and this being New England you can never rule out winter's last stand, but it feels like spring is finally here.

Since I finished talking, the doctor has sat silently as sunlight slices through the slats, pats of butter stacked against the wall. I rock side-to-side, leg shaking, toe tapping, a nervous habit. I don't know how long I've been talking, how long I've been in this place. It has been a while. My propensity to daydream and slip from time can take me far away. The pictures on the wall are familiar, in that cheesy overarching way, motivational couplets designed to improve self-esteem, restuff, sew up the scarecrow, get him standing on his own two feet again. A wispy house with a delicate frame, a single brush stroke evoking legs and spine. Pray the wind doesn't blow.

"That is quite a story," Dr. Walker says.

Part of what I enjoy so much about being a writer is the way storytelling can melt away the hours. I wish I could call it catharsis, say I feel this great weight lifted. I do not. The people I care about are still dead. Much of the mystery remains unsolved, and probably always will. That's often the case in the books I write. I favor the ambiguous over the absolute. Leave the center open to individual interpretation.

Few things in this life are etched in stone, secured one way or the other. Though I tend to think in black and white—gray, in all its resplendent shades, is more often the case.

"How are you feeling?" Dr. Walker asks.

"Anxious."

"How long have you had this anxiety condition?"

"Long as I can remember." I want to laugh it off. "When I was little, every year around Little League tryouts I'd get the runs, I'd get so nervous. My mom used to tease me about it." I wait. "But not in a mean way."

"You miss her?"

"Of course. I don't care how old he gets, a boy should never live without his mother."

Dr. Walker smiles, kind, warm, maternal. She lifts the cup of tea off the end table. Steam still rises. *How long have we been sitting here, if her tea is still hot?*

"What do you hope to get out of this?" she asks. "Coming here."

"I've been in therapy most of my life. I don't do well without structure and routine."

"You don't strike me as a person who follows rules."

"Oh, very much. Rules, contrary to popular opinion, are meant to be followed. That's why they are called rules and not suggestions." I know I've used that line before. I tend to repeat myself. There are only so many ways you can rephrase the truth.

"Are you planning on staying in Connecticut when you get out?"

"Not sure. Mel McPhee wrote me. She's in Belize. Says I should visit."

"Will you?"

"I don't know. I keep thinking about my ex-wife, the choices I made. Or didn't."

"Children?"

"That's the big one," I say. "I think we'd still be together."

For some reason this response puzzles the doctor, but not in the way one might expect, more like a dim bulb has illuminated a room I don't have privileges to enter.

"You never call your ex-wife by her name. Do you notice that?"

"My wife?"

"Your ex-wife."

"She's my wife. Was. Whatever. Ex-wife. Father, son, uncle. Pronouns. In fact, in real conversation we seldom use each other's names. That's a bad habit for writers."

"Speaking of your uncle. He seems to have faded from the story. Like he disappeared when it became convenient."

"Not at all. He returned in the end. It was like I said. Uncle Iver takes trips north that time of year. I let my imagination run wild." I am distracted by a bluebird on the windowsill. "What can I say? My friend played me. Jim did a bad thing a long time ago. But I don't think he helped Jack's stepfather kill them."

"You believe that?"

"Jim was a lot of things. But he wasn't a murderer. He was an over-sexed teenage boy who got drunk and did something unspeakable. He said it wasn't rape but it was. We get what we deserve."

"And Ron?"

"You mean what's going to happen to him? Not for me to say."

I know the police talked to Ron. Wayne Wright filled me in, visiting me, sharing what he could. Wayne is a good cop and a friend. This has been hard on all of us. You start out as little kids playing games, cops and robbers, good guys and bad, and then you get older, grow up, and you are still playing the same game.

"Is that the end of your friendship?" Dr. Walker asks. "With Ron?"

"I don't know how to answer that."

"Yes, no?" Dr. Walker smiles. "It's not a trick question."

"I knew Ron and Jim a long time. They were my friends. What they did was horrible." I hesitate. "For some reason, I don't blame Ron like I do Jim. I don't know if it's rationalizing, making it easier because Jim is the one who ran, who is gone."

"Ron isn't as guilty in your eyes?"

"I can't answer that right now." I rub my eyes. The doctor has a housecat in the office. I am allergic to dander. The more I rub my eyes the more they begin to water.

The doctor passes the tissues.

I take one, adding, "I'm not crying."

"Would it matter if you were?"

"No," I say. "But I'm not. Sometimes allergies are just allergies."

"You have a very pragmatic approach," the doctor says. The statement is cool, detached, analytical.

I'm not sure how I feel about that, like I am being studied, a bug under her microscope. I have shortcomings and problems—my anxiety disorder can be crippling at times, and, yes, during panic attacks, it has the capacity to distort my thought processes. To combat this, I strive for normalcy by trying to control my environment. Some, like my ex-wife, label that approach rigid, inflexible. I see it as a form of self-preservation.

"When I was reading up on your case," the doctor says, "what struck me is how compartmentalized you are. It's borderline robotic. You possess an uncanny ability to delineate with extreme prejudice. As though you remove yourself from the action you are describing. I am guessing that, as a writer, this skill comes in handy. But I'm wondering how it affects the rest of your life." She waits a long time, so long I deduce the manipulation behind it.

I've played this game before. I can play it again. It's all a game, this life of the mind. Hide and seek, show and tell. Subterfuge.

Dr. Walker opens a chart, peering down the tip of her readers, checking notes. "This story you've told me … was … interesting."

"I wasn't trying to entertain you. It's what happened."

"Yes," Dr. Walker replies, lips tensed into terse grin. "I have no doubt it was the absolute truth. I've read the official reports from the police and detectives. I am not, in any way, accusing you of embellishing."

"Good. Because I didn't."

"Yet, you told it like a writer."

"Spoiler alert, doc." I spread my arms.

"Art, writing, creation, these are important to you."

"It's what I chose to do with my life." I'm struggling to see where she is going with this.

"It says here you feel so strongly about the connection between life and art that you think…" She cuts herself off, pretending to read what I know she's already memorized. "You once gave yourself a serious condition, one that required major surgery to…" Again, she pauses, though she knows damn well what she is about to say. "—The saphenous vein." Pause. "You believe you sustained this injury (pause) after you wrote that particular plot point (pause) in a book?"

The way she says it makes me sound crazy, like I believe I am Nostradamus, Rasputin, some confidence man, a soothsayer. Yes, it *is* a sincere belief of mine, that art and life are intricately linked, that the artist can, by tapping into a modern audience's mindset, the goings on in the world, alter fate, impact his or her very own physiology, to a limited degree.

"Yes," I agree. "Also, no," I add, clarifying. "In that particular book, or rather in subsequent interviews, I merely pointed out the strange confluence of events. That particular instance was … odd. I wrote about something. And then that something happened. It could also be a coincidence."

"But you don't believe in coincidence, do you?" Before giving me a chance to respond, the good doctor turns behind her, bending over. She scoops a hefty load, bringing back a big stack of books. My books. *All* of them. "There's a line you write," she says. "One that you repeat. Quite often."

"A line I repeat?"

"In your books."

"You read my books?"

The doctor smiles, making a show of presenting the stack. "Each and every one."

That a doctor with her credentials would take the time to read one book is flattering. That she's read them all? Downright humbling.

Then I stop being flattered and start growing annoyed. She hasn't read my books for pleasure. She's read them to use against me. The gesture smacks of manipulation. And how could she have read so many books so fast? True, I tend to write shorter books, but nevertheless it is a serious undertaking, commitment. It makes me wonder how long I've displaced myself, how long I've been unstuck in time this time.

"Though," Dr. Walker says, picking up her own conversation, "I admit this genre, crime, isn't my usual milieu. I tend to gravitate toward the more academic." Before adding, in an attempt at levity, "Books that aren't as exciting as yours."

"You don't have to do that," I say. Leaving her to infer whether I am talking about studying my work or her patronizing me.

She flips to a dog-eared page, a savage way to mark a book. "In the world of investigation, there is no such thing as coincidence." She closes that book, then opens another to reread the same phrase. Finished, she closes that one, picks up another, opening to a new mangled page to tell me what I already know.

"Stop. I know what's in there. I wrote the damned things."

"So you are aware how much you repeat yourself."

"We all have phrases, stories we tell, often. Favorite anecdotes. Writers are no different. We repeat lines, descriptions, have an authorial fingerprint. Like how a computer figured out who wrote *Primary Colors* by using algorithms—"

"True. But it's human nature to forget how often we repeat ourselves."

"Not me. Nothing I write is by accident."

"Are you sure about that?"

"What? That I'm in total control? Of course!"

The doctor waggles her finger, a tsk-tsk dismissal from a superior. I do not like it. The doctor leans back, adopting a far too casual position for a therapist. In that moment, Dr. Walker seems to grow younger, resembling a hotshot, up-and-coming executive. I wouldn't put it past her to pull out a box of cigars, clip an end, and puff her privilege. In the yellow sunlight, the strands of gray shine luminous blonde.

The doctor checks the clock, a pointless gesture. We know how much time is left. We are both running out of it, and yet have all of it that we need.

Dr. Walker's stare intensifies. "If you are," the doctor says, reading her notes, "'in total control'—"

"I am."

"Why would it stop there?"

"Stop where? I'm not following." I feel the sudden, pressing need for a cigarette. I want my wool cap and beard back. I feel naked smooth shaven. I need a goddamn good IPA.

"Reading your files—which are extensive—"

"I've been in therapy most of my life."

"Including other hospital stays—"

"When it got bad, sure. But that was a long time ago—"

"—I walked away with the impression that you think you create your own reality."

"Don't we all?"

"I don't mean it like that," she says. "And I don't think you do either. I think, like the saphenous vein incident, and countless other examples you include in your books, these odd confluences of events, the deaths predicted, the pasts erased, altered, changed." Again, she gazes at my collected works, forlorn and inquisitive. "I think you believe that, one, the art, shapes the other."

"I do." There is nothing "crazy" about noticing, appreciating—even honoring—the symbiotic relationship between art and life. Countless adages, maxims, axioms, clichés and tropes attest to this fact. Life imitates art and vice versa.

"In a sense you are writing your history." She pauses, pensive. "And your future."

I do believe that. It would be hubristic to deny the reliance of one on the other. I expressed this to the doctor. Perhaps not as well aloud as when I have the chance to edit my words. Talking has always been much harder for me than writing. I am not sick, not insane. I simply have a viewpoint that is different than yours.

That isn't good enough for the doctor.

"No," she says. I wait for her to say my name, the ultimate power move, saying someone's name, over and over. Saying someone's name in dialogue establishes dominance, belittles.

"If you create worlds," the doctor continues, "where's the evidence to say you didn't create this story too?"

I've had enough. I agreed to come here for help, not to be accused of making up a story as heinous as this. Not when every word I've uttered is one hundred percent factual and verifiable. "If you are imply-ing that Jim, Ron, Jack's stepfather—Annabelle and Ava…" I stop, cool my jets, let the calm wash over. "Charges have been filed, the matter investigated. Feel free to call the Berlin Police Department."

Dr. Walker pats the closed manila folder. "I have access to every-thing *you* do."

Why are these folders always manila? Every time there is an authority or expert, the folders must be manila. Same size, shape, color, all hoarding secrets.

"Why must it stop there?"

I turn toward the door, ready to leave. *Where do I think I'm going?* I can't get the words to form, tongue-tied, throat dry. I'm parched—I need a drink—I am in desperate need of fresh air and a cigarette.

"If you're trying to say something, doc," I manage to squeak out. "Say it."

"Under this belief system of yours, what's to say you aren't a charac-ter in your own book?"

I stare back slackjawed—I like Dr. Walker—but I can't hold my tongue any longer. "That has to be the dumbest fucking thing I've ever heard."

"Perhaps you're misunderstanding."

"Okay, I hate to use clichés, doc, but explain it to me like I'm a five-year-old."

"What's to say this story you've told—"

"Stop calling it a 'story.' Call it what it is! The truth!"

"Yes, the truth. Here. Now. For us. How do you know that there isn't another writer, far from here, making you a character in *their* story? And that maybe in that story, which is written by another writer, you have a very different life."

I spit an unhinged laugh. "A parallel universe?"

"I'm using *your* words." She is so deathly serious. "Another writer. An unnamed narrator. Much like you. But not you. One who made different choices, has different friends. Perhaps in that world no Rodgers Twins existed, or if they did, they were never abducted. Had different names. They grew up happy and healthy. Maybe your friend Jack is still alive."

"Oh, so somewhere else, I'm, like, a better man?"

"Not necessarily better. Just one that made different choices. Yielding different outcomes. You talk so much about not having children. When you speak of this, I get the sense you regret it."

"Sometimes I do."

"Maybe this other man," Dr. Walker says. "Maybe he has children, is married, still living out west."

For some reason the suggestion that I could be somebody else starts to break me. I don't consider myself an unhappy man. But we all want a better life, we all want more; we all recognize the possibility of the ultimate fantasy: having it all. I grab the goddamn tissues. The allergies are back.

"Sure, doc," I say, playing along. "So how do we find this other man?"

"I don't know," Dr. Walker says, receding with a smile. "You tell me."

ACKNOWLEDGEMENTS

As always, thanks to my lovely wife, Justine, and the boys for giving me the time to go insane and make up worlds.

Thank you to Square Tire © and owner Michael Torres. Appreciate your letting me join you on this crazy ride.

Thank you to my agent Jill Marsal, who never stops believing in me. Thanks to Lisa Daily and Christian Storm, publicist and designer extraordinaire, respectively.

And the rest: my editor, Chris Rhatigan, and all my beta readers—Celeste Bancroft and the Gang; Michael N. Thompson, Michelle Isler, and Shannon Wise. I'm sure I'm missing a name (or three). But, trust me, I appreciate all the love, help, and support.

Thanks to Brian Panowich and the rest of the crime-writing community members who have stuck by my side.

I'd also like to say a very special thank you to all the people who allowed me to use their real names in this work of fiction. I can't stress this enough. *Say My Name* was a fun, if disturbing, book to create. At the risk of repeated redundancy—I want to be sure we are all on the, well, same page. Guys like Jim Case, Ron Lamontagne, and Wayne Wright are real friends who granted me permission to use a variation of their person. None of the crimes this writer conjured are reflections of actual character attributes. (Except maybe the part about being bald.) I am in your debt. And thanks to those who allowed me to use fictional variations of their name. Without that vital touch, this story lacks the requisite verisimilitude.

Lastly, I want to thank Jack Lotko's window, Tracy Devlin Lotko. Sadly, that part of the story was true. We lost Jack to cancer a few years back. Jack and I weren't close in high school, but later in life we managed to strike up one of the most meaningful relationships I've ever had. Jack was an avid supporter of my work, and I wanted to find a way to honor my dear, departed friend. Being a crime writer, I found my choices rather limited. Though I think Jack, who was as docile and kind as they come, would've gotten a kick out of being portrayed as the town "bad boy."

Love you, buddy. You are missed.

Keep reading for exciting
follow-up to *Say My Name*

Available soon

CHAPTER ONE

January 8, 1998, 1:24 a.m.
The Morning of the Disappearance

Sitting in a bitter and desolate roadside parking lot in Briarboro, Vermont, just over the border from Massachusetts, Brooke Mulcahy used the flickering motel sign to read the unfurled, tattered gas station map. Oil stains, creases, and Native American etymology wasn't making it easy. Snow slanted through lamplight splashing down from tall poles. The winds picked up. The late hour meant all the rooms were silent. Judging by the lack of cars in the parking lot, there weren't many guests registered. Then the motel sign flickered once more and went dark for good. Brooke had never felt more alone.

The motel billboard advertised cheap rates. Given the time, she considered calling it a night. Get a room and some rest, resume her journey in the morning. If she gave into the fatigue now, she might change her mind later. It had taken too long to decide to leave. Clear-headed rest might impede the inspiration. She had to keep going.

The weather report projected a furious swath passing through the Berkshires en route to Cape Cod, where a low-pressure system and rapid drop in atmospheric pressure predicted a bomb cyclone. A Nor'easter on steroids. The front wasn't supposed to be this high up, targeting Eastern Mass, Boston, and Rocky Cove, her hometown, the shoreline, coasts, and beaches. The weather report got it wrong.

She thought she'd gotten out ahead of it. Brooke hadn't been on the road long before heavy snow started to fall. Not enough time had passed to put sufficient distance behind her. Brooke didn't want to be driving blind in a snowstorm without any idea where she was going. Each minute she waited was another minute wasted.

Pick a destination.

Smoothing the wrinkled map on the dash, Brooke zeroed in on Niagara Falls and the greater Buffalo area. She remembered vacationing there with her mother and father before everything fell apart. The trip was one of the few pleasant memories she held onto. She wasn't wedded to the region, and was also considering Chittenden, Winooski, and the tinier, insignificant dots on the map like Ashton, New Hampshire. She didn't give a shit. *North.* That's what the little voice in her head kept repeating. She'd venture into Canada if she had to. Brooke hadn't brought any documentation with her. Did she need paperwork to cross the border? No, Canada didn't require passports, did they? She was pretty sure they didn't. Brooke hadn't thought this through. Not really. Not well. For months—and these last few weeks in particular—the desire to get out of Rocky Cove had been weighing on her. The *need* to leave, however, had come on fast and undeniable, the culmination of a crushing defeat on the heels of a lifetime of disappointment, a final push past the tipping point and over the edge. Then again, it hadn't taken much. Brooke believed in signs, in fate. Be open and receive the call. She got it last night. So she packed a few clothes, important medications like birth control pills and antidepressants, sentimental belongings—necklace, old letters from her mom. She made one last stop to see the only person who mattered, her best friend Aaron, promising that she'd be back. It's not a lie if you believe it.

Near the motel walkway, Brooke spied a payphone. She considered calling Aaron once more. By now Mike had to be on the hunt, raging and out of control, and sooner or later he'd go to Aaron. Which was why she couldn't tell him where she was going. If he didn't know, then he didn't have to lie. Mike hated Aaron. It didn't matter what she said, how she and Aaron were just friends (Brooke *wished* she thought of Aaron that way). Mike was jealous of their relationship. If he thought Aaron knew something, he'd beat the shit out of him first, ask questions later. Mike could already be at Aaron's, waiting for her to call. She couldn't risk it.

There's no such thing as a quick fix. Geographical cures don't work—Brooke had picked up that much in her classes and training. At least you give yourself a fighting chance. Rocky Cove, Massachusetts, wasn't the mean streets. She'd grown up in a stolid middle-class neighborhood. That didn't mean she had it easy. Everyone has a story. And Brooke didn't want hers ending with another used-up girl, clutching her fading beauty like smoke, getting nailed against dumpsters behind townie bars.

There was a span, right around graduation, where Brooke felt genuine hope. She'd be going to college. The first one in her family. No Mulcahy had ever gone to college. Generations of Mulcahys were born to toil in factories and die unfulfilled. She didn't care that it was a state school, or that she wasn't sure what degree she wanted (nursing seemed as good a guess as any). Brooke was breaking the cycle. And that felt like progress. She had a direction, and by moving forward, she'd be leaving something behind. There was nothing left worth holding onto in Rocky Cove.

Brooke's problems didn't begin when her mother left. But they got worse when Connie returned. Brooke was sixteen when Connie came back, out of the blue, brand new baby brother Bobby in tow, as if ten minutes had passed and not ten years. Of course, Paul wasn't turning her away—her father never loved anyone else. And that was before Connie told them she was sick. Eleven months later, she'd be gone again, this time for good, the cancer finally delivering Connie to Jesus and that eternal life she craved. All Brooke got out of the deal was Bobby, a cross-eyed interloper who'd been nothing but a pain in her ass since day one.

Brooke knew she couldn't pin everything wrong on her bastard half-brother. She'd been going down a bad path for a while, too many drugs, bad guys and worse decisions digging a deeper hole. Now she was so low down, covered in dirt, suffocating—recovery was a pipe dream. There was no one person to blame. Not Mike. Not Bobby. Not Connie or Paul, not her married basketball coach, Rod Collins. This moment, this snowy night, presented a bona fide crossroads—a head-on collision in the ongoing war between the two distinct parts of Brooke Mulcahy: the one that was screwing up, and the one that knew she could do better.

Brooke was tired of thinking about where it all went wrong. Who cares about the exact order of events? Born under a bad sign, rotten luck, shit circumstance, this guy or that, sex turning the male species into lunatics. She was still stuck outside a low-rent random roadside at close to two in the morning, one state over, and not feeling any safer. Stasis equaled surrender.

It doesn't matter where the time goes. So long as it's gone.

Ice started mixing with the frigid rain, joining the snowy slop dumping buckets of muck, slicking the streets and speeding up the clock. Brooke pulled off the shoulder and back onto the road, feeling her tires try to gain traction, slipping and sliding. She intended to hop on the highway. The map showed Route 23 was a quicker shot than Interstate 91. The rural road should be clear of traffic this time of night.

With each mile, Brooke felt as though she were being lifted from the earth, unburied, dirt washed off and sprayed clean, rebirthed. Ascending, she felt her throat open, passageways unblocked. Even though it was a blizzard, Brooke unrolled the window, stuck out her head, and inhaled deep. The icy air tasted sweet.

Rescued from the grave, she could breathe again.

CHAPTER TWO

NOW

The radiator clanks, water in old pipes gurgles, and the heater thrums back to life. Fake ficus leaves tremble beneath the soft billow of tepid air. I stare off into space trying to both remember and forget. I'm so sick of talking about where it all went wrong.

"Robert?" Dr. Amy says, as if I've been slacking.

I've run out of things to say. Twenty-plus years of the same routine, rehashing tragic upbringings and paying a stranger to listen to you complain. You can't reinvent the wheel, and no one needs another origin story. My stepsister—my half-sister Brooke—disappeared one snowy night over two decades ago. Talking about her fifty minutes each week isn't bringing her back. I've accepted I'll never know what happened, how badly it ended for her. The only thing state troopers found: Brooke's abandoned, cracked-up car on the side of a snowy rural road. No tracks. No body. Nothing. The blizzard that sent her car careening in a ditch was the worst in years. Hope faded, leaving only the possibility of closure. After this long without a single lead, I've accepted I won't find that either.

I catch Dr. Amy glancing at the tiny clock on her table, a tip-off our time is up. She turns over her notepad, purses lips, and furrows brow. I can't help but feel I've let her down. Like all my mental health practitioners, Dr. Amy focuses with such intent, trying to coax the words out of me, as if she can crack the deepest reaches of my subconscious through will alone. I wish it were that easy.

"We need to stop," she says, before passing along a folded piece of paper, a tally for the past month and a half of attempting to locate the underlying source of my discontent.

I write the check, tear away the two-hundred-dollar co-pay, and nod a terse goodbye. I step into the blustery parking lot. The January winds stir, threatening the worst is yet to come. Upstate New York this time of year is nothing but one storm after another. Where I live, in the valley of Diemen, cold rain breaks up the spurts of snowstorms. Miserable. My cell buzzes. My wife Stephanie has my schedule down to the minute.

"Hey, hon," I say, sliding on the iPhone, tapping the remote to unlock my Porsche, a recent purchase and the nicest thing I've ever splurged on, celebrating what's been a great year.

"There's a write-up about the awards dinner in the *Times Union*." She says this lacking enthusiasm. I don't let the apathy hurt my feelings. There is a natural competition in any marriage. When one shines, it's difficult for the other not to feel overshadowed. Stephanie brought her own money into the marriage—she's never lacked. But inheriting wealth and securing professional success are different beasts. Not that being a civil engineering professor is the mountaintop.

Since our son Peter was born, the precipitating event that cemented a lifelong partnership, Stephanie has been a stay-at-home mom. Now that Peter is almost thirteen, she could go back to work if she wanted to. She also doesn't need to.

Before I feel guilty about the grant, I remind myself I've earned it.

I settle into the stiff leather bucket seat, fire up the car, and wait for the butt warmers to work their magic. There is a lag before the call switches over to the sound system, downtime I use to plan the order of errands I must complete before tonight's ceremony.

"Did you hear me?" My wife's voice booms over the car's speakers.

I turn down the volume, forgetting having been engrossed by NPR and *All Things Considered*. "I'm leaving the doctor's," I say. She, of course, knows this. I allow the engine to idle, calmed by the purr of pristine, finely tuned German craftmanship. Regardless of a lifetime in therapy, I know I can be knocked off my axis without much effort— that raging little boy still lurks in there somewhere. "I'll be home—"

"I don't know how smart it is for them to keep broadcasting something like that."

"Like what?" I pat my pockets, seized by panic when I can't find my phone. Only to realize it's in my hand, which makes me chuckle to myself over both how absentminded I can be, and how dependent we've become on these damn things. A car backfires up the street, and even though Dr. Amy's office is in a nice section of town, I flinch. One of the unfortunate hallmarks of the type A personality: being wound tighter than a drum.

"How much money you are receiving," my wife says.

"It's an NEH award, Steph. We're not talking MacArthur." I try not to groan having to defend the obvious. I know my wife is playing Devil's advocate. Academia can be a prickly place, with so many hungry mouths to feed fighting for limited morsels. Even at an upscale university like Uniondale, these awards are few and far and hard fought to secure. The amount of money is rare for a scholarly venture; however, that is not the real allure. The prize comes with a sabbatical, granting that rarest of commodities: time.

I switch on the wipers to clear away the raindrops and fat snow-flakes that have already begun to melt. "Civil engineering lands a long way from rock star," I say, attempting levity, shifting into reverse, centering the camera. "This is dull, pedagogical research."

Stephanie sighs and tells me to drive safely. I hang up, steering down slick side streets, as I make my way to the office. Even though Uniondale is on winter break, I don't deviate from my daily schedule. I'd planned to get a start on the book but find my mind circling back to this morning.

As always, I woke before Stephanie, who likes to remain in a warm, toasty bed with thick comforters and high thread counts for as long as humanly possible. I prepared as quietly as I could, slinking downstairs and into the kitchen. There I found the boy, loading up his backpack for the day. Peter bobbed his head, the teenage version of hello, which is all I can expect from his age. Recent outbursts notwithstanding, Peter is far more self-assured than I was at thirteen. Of course, I didn't grow up with the stability we've given him. This has been one of my life's greatest achievements: breaking the cycle. Peter will never have to wonder where he will be sleeping tonight, if there will be enough to eat; he will never have to live in a house with one parent absent, questioning whether the other loves him.

As I made my coffee, we were aware of one another's presence but did not speak, two separate entities moving about this shared space, alone but together. This silent awareness comforted but also filled me with a pervasive sadness—the inevitable extraction, the father losing his son who was once dependent on him for everything; the son who, like all boys, once viewed his father as the strongest man in the world. Now that he is older, Peter can see I am just another man. We watched Die Hard together before Christmas. Just he and I. A special treat, since he's underage and it's rated R. He seemed to enjoy it. So, it's not like we don't have our moments.

Before he left this morning, our eyes met. That was our entire exchange, surrounded by ticking clocks, percolating coffee, and knives scraping across toasted bread, wordless. I don't know why I am reviewing the interaction through such a melancholic lens. We are still father and son. We remain close in our own way—we have dinner together most nights—but he is on his way to being his own man, going the route I once did, where he will have to face difficult situations and make hard choices, some that have dire, life-altering consequences; and that is a hard concept for a father to accept. Because it works the other way too, that dependency.

By the time I head up the stairwell to my office, I'm gripped in the throes of despondency. Time has coalesced these worrisome, fretful thoughts.

Work is the great distractor. Pulling up a folder on the computer, I prepare to dive into the project the NEH is paying me handsomely for. I have several ideas for where to start—I've researched the project for months, compiling extensive outlines, motifs, and conceits that will show how cities, ancient and modern, are living, breathing entities. That's my thesis: the reciprocal relationship between man and his creation. The possibilities are endless. I am so excited; I can't contain my enthusiasm.

Before I get a word on the page, I realize someone is watching me.

A young woman stands in my doorway. She possesses a vague familiarity, though I know she is not a student. It's the raven-black hair and penetrating green eyes, the way they seem to be able to stare through me. Also, how tall she is—thin, sinewy. Like Lori Singer in that old Kevin Bacon film from the 1980s, *Footloose*. She must be at least five foot ten. Déjà vu. That's what I will say later, when I look back and reflect on a moment no longer defined by the present, because time isn't always linear. It can loop back on itself, reshaping moments, altering our perceptions, until we, quite literally, rewrite our own history.

"Bobby?" she says. "Er, um, Mr. Kirby?"

I take off my glasses, blink, a pointless delay of the inevitable. A part of me knows what is coming next. Because I have replayed this by now, returned to the moment, processed what she is about to say, her having already said it; it's been sorted and slotted into its appropriate mental file.

"Yes," I reply with professional decorum. "I am Dr. Kirby." There is no one else on the department floor. The university is still on winter recess. It is doubtful anyone else is in Willard Hall. We are not a commuter school, Uniondale a ghost town over the long breaks. "How can I help you?"

The girl shuffles, bites her lip, checks down the hallway as if listening for footsteps that will not come. I feel like I am looking at a ghost.

"My name is Lily," she says, stilted. "I'm your—I'm your sister Brooke's daughter."

ABOUT THE AUTHOR

Joe Clifford is the author of several acclaimed novels, including *Junkie Love* and the Jay Porter thriller series. He lives in the San Francisco Bay Area with his wife and two sons. Joe's writing can be found at www.joeclifford.com.